Katie's
Choice

AMY LILLARD

Katie's Choice

B&H
PUBLISHING GROUP

Nashville, Tennessee

978-1-4336-7753-3

Published by B&H Publishing Group
Nashville, Tennessee

Dewey Decimal Classification: F
Subject Heading: AMISH—FICTION \ LOVE STORIES \
DECISION MAKING—FICTION

1 2 3 4 5 6 7 8 • 17 16 15 14 13

To Rob. I love you.
Especially when we're lost in Amish country.

Acknowledgments

A ton of work goes into the "making" of a book. For those of you who believe writing is a solitary journey . . . well, it's not. This book could never have been if not for the wonderful encouragement from my agent, Mary Sue Seymour, and my editors, Julie Gwinn and Julie Carobini. Endless gratitude to my family and friends who continue to amaze me with their love and support. (This includes answering the phone even though you know it's me on the other end and I'm in "Amish" mode.) And a special thanks to everyone who patiently answered my endless questions about the Amish. I appreciate you all.

1

"Are you ready to go back out on assignment?" The phone line crackled slightly on the last word, but he thought Jolene Davidson, senior editor for *Around the World* magazine, had said "assignment."

Zane Carson sat up in a hurry. He'd been lounging on the couch watching reruns of *Happy Days* when he should have been at his physical therapy session. But he just wasn't up to another round of incredibly boring exercises with the commando instructor. No sir, he just couldn't do it again today. He'd been a little contemplative lately.

Okay, so he had been downright depressed. But who wouldn't be? One bullet and his entire life had been put on hold. His entire life had changed. He'd been sent home, grounded, and for once he'd started to think about the future. His future. His and Monica's.

"Of course I am," he lied. But what better way to prove to everyone that he was ready to hit the red zone than jumping on the horse, so to speak?

"Are you sitting down?"

"As a matter of fact, I am." Jo was always one for drama. If she weren't such a wordsmith, she could have been an actress instead. "Lay it on me."

"Oklahoma Amish country."

"Come again?" Surely he heard her wrong, because he thought she'd said—

"Oklahoma Amish country."

He leaned forward. "What are you talking about?"

"I'm talking about you . . . going to Oklahoma . . . and living among the Amish to get the inside scoop on what it's like to be part of such a community."

"Jolene, I am a war correspondent. That means I cover *wars*." He purposefully made his voice sound like he was talking to a four-year-old. When would they accept that he was ready to go back out into the field? Maybe *ready* was a bad word, but he needed to get back out there, if only to prove that he could.

"Now, Carson, this is an important assignment—"

"Jolene, there aren't many wars in Oklahoma, and there certainly aren't any in Amish territory."

"Country."

"Whatever." He flopped back on the sofa, then grimaced as he jarred his healing shoulder. "Aren't they conscientious objectors?"

"You've been calling every day asking for an assignment."

He hadn't called today and look where that got him.

"Now they want to give you one. You can't turn it down if you ever want to get back into the red zone."

She was right. But . . . "Did you say Oklahoma?" Did they even have an Amish community? Why not Pennsylvania? Everybody knew about Lancaster County.

"Everybody knows about Lancaster County. We're looking for something different—smaller settlement, tighter surrounding community. Alternate worship right there in the buckle of the Bible Belt."

Zane didn't know if he would call their manner of religion "alternate," but what did he know about such things? He'd never been to church. His parents had preferred to worship nature and his uncle hadn't had time for that sort of thing.

"I need you to do this for me." Those quietly spoken words held a wealth of information. "You do this and I'll make sure you get the Juarez assignment."

"I thought Douglas was in Mexico."

"He's ready to come home, but he's willing to stay until we can find a suitable replacement."

Juarez, Mexico. Where innocent people died for being in the wrong place at the wrong time. It was dangerous, very dangerous, this war on drugs. And exactly where Zane wanted to be. Jo knew that, and she used that information to her advantage.

He sighed. "When do you want me there?"

"Day after tomorrow."

That didn't give him much time. Zane pushed his fingers through his hair. It needed a cut, but it seemed like even that would have to wait. At least he was going back to work. Sort of. He really didn't consider an assignment like this *work*. How challenging could it be? Amish. Right. But with Mexico dangling in front of him, what choice did he have?

"You'll fly Chicago to Tulsa. There's a driver who will pick you up and take you to Clover Ridge. And . . ." she paused for dramatic effect. "I've arranged for you to stay with a host family."

"Wait. What? Hold on." Zane ran his hands down the legs of his faded jeans and tried to get a handle on the information she just dumped on him. "A driver? Why do I need a driver? What about a car?"

Jolene sighed in an aren't-you-just-the-silliest-thing kind of way that set his teeth on edge. "Zane, the Amish don't drive cars."

What had he gotten himself into?

"You're going there to learn how to live like them, give the world an inside perspective. You certainly can't do that if you're zipping all over the place in a rental."

That might be true, but he was sure he could get the feel for the lifestyle without being stranded in podunk Oklahoma with no means of transportation. But he knew better than to argue with Jo when she thought she was being brilliant. "Define 'host family.'"

"Basically there's a family, let me see here . . ." Zane could hear her shuffling papers. "The Fishers. You're going to stay with them, and learn how to live like the Amish."

"And what do they get out of the deal?"

She paused. "The satisfaction of helping their fellow man?"

He shook his head. "Helping their fellow man sell countless magazines and make lots of money. Isn't that a little . . . un-Amish?" Even writers were sometimes at a loss for words. But someone once told him that the Amish weren't interested in making money and getting ahead. They only earned what they needed to in order to care for their families. Or maybe he had read it in a magazine during one of his countless layovers.

"The mom has cancer. They're hoping that the exposure will help bring more people into the community and thereby raise enough money to cover the medical costs."

That seemed a little out of character too. But what he knew about the Amish could fit on the back of a postage stamp—with room to spare.

Host family usually meant an in-depth study, a series of articles, and quite a bit of time away from home. Zane glanced around his tiny apartment. He was so sick at looking at these walls. Maybe an assignment like this was worth getting out for. "How long are we talking about here?"

"Three months."

"Are you insane? Three months?" He flipped the calendar to October. Three months would get him back to Chicago at the first of the year. "I'll be gone during Christmas."

Jolene snickered. "I thought you might like to spend the holidays with someone other than me."

Truth was he'd never spent any personal time with Jo at the holidays, or any other time for that matter, but he was one of the few reporters at *Around the World* that had no family to speak of. No one would miss him if he were on assignment Christmas Day. Not even Monica. Well, she might miss him, but she would understand. Not that it mattered. It'd never been a big holiday for him before or after his parents died.

"And you're sure it's okay with them?" The Amish were a tight-knit group, and the last thing he wanted was to invade their inner sanctum. He'd been in war-torn countries with bullets whizzing past his head like fiery hail, he'd suffered discrimination of being the only white face in the jungles of Africa, but there was no way he'd overrun someone's private time with their family. That was not a road he wanted to travel down.

"Are you worried, Zane?" She said this, but what she really meant was, *Are you going soft on me?*

"Not at all."

"Good, then. They'll be expecting you on Thursday. I'll send over the specs on the angle we'd like to see. This is a serious assignment, Zane. We want it all—interviews, pictures, the works."

"Got it."

"In the meantime, it's probably best to start your own research. You'd better get on it though. You only have a day and a half to learn how to live like the Amish."

Soft music played in the dimly lit restaurant. Zane smoothed a hand down his tie, resisting the urge to loosen it. He was certain the maitre d' would frown upon anything less than perfection from his diners. And the noose was for a good cause. He glanced at his dinner companion.

To call Monica Cartwright pretty was the understatement of the century. With her silky, black hair, flawless complexion, and petite frame, beautiful didn't seem to cover it either. Gorgeous, stunning, breathtaking—those came close. Or maybe it was the way she carried herself, with a self-assurance that came from old money. Why she had set her sights on a footloose vagrant like him was beyond comprehension.

He wasn't going to examine it too closely, though, but instead ride it for all it was worth. He absently fingered the little black box he'd tucked away in his suit coat. Tonight was a special night. And he had yet to tell her about his sojourn into the land of the backward.

That wasn't fair. He was sure the Amish were good people, but he needed to be in the thick of things. That's what made him tick, made him feel alive. What had Jo talked him into this time? Amish. She had better deliver on Mexico the minute he returned.

"Zane?"

He lifted his gaze to Monica, only then aware he'd been staring at the menu without even reading it.

She shifted in her seat. "You're a million miles away." The immaculate navy blue cocktail dress hugged her like a second skin and matched her eyes to perfection.

"Sorry." He smoothed his tie once again. She was probably sensing his unease. He'd have to tell her eventually about his assignment. She'd be disappointed, but she understood the busi-ness. Even if the magazine she worked for was owned by dear old Dad, Monica prided herself on working her way into her current position as staff editor of *Talk of the Town* magazine. Of course, she wrote about Chanel lipstick and Louboutin shoes, not the harsh realities of war. But she understood.

Of all the days to get an assignment.

"It's all right."

He was about to spill the news when the waiter came to take their order. One prime rib and one frou-frou salad later, he couldn't hold it in any longer.

"I got an assignment today."

"Oh." Crestfallen was the only word he could think of to describe her expression. Of course, she thought he was going back to the Middle East.

"It's an easy assignment."

She chewed on her bottom lip for a moment, then gave him a sad, brave smile. "Where are you going?" For all her talk about accepting his job, he knew it wouldn't be easy for her when he headed off to Mexico.

"Oklahoma."

Her brows rose. "Are you joking?"

"I wish I was. It's a crazy assignment, but if I want to get back out in the field, then I have to go."

"I understand." She looked down, seemingly captivated by the pattern on the ends of their flatware.

He hated the resigned slump of her shoulders. "It's only for three months."

"That's not bad." There was that brave smile again.

He shook his head. "There's something else I want to talk to you about."

She took a sip of water, watching him over the rim.

Zane's hand started to tremble. *Surely a natural reaction.* After all, it wasn't every day a man got engaged. He pulled the velvet box from his suit pocket and placed it on the table in front of him.

Her sapphire eyes grew wide. "Zane, I—"

He shook his head, effectively cutting off whatever she was about to say. "Just hear me out." He took a deep breath, then flipped open the top of the ring box to expose the sparkling ruby and diamond engagement ring inside. Another breath. "Monica, I've always been something of a loner. I guess it's in my genes, but getting shot made me stop and think about the future. That's when I realized I didn't have one. At least, not one that I was looking forward to."

He cleared his throat and dropped down on one knee beside her. "Monica Cartwright, will you marry me?" His voice cracked on the last word, but she didn't seem to notice.

She looked from the box on the table to the knot in his tie, but made no move toward the ring. "I don't know what to say." She didn't meet his gaze.

"I believe this is where you're supposed to say yes."

"Oh, Zane." Her voice was filled with anguish and indecision instead of the happy love that he'd been expecting. She tugged on his sleeve. "Stand up. Stand up."

Zane rose, then sat in his chair, wondering where his proposal had gotten off track.

"What about your job?"

He shrugged, his shoulders stiff. Then he tried to laugh it off. "I'll need to keep it, don't you think? We'll still have bills to pay."

She dropped her gaze to her lap. "You'll be gone most of the time."

He reached across the table and took her hands into his own. "I was laying there in that hospital bed wondering if each sight was going to be my last and all I could think about was you. And the future. That's how those soldiers do it, babe. They can go over there and fight because they know they have someone to come home to. I need you to be my someone."

Tears filled her eyes, but she blinked them back. "I don't know, Zane. I—I just don't know."

This was not the response he'd expected. In all fairness he was asking a lot. For her to wait on him, to wonder and worry, raise their family and never know if he'd return in one piece. But they weren't the only couple facing the same prospects in this time of war. Others survived. They could too.

He picked up the ring box, snapped it shut, and pressed it into her hand. "You think about it while I'm gone, okay?"

She nodded and slipped the box into her evening bag. "It's not that I don't love you —"

"Shh. I know." He pressed one finger to her lips. "We'll talk about it when I get back."

Engaged. He was engaged. Well, almost engaged. He'd taken Monica by surprise was all. And now this assignment. He was counting on the old *absence makes the heart grow fonder* thing to kick in while he was gone. She'd come around to his way of thinking. He was certain of it.

Engaged. It was a weird thought. There was someone waiting for him to return. Someone who counted on him to come back and continue their relationship without question. The idea was as foreign to Zane as the landscape whizzing past.

As promised, a driver named Bill had met Zane at the airport. Bill was more than willing to talk about the weather, the trees, and how the University of Oklahoma football team was playing this season, but Zane didn't think it was the time to drill him for secrets into the culture he was entering. Bill wasn't Amish.

"Mennonite," he supplied with a smile and a glance in Zane's direction.

"And what would you say the primary difference is?" Zane asked. "Besides driving." He'd been a little surprised that the driver was also of the Anabaptist sect, though he wouldn't have known it if the chatty Bill hadn't volunteered the info.

"Well, now, there are quite a few differences. 'Course you got your Old Order Amish and your New Order Amish, they differ greatly as well."

"And Clover Ridge?"

"Definitely Old Order."

Zane nodded. Not that he understood any of what that meant. He wished he'd done a little more research. All he could remember about the Amish was the tragic shooting several years ago and that they seemed to be a loving and forgiving sort of people. He had been in Bosnia when it happened, so all his info had been filtered by the time it reached him.

"I thought Oklahoma was flat and dusty." Zane gestured toward the green grass. The sky was colored a pristine blue, and the hills seemed to roll on forever into the distance. Sort of reminded him of Oregon and the commune where he grew up. At least how he remembered Oregon.

Bill laughed. "Not this part. You're in what's called Green Country. Out in western Oklahoma, it's like that. Dry prairie. But neither side lives in teepees."

Zane turned to face him, questions on the tip of his tongue.

Bill's eyes twinkled.

Must be an inside joke, Zane thought, and leaned back in his seat.

The rest of the trip flew by in a blur of unexpected green. Bill pointed out a few more things along the way—mistletoe, the state flower, and the scissor-tailed flycatcher, the state bird. And in less time than it would have taken him to drive from his apartment to downtown, they were entering Clover Ridge.

The town was a mixed oddity of old and new. There was a McDonalds and a Walgreens, but somehow they had managed to keep the Walmart invasion at bay. A general store named Anderson's sat next to the post office, then a lumberyard, and a Dairy Queen.

But most interesting of all were the buggies hitched to horses and tethered in front of all the stores. At least they weren't in the drive-through line at Mickey D's, he thought, hiding a smile.

In no time at all, they pulled into a long dirt drive lined with wooden fences on both sides. Across the road from the turn, a field had been left fallow, the rich, dark earth looking like no soil he had ever seen. A small wooden shanty stood at the edge of the field, seeming too new for the rest of the farm.

"Here we are." Bill pulled the car to a stop in front of a rambling white house that looked like it had been added on to several times.

A big red barn stood opposite the haphazard structure, a pasture with no end spreading behind it. The yard itself teemed with life. Chickens, dogs, cats, geese, and even a duck strutted around pecking at bugs and giving the occasional cat a chase.

Bill didn't even honk the horn. At the sound of the car's engine, three people rushed from the house to the porch. Zane stepped from the car, looking from them to the stern-faced man coming from the barn, the obvious Amish patriarch.

Before he could utter one word of greeting, Bill raised his hand toward the elder man. "Abram Fisher. I've brought your new house guest."

Abram raised his hand in return. "Bill Foster. It is good to see you." The men shook hands and clapped each other on the back as Zane watched the group on the porch. A tall, slender woman stood in the center of the fray, most likely Abram's wife. What had Jo said her name was? Ruth, yeah, Ruth.

"You'll stay for *natchess*," Abram said, not quite a question, but Bill nodded in return. "Wouldn't miss Ruth's cookin' for nothin' in the world."

Abram shook his head. "Ruth's restin' more these days. It's Gideon's Annie who'll be preparin' your food for the evenin'. But a right fine cook she is at that." Zane couldn't help but notice the haunted look in his eyes at the mention of his wife's name and once again he worried that his staying with them might turn out to be more of a hardship than a benefit.

He mentally shook himself. Maybe Jo was right. Maybe he was getting soft. Normally he wouldn't care about such things. They had invited him here. They were getting something from the deal. He was just doing his job. And that's all there was to it.

"What say you, Bill Foster?" Abram asked. "What else do we need to pay you for your services this evenin'?"

Zane stepped forward and reached for his wallet. "I've got this." He pulled out two twenties and a ten, more than enough to cover the gas for the trip. He thought better of it and pulled out a couple more twenties. Surely that would pay for the man's time.

Bill shook his head and made no move toward the money. "I'd rather not have money, if you've still got any of them pickles."

Abram nodded. "That we do. A couple of jars of those, and I'll say we're even."

Zane looked down at the cash he held in his hand. Pickles? Was he serious? The Amish man and the Mennonite shook hands. Evidently they were.

"But—" he started, not really knowing what to do and how to protest that Bill hadn't taken his money in trade for services. Bill looked down at the bills in Zane's hand.

"That's mighty kind of you, son," he said, plucking it from his fingers and handing it over to Abram. "Perhaps this would be better used in Ruth Ann's fund."

"*Danki*, Bill Foster," Abram gave a nod of his head. "I'll make sure Annie gets it."

"Come on with you both." Abram pointed to the bags Bill had pulled from the back of the car. The men grabbed the luggage and started toward the house.

"By the way, I'm Zane Carson." He didn't know why he felt compelled to say anything. It wasn't like they had paid him the slightest attention, but he felt he should say something. Or maybe not. He adjusted the strap of his laptop bag and followed behind Bill and Abram.

"*Ach*," Abram said with a shake of his head. "That you are."

Zane didn't have time to think about the lack of greeting. All at once they were standing at the foot of the porch.

"Annie, I hope you've prepared enough, we've got guests for supper."

A petite woman with dark hair and unusual eyes nodded to Abram. "I have indeed. There is more than enough to go around."

Her accent was different from the others'. Abram's voice held the lilt of his German ancestors, but Annie sounded like a purebred Texan. And stranger still, Zane had a feeling he'd met her before.

"Abram," the woman on the porch said, "introduce the family and guests."

The eldest Fisher jerked his head. "Zane Carson," he said with a motion back toward him. "This here's my wife, Ruth Ann, and that's Annie Hamilton, my son John Paul. Gideon will be along directly with our son, Gabe, and his boys."

"And Lizzie," Annie said. "I mean, Mary Elizabeth, will be here too."

"Don't forget Katie Rose," John Paul added. "She's my sister."

Zane did a quick mental calculation and, depending on the number of boys that belonged to Gabe, there would be at least twelve people at this *natchess*, maybe more. He hadn't survived in the Middle East without being quick, and he could only assume that *natchess* was the next meal.

Everyone bustled into the house, the inside much warmer than the greeting he'd received from Abram. Yet, there weren't any of the vanity objects that dominated non-Amish housing. No pictures on the walls, no knickknacks scattered about. The floors were solid wood, covered only by a few homemade-looking rag rugs. There were no curtains on the windows, no cozy items strewn about. All in all he couldn't figure out why it seemed so welcoming.

Maybe it was the family. Despite Abram, Ruth Ann and Annie seemed to welcome him into the house. Upon closer inspection, he could see the ravages of cancer treatment on the Fisher matriarch. She wore a black bonnet that he was pretty sure hid the last remains of her chemo-ravaged hair. Her skin held a gray tinge, her cheeks puffy from the steroids, her eyes sunken. Her dress hung on her frame, but those mossy green eyes sparkled with a light that even medical science couldn't extinguish.

Annie was much younger and healthier, though Zane noticed she hovered close to Ruth as if to spot her in case she stumbled. Zane still couldn't shake the feeling that he knew her somehow. They say everyone has a twin. Well, at some point in his life, he'd run across Annie's.

"John Paul," Ruth commanded, her voice strong despite her frail condition. "Take Zane Carson's things upstairs and show him to his room."

"Thank you, ma'am, but I can get it."

Ruth shook her head. "John Paul will help."

The young man stepped forward and for the first time Zane noticed he wore faded jeans to rival his own. His blue shirt looked impeccably tailored, and he'd rounded out his attire with a pair of dirty running shoes. Had he not had the distinctive chili-bowl hairstyle, John Paul Fisher would have looked like any other teen-ager in countless other small towns around the country.

Yet the women had both dressed the same: dresses covered in some sort of apron and shawl, hair pinned back and covered with a small, white cap. Why did John Paul dress differently? Zane made a mental note to find out the first chance he got.

John Paul picked up Zane's suitcase and started toward the large set of stairs. "This way."

Zane grabbed his computer and followed behind.

"You'll be sharin' a room with me, since Gideon's Annie has the other." He nodded his head to the closed door directly across the hall. He pushed open the opposite door and ducked inside.

Two neat beds sat side by side in a surprisingly large bedroom. Each bed was covered with a quilt of vivid colors—black, red, yellow, orange, and green. A rocking chair had a strange-looking floor lamp next to it, the neck of it protruding out of an old propane tank.

"This one's the bed I usually sleep in." John Paul pointed to the one on the right, and it wasn't lost on Zane that he didn't call the bed "mine." "But I'm not here much." He shrugged his shoulders as if to say, "whatever."

"Then I'll take this one." Zane hoisted his laptop bag into the center of the quilt. "Tell me again, Gideon's Annie is who?"

"She's the dark-haired girl downstairs. She's intended to my older brother Gideon."

"Why do they call her by his name too?"

"You see, there's a lot of Annies, but she is—"

"Gideon's. Got it."

"Come next fall, they'll be married. Well, once she joins the church."

Zane sat down on the bed, briefly wondering if John Paul would mind if he opened his laptop and took notes while the young man talked. Probably. So he kept his expression blank as he asked, "She's not a member of the church?"

"No, she just moved here."

"From another community, you mean."

"From Dallas."

As in Texas? He wasn't so far off the mark after all. He was pleased to know that six months stuck in his own apartment hadn't dulled his instincts. "I wasn't aware they had an Amish settlement in Dallas."

John Paul shook his head. "Gideon's Annie isn't Amish. She's an *Englischer* wantin' to be Amish so she can marry my brother. She can't do that until she joins the church. And she can't join the church until she passes her lessons and proves that she's committed to our ways."

Now that sounded downright cultish, but Zane supposed love could do that to a person. "How did an Amish man meet a city girl from Texas?"

"*Ach*, man, now there's a good story," he said, sounding all the more like his father. "But it's better voiced by Gideon or Annie. I can tell you, though, that Annie, she wrecked her car on a snowy night this past spring. Gideon rescued her from the car, and she . . . well, I suppose you could say that she rescued him from his grief. His wife and son died over a year ago. Gideon never quite recovered. Until Annie, that is."

"I see." In the shoes he wore right then, he couldn't imagine how Gideon felt. How would he feel about the matter after Monica gave birth to his child?

John Paul sat down opposite him, and Zane nodded toward the young man's jeans. "So the men are able to dress like they want and the women wear the . . ." He motioned toward his torso and head.

John Paul laughed. "No. All Amish men and women dress the same as each other, but I'm in *rumspringa*."

"And that means . . . ?"

"I get a chance to go out and experience the world. I can wear what I want, drive a car, drink alcohol. Make sure I really want to join the church."

"And if you decide not to join?"

John Paul shrugged. "Then I can leave the district and go to live with the *Englisch*."

"Interesting." *More than, actually.* He would have loved to question John Paul some more about the rum-whatever, but they had been gone long enough. Time to get back downstairs and meet back up with his host family. He made a mental note to find out more at the first available opportunity.

"Is there a place I can plug in my laptop?"

John Paul grinned. "No."

"But the lamp?" He nodded toward the corner light.

"Runs off propane. Didn't anybody tell you? There's no electricity in Amish homes."

He had heard something to that effect, but it just hadn't sunk in. Or maybe it just didn't seem possible. "They were serious about that?"

John Paul's grin got a little bit wider. "Absolutely."

Back downstairs, it seemed that the house would burst with all the people who had arrived for dinner. Gabriel, it turned out, had five sons ranging in age from four to thirteen with his daughter Mary Elizabeth topping the list at fifteen. From her, Zane learned that *rumspringa* started at sixteen and could last as long as five years. Soon Mary Elizabeth would be joining the run-around time. By the gleam in her eyes, she could barely stand the wait. Gideon also arrived, looking as much like Abram as Gabriel did. Both Fisher boys were bulky and solid, with coffee-dark hair. Their mossy-green eyes were identical to their mother's, the one trait she seemed to have passed to her sons.

Zane couldn't help but notice Gideon and his intended were not very affectionate—at least not outwardly. He did catch them staring longingly at each other when they thought no one was looking. Maybe that was part of the culture as well. He wished he'd thought to bring his notebook from his case, but then again, maybe it wasn't kosher to take notes at the family dinner. Even if Bill the Mennonite driver was also attending. So Zane made do with mental notes, etching the questions into his brain so he could retrieve them later when he went to his room.

"Katie Rose," Mary Elizabeth said, grabbing the arm of a woman he had yet to meet. With all the milling bodies, it was no wonder he hadn't seen the Fisher daughter as she had arrived with her brothers.

She turned to face him, and Zane's greeting died on his lips.

Tall and slim, she looked as much like her mother as the Fisher boys favored their father. Honey-blonde hair, pale green eyes, with the barest hint of color high on her cheekbones.

And she took his breath away.

She exuded an angelic quality that even surpassed the peace and love that shone in Ruth Fisher's eyes. *Wholesome.* That was the first word to come to mind. She was what Monica would call a natural beauty. No makeup, no highlights, no artificial anything, and yet she was perhaps the most beautiful woman he'd ever seen.

"It's nice to meet you." Was that his voice? He nodded to Katie Rose, still trying to get his bearings, as he reached out to shake her hand.

"And you as well. Welcome to Clover Ridge." Katie Rose

smiled as she shook his hand, and Zane's breath stilled in his chest. Her fingers were warm in his, solid with just a few rough spots that told the tale of the life she lived. Monica would have been at the salon every day to have them removed, but they fit the natural beauty of Katie Rose Fisher.

He couldn't pinpoint what it was about her that seemed to seep into his bones. She was not his type, but the man in him could appreciate her beauty. The engaged man in him, however, knew to keep his distance. Now was the time to show his professionalism.

"Katie Rose is our teacher," Mary Elizabeth gushed. "Well, not mine anymore, but the other children's. She's wonderful."

"I'm sure she is," he said, realizing that he still held her hand in his.

Katie Rose pulled away, her smile unwavering. "I hope you enjoy your stay here."

"I'm sure I will." Zane did his best not to feel discarded as she nodded a "so long" and disappeared in the throng of her family.

Just when he thought the house couldn't get any fuller, someone called out, "Go get Noni."

From the back, John Paul brought in a stooped, elderly woman who couldn't have been a day younger than ninety. Arthritis had gnarled her hands into near talons, but her eyes still held the sharp edge of intelligence. She had a walking cane and a long black dress, her iron-gray hair parted down the middle pulled back and covered just like the young women.

Once they were all seated around the two large wooden tables, everyone bowed their heads. Everyone, but Zane. He looked around at their bowed heads, his gaze stopping on one of Gabriel's sons. Samuel? Or was it Simon? It didn't matter. Only the buzzing silence that filled the room as everyone prayed. For what, he didn't know. Zane had never been one to pray. At least not to a god . . . or *the* God. He just . . . never saw the point.

His gaze flitted from Simon to his aunt. Katie Rose had her head dutifully lowered, her eyes closed, and her hands folded neatly on the table. There was a peace about her that Zane couldn't place, and he pushed back thoughts of his earlier reaction to her. Her beauty had taken him by surprise. Where he came from, women did everything from color their hair to inject their lips in order to gain the aura that Katie Rose held by the grace of nature.

Professional, he reminded himself. *Be professional.* He was a little out of practice at living with other cultures. Six weeks in Chicago had done that to him. Maybe Jo had a point: He needed this assignment more than he realized. He'd definitely be in trouble if he lost his edge in Juarez. Better to get back in the habit of adapting to the Amish before he had to survive in the wild world of Mexican drug lords.

He cleared his mind of personal thoughts of Katie Rose and inspected her with a journalist's eyes. She, like the other women, wore a white kerchief-kind of hat perched on the back part of her head. Must be an Amish thing. He'd never thought about it until now, but in all the pictures he had seen of the Plain people, the women wore that same type of covering, or something similar. He made a mental note to ask John Paul about it.

Thankfully, Abram uttered *"Aemen"* and everyone raised their heads. Being at the table with so many people brought back memories of the cooperative where bowls of food were circulated and everyone served their plates before passing to the next person.

Someone burped. No one made mention of it, no one said *excuse me* or waited for another to do the honors. Another Amish thing? For so many people at the table, there wasn't a great deal of talking. Even the children were strangely quiet. Granted, what he had seen of Amish children tonight led him to believe that they were better disciplined than kids on the outside. Still, he couldn't help but believe that his presence at the table had something to do with it.

"How's your *natchess*?"

Zane's gaze jerked to Katie Rose. She smiled, and he realized her eyes were a lighter green than her mother's. And sweetly smiling instead of tired, as she waited for him to answer.

He realized he wasn't eating. Old habits and all. He'd never been a big eater. He was usually much more interested in what was around him than in food. But he had the next three months to absorb all he could of the Amish way of life. No sense in starving himself this early in the game.

"Oh, fine, fine," he answered, taking a bite to add credit to his words. "Very good, in fact. My compliments to the chef."

A few seats down, Annie blushed.

The meal was tasty. Some of the best food he had ever eaten. Maybe because it wasn't full of preservatives or lean on fat and calories. He could feel it clogging his arteries that very second, but he wasn't sure he cared. It was *that* delicious. "What do you call this?"

"Chicken pot pie," Annie answered.

"It's Annie's specialty," Mary Elizabeth said with a smile.

"And *onkel's* favorite," Matthew was quick to add.

Everyone laughed.

Another inside joke?

"There was fine weather today," Abram said from his place at the head of the table. "Tomorrow we'll start plowin'."

"Plowing?" Granted he'd been a city boy for the last twenty years, but he'd spent quite a few formative years in a commune. And he'd learned a thing or two about farming. One thing he knew was that it was October. Not time to plant anything.

"*Jah*," Abram said with a short nod. "Plowin'."

"You made out easy," John Paul added with a nudge to his side. "Last week we laid the manure."

"Seems like I came just in time," he said with a laugh. For the first time since he agreed to this crazy plan of Jo's, he realized the extent of what he'd gotten himself in to. Farming. And backward farming, at that. He rubbed at the dull pain in his shoulder. He supposed it was better than heading into a war zone. Safer, and not as stressful. A little cleaner and a lot cushier. But how was he supposed to live his life to the fullest on an Amish farm in the backwoods of backward Oklahoma? Three months, he told himself. Three months, and he was out of here.

❦

Abram Fisher had made a mistake. He was a godly man. He had learned humility. And he could admit when he'd done wrong. And this time he hadn't done right by his family.

He looked down the table to the stranger he had invited into his home—their home. He'd done it all for Ruthie. He was a selfish man, he knew. Every night he prayed to God to forgive him and his selfish ways and thoughts, but heaven help him, he wasn't ready to let her go.

But this *Englischer* with his hard eyes and unsmiling mouth was not a man he should have asked to come into his house. Not like this. But the deed was done. Zane Carson was staying, living among them, writing about what it felt like to be Amish.

Abram couldn't understand the draw of the outside world to their little community, but the *Englischers* seemed to be fascinated by the ways of the Plain folk. It beat him as to why. They all acted like Plain folk did something special. More special than just follow God's plan. Everything was right there in the Bible for everyone to see, to use. T'weren't any more special than that.

But with Ruthie's cancer treatments draining the funds from the district, Abram had to do something to put it back. The only thing he could do was take the fancy, fast-talking editor lady up on her plan. Invite a reporter to come into their midst, live with them, work beside them, and then write a bunch of stories about the experience. She assured Abram that the articles would bring tourists from all over to sample the wares, tastes, and simple life that was offered in Clover Ridge. More visitors meant more money for the town, and more money for the town meant more funds in the emergency coffers. More money for cancer treatments.

So he had done it for Ruthie. Everything for Ruthie.

2

Shortly after dinner, the women served pie, and Zane had to admit that the food was sure better here than it was in the Middle East. Annie's chicken pot pie beat out military MREs any day.

After everyone had eaten their fill of dessert, the whole clan had gathered around and listened as Abram opened a well-worn Bible. His reading was stilted and slow, much slower than when he spoke, and Zane realized: he was translating the words to English so that he, too, would be able to understand. Zane felt like the belly of a snake, trying to devise ways out of sitting through a Bible reading. Nothing about the idea appealed to him.

He supposed that was a natural side effect of being raised by agnostic parents. It wasn't that the Bible didn't have interesting stories and a strong moral code to live by. It was the whole heaven-hell thing that bothered him. A higher power who got to determine where you spent an eternity depending on a mood? That didn't seem quite fair. And Zane wanted no part of it.

But he acted the polite guest and sat patiently while Abram read, and everyone else sat in rapt attention. With their minds focused on the reading, Zane used that opportunity to study this family who had taken him in.

Ruth Fisher looked gaunt in her clothes. Tired and sad, but with her back ramrod straight as if to show the cancer she couldn't be beat. Next to her sat Annie, with her dark, dark hair. It was pulled back like the other women's, but Zane could tell that hers wasn't nearly as long as the Fisher girls'. He remembered John Paul telling him that Annie was an Englisher who'd only recently come to live among the Amish. Maybe that was the reason she seemed so familiar to him. Whatever it was, one thing was apparent—Gideon's Annie was a kind soul. She clasped Ruth's hand in between her own, offering comfort and support by her mere presence.

Gabriel's boys sat lined up in a row from tallest to smallest, with the exception of the youngest, Samuel. The redhead was perched on Katie Rose's lap, a thumb in his mouth and his other hand playing with the untied strings of her little white cap.

John Paul and Mary Elizabeth sat side by side, each seemingly captivated, both pretending to want to be there when in fact they'd rather be any place else. Zane had been young once, and he could see the signs. He had to admire how respectful the teenagers were to their elders.

Gideon sat across from them. The next to the oldest, Zane remembered. He continually looked from his father to his intended to his mother and back. His green eyes flicked over each one in turn, lingering slightly longer on Annie's pixie face before looking away again.

And Noni. The old woman had spunk. She hadn't said two words since John Paul had led her into the room, but Zane could tell. She had that feisty look that made him imagine she would clonk Abram on the head with her cane if he messed up the reading. They had only introduced her as Noni. He had no idea if she was Ruth's mother or Abram's, and the fact that he couldn't tell by the family's treatment of her was proof positive that the Amish had communal living down better than the hippies.

Zane smiled and made another mental note to find out whose mother Noni really was. Just so he'd know. Staying with the Amish in Oklahoma might not be as exciting as the war-torn Middle East, but he couldn't say it was going to be boring. Not in the least.

Thankfully Abram didn't read too many verses, and soon he was closing the book on a chorus of "*aemens.*" Though early, the Fishers who didn't live in the house packed up and left, while the ones who were staying tidied up and prepared to go to bed.

Zane said good night to everyone, and he and John Paul climbed the stairs.

"Bathroom's down that way. Best brush your teeth and ready for bed. Sunrise comes mighty early."

"Sunrise?"

John Paul smiled at him.

Zane laughed. He was joking of course. Who got up at sunrise? At least one of the Fishers had a sense of humor.

Zane grabbed his toothbrush and a pair of pajama pants and headed down the hall where John Paul had directed.

To call it a bathroom was beyond generous. The room was barely big enough for a person to stand, much less bathe. It had a tiny sink, mirror, and tub. But there was hot and cold running water, so he shouldn't complain.

"Three months, Carson," he muttered under his breath. Three more months, and he would be back in Chicago, then out into the field—on the border where he wouldn't know where he would spend the night, much less have water that came out of pipes. And he would have Monica to come home to. He could manage three months of Amish living. No sweat.

He slipped on the drawstring pants, grabbed up his T-shirt and jeans, and headed out the door, whistling under his breath as he made his way down the hall.

John Paul grabbed his arm and dragged him into the room, quickly closing the door behind them.

"Uh . . ." He nodded toward Zane's bare chest, his gaze lingering on the jagged scar on Zane's shoulder. It wouldn't be long before the questions came. "It's probably not a good idea to go around like, uh . . . that."

Zane glanced down and back up. "Sorry. I'm not used to . . ."

John Paul nodded, letting him off the hook of finishing that statement. There was a lot he wasn't used to. Being in an Amish farmhouse topped the list quite nicely. He also wasn't used to conservative ways, people offended by the sight of a man's naked chest, and a host of other things he was certain to encounter over the next three months.

He was chagrined at his lack of research. He wouldn't have dared enter a third world country without detailed knowledge of the culture. A man could get killed or worse for nothing more than shaking hands with the wrong person. He should have asked for a couple of more days to research his target, but he'd been too caught up in the excitement of going back to work to care one way or the other.

And if he decided to be honest with himself, he hadn't taken the job all that seriously. It was only the Amish. Yet the people were becoming real to him now, caring souls who had taken him in and who wanted to teach him about their culture. He had shown them nothing but disrespect by not caring to learn any of their culture before arriving. Something he needed to correct ASAP.

Zane pulled on the black T-shirt he'd worn during the trip and booted up his computer. Good thing he had charged it before he left Chicago. Now all he had to do was get as many notes down as possible before his battery died.

"Tell me about Noni."

John Paul shrugged. "What do you want to know?" There was a slight edge to his voice.

He decided a general question was in order. "Is it normal for grandparents to live in houses built on to the back?"

John Paul nodded. "Of course."

"And Katie Rose is your sister, but she lives with your brother."

John Paul nodded. "When Gabe's wife died, he needed some help. Katie Rose moved in to cook and clean and help with the boys. 'Course Mary Elizabeth was just barely ten at the time. So Gabe needed every hand he could get, what with the baby and all."

"Baby?"

"*Jah.*" John Paul nodded. "That's how Rebecca died, havin' Samuel. With no *mudder* to look after him, someone had to take care of him."

And with him having Down syndrome . . . "But now Mary Elizabeth is older. The boys are older. And she still stays there?"

"I don't suppose it would be easy for her to leave, not with Samuel still needin' her."

He didn't suppose it would. The boy had stuck to her like bubble gum on a hot summer day. It also seemed like just the way the Amish lived their lives. Katie Rose helping out Gabriel. Annie living with the Fishers until she could join the church and marry Gideon. And Noni living in the same house instead of being shipped off to a nursing home at the first opportunity.

"What happens if Katie Rose decides to marry?"

"I don't suppose that'll happen."

"Why not? I mean . . ." He was about to say that she was incredibly beautiful and worthy of any man's attention, especially an Amish man who appreciated the simplicity of her manner, the openness of her smile. But if John Paul thought Zane's bare chest might be offensive, he was sure not to like comments about his sister's attractiveness.

Zane was still a little stunned at his reaction to her. Even without a speck of makeup, and her hair pulled back into a tight bun, she was breathtaking. Not that he preferred his women painted up and fake, but he did appreciate a woman who took care of herself and wasn't afraid to let the world know how hard she worked to look good. A woman like Monica. Still, Katie Rose had done none of that, and he had noticed her.

Her lingering memory—it had been an hour since he'd last seen her—was proof that he'd been cooped up too long. For all practical purposes, he was an engaged man. But evidently he needed a break and should have taken one before accepting this assignment. A night out on the town was just what he needed, but between the days in the hospital, the weeks in rehab, and the countless hours in waiting rooms, there just didn't seem to be the time. Now he was paying for it, lusting after a sweet Amish woman who gave everything she had to her family and after he had proposed to another. He was slime.

"She seems like a nice girl," he managed to choke out around the lump in his throat.

An Englisher guy would have shrugged off the compliment and went about his night, but John Paul stopped. "The best." His green eyes, only shades darker than his sister's, studied Zane.

"Yeah," was all he could manage. He dropped his gaze to his keyboard, even though he had nothing to type. Maybe he should send an e-mail to Monica. "What about—"

"That's enough for tonight. See ya."

Zane looked up. "You're leaving?"

"I told you, I'm in *rumspringa*."

"And that means you can go out at this time of night?" For

all intents and purposes it was early. In Chicago, things didn't get started until nine o'clock. But this wasn't Chicago.

"Yeah, city boy, I can." With a jaunty wave, John Paul closed the door behind him.

Zane stared at the door and pondered the riddle that was the Amish culture. They dressed alike—well, mostly—they kept to themselves, and seemed almost cultish in their support of each other and their community. Yet they let their children run wild for years, then expected them to come back and rejoin the fold. He shook his head at it all and made a mental note to find out how many of the Amish teenagers found their way back to their church and how many of them headed for something more.

His computer chimed, bringing him out of his thoughts. He had a message from Monica. She was online now, and he could easily engage her in a chat. Instead he opened his e-mail and read the words of encouragement and well wishes she'd sent. "I hope you got there safe . . . let me know how things are going . . . don't forget me . . . miss you already . . . love you, Monica."

No mention of the ring. Or accepting his proposal. But it was only a matter of time.

He hit *Reply* and started composing his e-mail. "Got here safe. Sorry I didn't call. Busy night trying to settle in. This is going to be quite an adventure."

As he typed the words, the angelic face of Katie Rose Fisher floated into view.

※◎ ◎※

Ruth washed her face in the bathroom sink, then padded her way to the bedroom she shared with Abram. How many years had it been? Thirty-six if she counted the first year they were married. They had adopted the traditional way and spent the first year of their marriage traveling from one family member's house to another until they moved back in with her *elders.*

Thirty-six years together and never had she felt this self-conscious around her husband. It was wrong, she knew, and everyday she asked God for guidance and deliverance from her prideful thoughts. She had suffered through the surgery, accepted that her body was forever altered. She had accepted it as much as a person possibly could. But each day she was more and more aware that her bones practically showed through her skin, skin that was pale and waxy, as her hair fell out in huge clumps.

"Time for bed," Abram said, standing on the opposite side from the door.

"*Jah,*" she said, touching her bonnet only briefly. Not too long ago this was the time of night when she would brush her hair, running her fingers through it to keep it healthy and whole. But after this last treatment, she barely had any hair to speak of.

Lord, I did as You commanded. I'm fightin' this cancer, but I'm not able to fight these unholy thoughts. Help me, Dear Lord, to change these thoughts and accept this change without grief. Aemen.

She didn't want to feel this way, to be vain and proud, but how could she not lament her hair? The Bible said a woman's hair was her crowning glory. All the glory was to go to God, but she had no glory left.

She extinguished the lamp and pulled back the covers on her side of the bed. She slipped between the sheets and turned away.

"Ruth?"

She didn't answer, hoping he would just go to sleep. The medications had left her moody and tired, and she wanted nothing more than to be left in peace. Just what did the Lord want from her to fight this awful disease? Why didn't He just allow her to die with dignity?

Shame washed over her at the thought.

Abram touched her shoulder, his hand calloused and warm. "Ruthie?"

She choked back a sigh at the comfort his touch brought. She was weak and unworthy. Not quite whole and not quite healed. Undeserving.

"I'm tired, Abram." She pulled the covers upward, until he relented, retreating back to his side of the bed they shared. Then she silently cried herself to sleep.

———— ❧ ❧ ————

Zane felt a hand on his shoulder and a not-so-gentle nudge.

"Day's comin'. Get up. *Mach schnell.*"

"Huh? What?" He pried his eyes open, but had to blink to make sure he was seeing everything correctly. John Paul stood over him, a big grin on his face and not looking at all like he'd had less than—Zane checked his watch—five hours of sleep.

"*Guder mariye*, sleepy bones. The cows are a'waitin'."

Zane resisted the urge to throw the covers back over his head and pretend he wasn't home. He really thought they'd been joking when they said their day started before the sun. He wasn't a slacker, but at least he let the sun make an appearance before being forced out of bed.

"The cows are waiting on what?"

"Us." John Paul pulled the covers to the floor, and Zane pushed himself into a sitting position, still wiping the webs of sleep from his brain. He shouldn't have stayed up so late logging in the countless questions he had for the Fishers. Sometime around midnight he had powered down his computer, dry-swallowed a sleeping pill, and tried to let the day ease away. Considering the foggy state of his brain he should have probably only taken half the tablet, but how was he supposed to know that early meant *early?* Besides, he

couldn't rest without one. Between the nighttime pain and disturbing dreams of war, medication was his only solution for a restful
sleep. *Note to self: Go to bed at a decent hour tonight. Morning comes
before sunrise to the Amish.*

Zane staggered to his feet, still rubbing his eyes awake. "We
have a date with the cows?"

"Every mornin'. Gotta milk the cows, slop the hogs, feed the
chickens and the horses, the cows, goats—"

"How many animals do you have on this farm?"

"More'n enough. That's why you'll earn your keep while you're
here."

"Right." Zane pulled his suitcase from under the bed and
rummaged around for a clean pair of jeans and a T-shirt. Maybe a
jacket. Oklahoma wasn't nearly as chilly as Illinois, but there was a
definite nip in the air.

"Oh, and *Dat* said to wear these. He said if you were goin' to
live with the Amish, then you are goin' to look like the Amish."
John Paul pitched a bundle of clothes toward him. Only his quick
reflexes kept them from landing on the floor. "Be downstairs for
breakfast in five minutes." He winked and then closed the door
behind him, making Zane wonder if he had been to bed at all. Ah,
the joys of seventeen.

With a shake of his head, Zane shook out the clothes and laid
them on top of the bed.

Was John Paul kidding? Or rather, Abram? Did they really
expect him to go around in these . . . pants? They weren't so bad
by themselves, but when added to the suspenders and the dress
shirt, then he was sure he'd look like an escapee from a theatrical
production of backward lame-oids.

Maybe he could plead *rumspringa* and wear his jeans like John
Paul? And then he remembered the hard line of Abram's mouth
from the night before. Doubtful, very doubtful.

Or maybe he should just buck up and wear the crazy black pants with the flap in the front and rows of buttons across. He'd promised to come here and live like the Amish, work with them side by side, and get to know what it was like to be part of their community. He sighed once again at the crazy outfit. He'd worn worse. It was only for three months, he told himself again.

Then a foreign correspondent's mantra came to mind: *When in Rome . . .*

Zane quickly dressed, looking down at himself in horrific amazement.

He felt ridiculous. Who dressed like this these days? Okay, stupid question. The Amish dressed like this, but for the life of him he couldn't figure out why.

Zane had never considered himself tall. He was almost six foot, but he was apparently longer legged than the pants' previous owner, and two inches of white sock glared in between the hem and the laces of his black work boots.

Like anyone was going to see him. He donned the dressy blue shirt, grabbed his camera, and made his way down the stairs.

The enticing smell of bacon hit him before he even entered the room. It was barely five a.m. and the house bustled. Ruth stood at the stove, flipping the irresistible strips, a black bonnet covering her head again this morning. Annie hovered behind her. Zane couldn't tell if she was trying to help or flat-out take over. She reached toward the stove, and Ruth swatted her hand away.

Annie sighed. "You should sit."

"You should check the biscuits." Ruth might be engaged in the battle of her life, but she still had some spunk. Dark circles underlined her tired, puffy eyes, but her wan smile served as a testament of her courage.

Zane had liked her immediately. Almost as much as he liked coffee. He looked around, realizing there wouldn't be an automatic drip machine waiting on the counter, and focused instead on the stove. Ah-ha. An old-fashioned enameled coffeepot sat in plain sight, a puff of steam rising up and competing with the bacon for the most tantalizing smell of the morning.

"*Ach*, milk time." John Paul slapped a round brimmed black hat on Zane's head and grabbed him by the arm.

"But coffee—" Zane protested as he was dragged toward the back door of the house, so close to the beloved coffee, but too far away for a snatch and grab.

"Amish cows don't wait for *Englisch* habits." John Paul laughed, then frowned at the camera Zane held. "And you won't be needin' that." He plucked the Nikon from Zane's fingers and deposited it on the big wooden table.

Zane caught one last glimpse of the coffeepot before he was forced out the door.

A fine sprinkle of dew covered the grass. Stars twinkled above them, but already the sky had lightened to a deep shade of purple as morning approached. Zane had seen the sun rise from points all over the globe, but there was something unique about this cool, misty morning. He couldn't say what it was, just a specialness lingering in the air.

Maybe because it reminded him of his childhood. He was old enough when his parents died to remember their faces, but not many other details. Few photographs were left behind to jog his memory. He did know he was a perfect genetic combination of Thalia and Robert Carson. He'd gotten his fair coloring from his mother. She could sit on her long blonde braid, and her blue eyes sparkled when she laughed. She hadn't been overly maternal, but he always felt loved. His father had a thick beard he wore year round in the cool temps of the Cascade Mountains. His hair had been dark, his eyes deep brown, a definite trait they shared. His father had a booming laugh which he used often, content as he was to live off the land and not compromise his integrity by "working for the man." Or at least, that's what his uncle said when he came to get Zane after the fire.

He shook away those thoughts before they turned down a path he didn't want to walk today and instead focused on the way to the barn.

"You ever milk a cow, city boy?"

"No, but I've milked a goat." *How different could it be?*

John Paul stopped in his tracks, and for the first time since Zane had arrived he felt like he had the jump. "For sure?"

"I'm more than just a pretty face."

John Paul laughed and slapped Zane on the back. "You'll do, city boy, you'll do."

"So what do you think of the *Englischer*?"

Katie Rose shrugged at her niece's question, then nodded toward the mound of dough rising on the butcher block countertop. "That needs punchin' down."

Mary Elizabeth popped the last bite of cookie into her mouth and wiped her hands on the damp dish towel. "He's cute, don't you think?"

Cute wasn't the word that Katie Rose would have used to describe Zane Carson. He was . . . disturbing. Those knowing brown eyes, deep and bottomless, seemed to search her soul. He had taken her hand and stared at her, not lettin' her go when decorum demanded. And that was disturbing.

Katie Rose shrugged. "I guess. If'n you like *Englischers*." She couldn't say that she did. Not that she disliked them, but they were outsiders not prone to the traditions of the Plain people. And men in general, well, she had accepted the plan God had for her.

When Samuel Beachy had left to discover the ways of the *Englisch* world, she had been devastated. She had loved him so very much. It wasn't always the way of the Amish to love before marriage, but they had been truly blessed. Then Samuel had come to her one night and confessed that he wasn't ready to join the church, that there was a great big world outside their little community. The time they were allowed to experience it just wasn't enough to see everything that he wanted to see. He left the next morning before anyone was awake, leaving a note for his father. The bishop had been crushed that his eldest son had left, but Katie Rose hid her mourning behind a smile. After a few years, the smile became genuine instead of forced, no longer a place to hide, but her makeup as a person, as a Christian.

Without Samuel there, Katie Rose joined the church and took over teaching the children in the community. That was where she belonged. In time she knew that this was God's plan for her. Teach the children and raise little Samuel for Gabe. She was happy with her life. It was fulfilling. She didn't ask for more, to do so would be ungrateful. She had plenty to fill her prayers—her mother's health, peace for Gideon, knowledge for Annie, safety for John Paul. More important prayers than her personal wants.

"I thought he was really handsome."

Katie Rose did too, but no way would she admit to that. "When did you start carin' about such things, Mary Elizabeth?"

Her niece blushed. "I am almost sixteen."

"You just turned fifteen."

"A year, then. Won't be long before I can attend a singin'."

Katie Rose shook her head. "You'd better not let your father hear you talk like that."

"Isn't that what we all long for? To be old enough to start to enjoy the world? Maybe take a carriage ride with a boy, drive in a car—"

"You know there's more to life and courtin' than that. It's a special time to pick a life partner. Someone special you can share your life with, raise a family, carry out God's work."

"I know it's just . . ."

Katie Rose stopped kneading the dough and gave her full attention to her *nichte.* "It's just what?"

"Nothin'," she mumbled.

Katie Rose let the subject drop and instead gathered up the plastic bowl of bread dough. "Help me get these into the buggy. It's time to go to *Grossmammi's* house and make pickles."

"That handsome *Englischer* will be there, too."

It was the one thing Katie Rose hadn't been able to get out of her mind all morning long.

Zane pulled off his hat and wiped his sleeve across his forehead. Oklahoma was definitely warmer than Chicago this time of year. Or maybe it was all the physical work. Walking behind a plow pulled by two sturdy horses was no joke. Evidently the part about the Amish not using tractors in the field was as valid as their aversion to electricity. Zane's arms shook from the effort of holding the reins to guide the beasts, his shoulder ached, his legs were stiff and tired. Surely they were about to stop for a break. Snack . . . lunch . . . anything to get him out of the sun for awhile with a cool drink of water to wet his throat. But he wasn't about to ask when they were stopping. After all of John Paul's ribbing about him being a city boy, Zane was determined to hold his own among the men.

Gabriel and his oldest sons had arrived shortly after breakfast, followed closely by Gideon. Before the sky was even light, they had set out to the fields. Only Abram had not joined them. John Paul explained that he had a meeting in town with a man selling seeds for a new blend of wheat. That's what they were planting. Winter wheat he called it, which explained the crazy planting schedule. Despite the hard work everyone had put in that morning, no one else looked ready to drop.

Zane plopped the hat back on his head, took a deep breath, and forced his feet to make one more step. Then another. He had prided himself on being strong. He had trained long and hard, toning his body for the hardships of his job. He went into countries sometimes with nothing more than the clothes on his back and what he could carry in a knapsack. That required strength of character—mind, body, and soul. In between jobs, he worked out tirelessly in the gym, lifting weights, running on the treadmill, even hitting the hiking trails in order to keep himself strong, his stamina high. But since the accident, he'd let himself slip, fighting the physical therapy, allowing himself to sit too long on the couch and wish for an assignment, a future. And look where it had gotten him: Amish country, sweating like a pig and wondering where the strength for the next step would come from.

"Ho, now!"

He turned as Abram came striding toward the fields. In all of Zane's efforts to remain upright, he didn't hear the buggy turn down the drive and the patriarch of the Fisher household return.

Zane clicked the horses to a standstill, grateful for the excuse to rest, if only for a moment.

Abram stopped to talk to John Paul first, then he motioned for his other sons to join them. Zane stayed where he was, not wanting to intrude on the family moment. Could it be that Abram had other news to share with them than just information on the seeds? Maybe something to do with their mother's condition? Very possible, he thought, as he watched John Paul's head droop. The other men stared at the soil beneath their feet as their father continued. Then as a group they approached Zane.

"Zane Carson," Abram said.

Zane hid his smile at the title. That was one thing he had picked up in the short time he'd been with the Amish. They liked to use full names. What was it John Paul said about their names? That they used a lot of them over and over until it got so confusing that they used nicknames to differentiate? He'd lay money down that there wasn't another Zane in all of the district.

"Zane Carson, it seems my boys have not forgotten their sense of humor, but this time it's been aimed at you."

A smile flashed across Gideon's face before the man successfully hid it. "We're sorry," he said.

"It was all in fun," the stern-faced Gabriel added.

Abram braced his hands on his hips. "Fun for who?" The brim of his hat shaded his eyes, but his posture was unmistakable.

John Paul stepped forward. "Don't get mad at them. It was all my idea."

Abram's expression didn't soften. He looked as stern as ever. "You treat our guest with the respect that he deserves. I'll not have him goin' 'round tell tales about unfair treatment in my household."

John Paul's shoulders slumped under the weight of his father's scowl. "It wasn't supposed to be for long. It's just once we started our own plowin' we plumb forgot that we'd—"

"Given him your *grossdaadi's* plow?" Abram shook his head in apparent disbelief. "It's a wonder Zane Carson still has arms for hangin' at his sides workin' with that old thing."

That's when Zane noticed that the plows pulled by the other men were bigger than the one he'd been behind all morning. A lot bigger. And newer.

"Now say what you've come to say."

Each man in turn shook Zane's hand and apologized for the part they'd played in the joke. Zane was uncomfortable accepting their words; it was all good-natured ribbing. He supposed he had it coming. He had invaded their world, and they wanted him to know that he didn't belong. Zane had been through worse. Much worse. For now he'd accept their apologies and would bide his time for the right moment to return the favor.

"Now, Zane Carson, go on up to the house. John Paul here will finish this field with the plow he expected you to use while you drink lemonade with the womenfolk. These boys'll finish the plowin'. Tomorrow, we plant."

Zane thought about protesting, but something in the set of Abram's jaw kept the words at bay. He nodded once toward the four men, then started for the house, a cold drink of something wet filling his thoughts.

The sun beat down on him as he made his way across the freshly turned earth. Zane felt a sense of accomplishment as he stepped over the soil that he had readied with nothing more than steel and the pull of horses. As a child at the cooperative, he'd been called to hoe the garden, pick small vegetables and fruits, like cucumbers and strawberries, and of course, milk the goats, but he'd been too young to realize how satisfying a day's hard work could be. He'd been too interested in getting to the end of the chore so that he could go fishing or swimming, two of his favorite pastimes as a child.

Funny, but he hadn't thought about those days in a long, long time. Maybe because so many of his formative years had been lived in Chicago with his uncle. And yet he'd thought about those first years in Oregon with every other breath since he'd arrived in Oklahoma's Amish country.

With each step fueled by the need to sit, rest, and drink something cool, Zane crossed the bustling yard and bounded onto the porch. As he opened the door, he was immediately assaulted by the smell of vinegar. Zane pulled off his hat as he had seen the other men do, blinked a couple of times for his eyes to adjust to the dim interior of the rambling farmhouse, and resisted the urge to cover his nose. The stench burned his sinuses with each breath, yet he couldn't imagine that he smelled much better.

He'd expected to step into a quiet kitchen, fan lazily turning, refrigerator humming, lemonade waiting for him to come and drink it. A beautiful fantasy really, most likely fueled by his writer's imagination and sunstroke. He had never really wondered how the fan would turn without electricity, or how Amish kept perishables cold. As for the pitcher of lemonade? Purely wishful thinking.

What he did find was half the women in the county bustling around like crazed cooks while Gideon's Annie barked orders like a drill sergeant.

Yet only one woman captured his attention. Katie Rose stood in the middle of the chaos, as angelic as last night, as peaceful as a spring breeze. She seemed the epitome of the Amish: serene, composed, and godly. He'd never had a thought like that before about a woman, and it surprised him. She exuded some sort of quality that had him wondering about a higher power. Or was it just the belief in such a being that could make the difference? He shook the thought away. He'd never been one to focus on the supernatural. Katie Rose's look of serenity came from clean living and lack of cosmetics. That was all.

He cleared his throat, hoping to gain someone's attention.

But not that of the entire room.

All eyes turned toward him, and whatever the ladies had been doing, forgotten, if only momentarily.

"I'd like to get something to drink, please." This would have been so much easier if the kitchen had been empty, even if the lemonade hadn't been waiting on the table for him. As it was, he was reliant on the women before him since they filled up every available space, leaving him no room to maneuver.

Mary Elizabeth nudged Katie Rose in the ribs and nodded in his direction. "*Aenti*, would you get our guest a drink?"

Katie Rose turned toward the rectangular box in one corner of the kitchen, her expression indifferent.

Zane shifted from one foot to the other, ignoring the strange looks he received as one by one the women returned to their duties.

He wasn't entirely sure why Katie Rose was the one chosen to get him a glass of lemonade. It wasn't her home, and he certainly wasn't Mary Elizabeth's guest since she lived with Gabriel still.

He watched Katie Rose with hooded eyes as she poured him a tall glass and brought it around the counter toward him.

"For you, Zane Carson," she said, handing him the drink, her eyes not meeting his.

"Thank you."

"*Danki*," she said quietly.

"Does that mean 'You're welcome'?"

"It means 'thank you.'" She turned toward the other ladies, and Zane had to fight the urge to reach out for her like Samuel and tag along behind her. *Ridiculous.*

He looked for a place to sit, preferring the company of the busy women to his own. It had nothing to do with the willowy blonde. Nothing at all. He pulled out a chair from the table and moved it to an out-of-the-way corner where he could watch without getting in the way. Four ginormous pots bubbled on the stove, rows upon rows of jars lined every available countertop space, and the table was covered with mounds of cucumbers.

"Pickles!" he said, sounding so much like the man who hollered "Eureka" that he almost laughed out loud.

Gideon's Annie turned to him, her orders put on hold momentarily. "Yes?"

"You're making pickles," he reiterated, only quieter this time.

Annie nodded. "That's right."

"A lot of pickles."

"They're for Ruth."

Zane glanced about the room. Ruth Fisher was nowhere in the fray of busy-bee workers. "I take it Ruth likes pickles."

"They're to help pay for Ruth's treatment."

He knew firsthand that was going to take a lot of pickles. He'd watched his uncle battle cancer and lose, his half-a-million-dollar life insurance policy barely enough to cover burial expenses after the doctor bills had been paid.

Mary Elizabeth nudged her aunt once again. "Go explain it to him."

"It was Annie's idea," Katie Rose protested.

"She's busy," Mary Elizabeth explained. "And you know more about the operation than anyone else. Maybe if he puts it in his magazine . . ."

Mary Elizabeth didn't need to say anything else. They all hoped that exposure in his story would spur pickle sales, so Katie Rose's love for her mother convinced her to give him her attention.

He tried not to appear too pleased. After all, it was only for a story.

Katie Rose came around the counter again, Samuel watching her from his perch on the corner stool. He had a piece of string in his hands, making familiar designs that Zane remembered from his own childhood. Some things didn't change.

She pulled out her own chair, placed it as far from him as she could get and still be heard over the din, and took a moment to rest. He knew that Amish women worked hard, but a pickle-making production as big as this one had to require a ton of energy.

Finally, Katie Rose spoke. "Well, I guess you could say that it all started when Annie came back to us."

"Came back?"

She nodded, but didn't elaborate, her gaze fixed on her lap.

"She put her car up for sale and gave the money to the community fund. That went a long way to helpin' pay for *mamm's* treatment. But it wasn't enough." She looked up and met his eyes, and he tried not to notice how the green of her dress reflected in her gaze. He didn't need to notice such things.

He cleared his throat. "And the pickles?"

Katie Rose shrugged. "It was Annie's idea. See, *grossmammi* makes the best pickles this side of anywhere. Annie decided that we could sell the pickles and raise money. So she started us a website. We take orders online, fill them from this kitchen, and ship them out all over the country."

"Wait. Online? As in the Internet?"

She nodded, and Zane sat mesmerized by the gentle sway of the strings on her little white cap.

"But I thought . . ." John Paul said there was no electricity, that meant no computers and, in turn, no Internet.

"We don't have a computer here at the house. Gideon takes Annie into town a couple of days a week. She uses the computer at the library. Bishop Beachy turns a blind eye because she hasn't joined the church yet. And he knows we need the money."

"So you ladies make pickles each week, send them out the following week, and start all over again after that?"

"*Jah.*"

"Those must be *some* pickles." He couldn't imagine. Weren't homemade pickles supposed to be . . . well, disgusting?

Katie Rose rose from her seat and wound her way through the other ladies to the refrigerator that sat in the corner of the kitchen. He made a mental note to ask how the crazy thing worked. It seemed that the Amish may not have electricity, but that didn't mean they were without creature comforts. Or maybe he should say "necessities." There was a difference, after all.

She handed him a jar and a fork and waited patiently while he sampled one of Noni's famous pickles.

One thing was certain: they did indeed warrant celebrity status. They were cool and crunchy, with just the right amount of everything—salt, dill, garlic, and some unknown ingredient that made them different from any pickle he'd ever tasted. They were . . . perfect. No wonder they had jars spread all over the house. What a great addition to his feature.

"Let me get my camera and—"

Katie Rose shook her head. "It is against the *Ordnung* to have photographs."

He studied her face to see if this was another chapter of the Fisher family's book of practical jokes, but she seemed serious enough. "For real?"

"I'm not sure what that means, but yes . . . I think. We do not allow our faces to be in photographs."

"What about "

"You may take a picture of the kitchen, but none of us. Maybe the barn and the animals. Anything more, and you'll have to speak to *Dat*."

"Okay." He'd love to get a picture of the kitchen, but what good was that without at least one cook? He made a mental note to talk to Abram about taking a picture of the women as they made their pickles. Maybe if he photographed them from a side angle or from behind . . .

He'd ask. After all there would be a few more pickle-making days before this assignment was through.

"So once the treatments are paid for, the pickles will stop?"

Katie Rose smiled like Mona Lisa. "We'll only make enough for our family and any others for trade."

"Trade?"

"Noni makes the best pickles, but Aaron's Rachel's Sarah makes the best applesauce. So we swap."

He popped the last bite into his mouth. Before he could ask her what that meant and who Aaron, Rachel, and Sarah were, she stood, and with a quick nod, excused herself.

Zane watched her go and tried not to be so pleased that, despite the fact she lived in another house, he would see her next week. He'd just have to make it a point to be closer to the house on pickle-making days.

3

"You know today was all in fun, *jah*?"

Zanc sat on his bed, typing in questions, notes, and anecdotes from the day as quickly as he could. The battery light on his computer blinked out a warning. He probably only had about fifteen minutes left before the thing died, and he'd have to resort to pen and paper to record his thoughts. It wasn't the worst thing that had ever happened to him, but he could type much faster than he could write in longhand. In cases like that, he often lost the idea before he had a chance to get it down on paper.

He glanced up, wasting precious electronic seconds as he turned his attention to John Paul. The teenager stood in the doorway of their shared room, a tentative smile on his face.

"Yeah, but you know what they say?"

John Paul shook his head.

"Payback's a . . ." he caught himself before actually saying the word. How many times had he used profanity and never given it a second thought? It was a harmless word, not meant to hurt or

degrade, but saying it in the house of a devout man like Abram
Fisher gave Zane pause. "Paybacks are not fun."

"What does that mean?"

Zane shrugged and shot his roomie a cryptic smile. "Whatever
you'd like it to mean."

John Paul squinted those mossy-green eyes, but didn't ask any
more questions.

Zane turned back to his dimming screen as the warning light
turned from flashing yellow to urgent red. He growled under his
breath. He had only seconds left.

"Somethin' wrong?"

"My battery is low. Well, about to die. And I can't charge it here."

"Maybe we could rig up somethin' with the propane generator."

Visions of his computer catching on fire and blowing up flitted
thorough Zane's mind. "That's okay. I can make do." Too bad he
hadn't brought his tablet with him.

"Or I can take you to town tomorrow. After we get the seeds
in the ground."

That's right. Tomorrow was planting day for the winter wheat.
"How long does it take to get to town in the buggy?" It was probably an hour at least.

John Paul shrugged and a mischievous grin spread across his
face. "Won't take any time at all in my car."

"You have a car? Wait. A real car?" Who knew the Amish
could be so much like the rest of the world?

"I told you, I am in *rumspringa*. I can own a car, go to the movies, all the things you *Englisch* do. And that means I can take you
to town tomorrow afternoon. I am sure Mr. Anderson will let you
charge your computer at the general store."

Zane hit *Save* just before the screen went black. It was nothing
but an oversized paperweight now. "Thanks, John Paul. That'd be
great."

Great was not the word that came to mind as Zane held on to the passenger door for dear life.

He should have run the other direction as soon as he laid eyes on the ancient Ford. But need and necessity won out, and he'd climbed into the passenger's seat.

That was his first mistake.

"Are you sure you don't want me to drive?" Zane asked for the third time in not so many miles as John Paul rounded a particularly sharp corner. Gravel flew in all directions as he spun into the grate at the edge of the road.

John Paul shot him a grin that said much more than words. "I only get to do this for four years. I'm not missin' any chance I got."

Four years with this guy behind the wheel? Lock up your children and dogs. No one was safe.

"What happens in four years?" Zane asked, focusing his attention on something other than flat-out fear for his life.

He immediately regretted the question as John Paul slid his gaze from the road to study him. "I'll join the church."

Zane pressed his feet against the floorboards as if sheer will alone could slow the car. "You might want to, uh—" He nodded back toward the road and the creature that had unfortunately ambled out of the woods and into the path of John Paul's car.

John Paul swerved toward the other side, sucking Zane off the door and throwing him against the driver's seat. He grinned as if to say, "What's a guy to do?"

"I thought *rumspringa* was a chance for you to decide whether or not you wanted to join the church," Zane asked, once John Paul straightened the car from its death spin.

"It is."

"But if you already know you're going to join, what's the point?"

"I would not miss this for the world."

Zane braced himself again as John Paul took a turn too fast, but at least now they were on blacktop. Or did that just make it worse?

Suddenly, a familiar white sign came into view, and Zane uttered a few words of gratitude to whoever was listening. They had made it to Clover Ridge without an accident. But the trip had taken longer than he thought it would. Or maybe the imminent threat of death and maiming made it seem that way.

John Paul probably took him the long way around out of sheer orneriness, but Zane wasn't convinced the crazy driving was anything other than that—a man who had no business behind the wheel. Four more years. Thankfully he'd be back in Chicago soon.

His Amish roommate pulled to a stop in front of the general store, a few slots down from a hitching post where two buggies were tied. The horses neither shied nor glanced in their direction, a testament to their training. Or maybe the horses were as crazy as John Paul.

Zane unfolded himself from the car, making a mental note to not challenge the powers that be by getting into the car with the crazed teenager again. He grabbed his laptop case and followed the laughing John Paul into Anderson's.

As he stepped into the cool interior of the store, Zane felt as if he'd slipped back in time. Only the hanging lightbulbs and the gently whirring fans were testament to the age of electricity. The planked floor beneath his feet had been swept clean and lightly polished to show off the beautiful oak grain. Merchandise climbed the sidewalls, but in the center of the store, wares were displayed on shelves no more than shoulder high. Across the back stood a candy counter straight out of the '40s with jars of sweets and a soda fountain lining the wall behind. A pretty young Asian girl sat at one end of the counter, flipping through a magazine, her face hidden by the dark curtain of her hair.

"*Oi*," John Paul said by way of greeting. He waved to a man in a white butcher's apron. "Coln Anderson, come meet our *Englisch* guest."

The proprietor wiped his palms on his apron then reached out a hand to shake with Zane. "You must be Zane Carson."

Zane nodded, a bit taken aback. Small community if news of his arrival had already gotten to town *and* included his name. "Nice store you've got here."

Coln smiled, nodding his thanks. "It's a joy and a blessing."

"Mr. Anderson, Zane Carson needs to charge his laptop. We were wonderin' if'n you would allow him to do that here."

"Of course, of course. Right this way." He led them to the back of the store and behind the candy counter.

Evidently this wasn't the first time the request had been made. Someone had set up a table next to the outlets. A cell phone and a Nintendo DS lay side by side, and Zane wondered if they were part of someone's *rumspringa* splurge. He thanked Coln for his generosity and plugged in his laptop and cell phone. "What do I owe you?" he asked, turning to face the man.

"Not a thing," Coln answered. "I'm just glad you came to help."

Zane wouldn't exactly call what he was doing "help," but many believed that his stories would bring business into the community. He made a mental note to provide some sort of thanks in his articles when a jar of candy caught his attention. Candy he hadn't seen in ages. "Are those . . . Astro Pops?"

If Coln was surprised by the question, he didn't show it. "Yes, they are."

"I used to get these when I was a kid." Wonderment and memories filled his voice. On the infrequent trips they made to town, his father would take him to the apothecary and get him an Astro Pop. Just the thought of them brought back memories of his dad, his childhood, and all the good they had shared before his parents died.

Without hesitation, he reached into the jar and pulled out a handful of the tri-colored suckers.

"Where to now?" John Paul asked as they walked back out into the fall sunshine.

Zane reached into the brown paper sack containing the Astro Pops and retrieved one. He offered the bag to John Paul, who shook his head. "*Danki.*"

That's when Zane realized that he was stranded in town with no way home except the deathtrap car and John Paul, NASCAR driver in training.

He unwrapped one of the candies. "How far is it to the school?"

The words popped out of his mouth before he had considered them. He was interested in seeing the one-room schoolhouse he'd heard about for the novelty of the visit. *Not* because of a certain jade-eyed teacher.

"It's a couple of miles that-a-way." John Paul pointed in the direction they had come from.

"It might be fun to see. For the feature," he added.

He popped the sucker into his mouth, hoping it would stem the flow of inerrant words. The Astro Pop tasted even better than he remembered—pure corn syrup with just a touch of flavoring. It was kind of like eating a candied apple without the apple. Zane smiled at the memories that something as simple as candy could evoke.

"Get in. I'll take you there."

It wasn't exactly what Zane had in mind, but there was no way around it. It would have made more sense to Zane if John Paul had poked around like a grandma driving as slow as the clomp of horses

44444444444444444

pulling a shiny black buggy. Next time, he thought, he'd beg a ride in the old-fashioned way. For research's sake.

Plan in mind, Zane held on tight as John Paul sped away from town.

The one-room schoolhouse was beyond picturesque. Painted antique red, it sat on a hill in a little field, surrounded by minimal playground equipment and a large oak tree complete with tire swing. It was nothing like he'd ever seen and so different from what he had imagined. He'd expected . . . well, a school—bustling hallways, multiple teachers, cafeteria. School. Instead, he felt like he'd stepped onto the set of *Little House on the Prairie*. The feeling intensified as he watched the children in their old-timey Amish clothing file out the door. The only thing missing were the lunch pails of yesteryear. These kids carried regular insulated lunch boxes like the rest of American schoolgoers. Strange how differences and similarities melded together.

"Looks like we got here just in time."

Katie Rose stood on the school porch handing papers to the children as they headed out for the day. "And don't forget, sixth grade, you have a readin' test on Monday."

One tall boy with too-short pants waved in recognition to her words. "*Jah*, Katie Rose. I'll study hard."

The fact that only one child responded to her warning made Zane wonder if there was only one sixth-grader in the crowd of milling children. He made a mental note to find out more about the tiny school.

"*Goedemiddag, shveshtah*," John Paul called out what Zane surmised to be a greeting.

"*Goedemiddag, bruder*," Katie Rose returned. She kept her gaze firmly locked on the children as they disappeared down the road.

Zane thought he recognized a few of Gabriel Fisher's boys in the mix, but he didn't stop them. He had learned a thing or two about Amish life since he had been in Oklahoma, and the boys would have a chore list as long as their arm to complete after they got home. He surely didn't want to slow them in their attempts to get everything done before they enjoyed whatever after-school fun activities Amish children liked to indulge in. He made a mental note to find out what those activities included. It would make a great side note to his feature.

"*Wie geht?*" John Paul called.

"*Gut, gut,*" his sister answered.

"English?" Zane protested lightly around his Astro Pop. He hated the fact that Katie Rose still wouldn't look at him. What had he ever done to her? Nothing. He was English and different from her, but that didn't mean they couldn't have a working friendship while he was here. It was going to be a long three months if she kept this up.

"I asked her how everythin' was, and she replied—"

"Good. That one I know."

John Paul nodded his head, as if impressed with Zane's efforts.

They crossed the yard under the oak tree, and Zane experienced another blast of nostalgia. Swinging from a rope and splashing down into an icy cold, clear-as-air creek. He must have been about eight. His stomach dropped at the mere thought of letting go of the rope and flying through the air. Where had the time gone? He hadn't done anything like that in years. Something he needed to correct and fast. Perhaps on this trip. What better place to get his feet wet than rural Oklahoma?

Katie Rose stood on the schoolhouse steps as her brother and the *Englischer* approached. As usual, Samuel had his hand fisted around the folds of her skirt as they stood outside in the beautiful Indian summer sunshine.

"Zane Carson wanted to see the school," John Paul explained.

"I was just leavin' for the day. But you can come in if you like." Only politeness forced the words from her lips. She wasn't in a hurry. There was nothing more urgent waiting for her at home than starting supper. But she didn't want to be around the *Englischer* any more than necessary. And a tour of the empty schoolhouse was *not* necessary.

"That's okay," Zane Carson said. "Maybe another day."

"*Jah.*" Secretly she hoped that day wouldn't come. The thought made her feel rude and ungrateful. This man had come to help bring people to Clover Ridge, visitors that would spur their economy and indirectly fuel the coffers that paid for her mother's cancer treatment. She should be more thankful for the blessing. But when she looked into those brown eyes she had to fight the urge not to run as fast as she could in the other direction.

A tug pulled her skirt. She looked down into Samuel's green eyes. "Wose," he said using his abbreviated version of her name. "The boys." He pointed to where his brothers walked across the playground toward home.

"You want to go with them?"

He nodded.

"*Jah*, then," she said. "*Geh.*" She resisted the urge to pat him on the head or kiss his cheek like she wanted to. He would always be like a baby to her, sweet and innocent, but more than anything he wanted to grow up confident and capable like his *bruders*.

She watched him until he caught up with the others, love filling her heart. What a blessing he was despite the tragedy of his birth. Another of God's lessons she had yet to understand.

John Paul tugged on the *Englischer's* arm. "Come on, then."

She thought she saw fear flash in Zane Carson's eyes before he turned his full attention back to her.

He turned his gaze on her, his brown eyes were warm and inviting. "How are you getting home, Katie Rose?"

She hated the heat in his stare, so she turned away and instead watched after the *kinder* as they ambled down the road. "I usually walk with the children," she muttered, hating the lack of conviction in her tone. Why did this stranger affect her so?

"Oh, yeah?"

"I . . . I should be goin'." She pulled the schoolhouse door shut, realizing that she had left her lunch box on her desk. Nothing inside couldn't wait until tomorrow, and she had to get away from Zane Carson as soon as she could. Immediately. Sooner.

"How far is it? Home, I mean. To Gabriel's house."

"Not far." She hoped the *I'll be fine. I do this everyday. Please don't invite yourself along* was evident in her tone. It would have been downright ill-mannered to say the words. Especially since this man had come to help and at the invitation of her *elders*. But she needed to breathe air which he didn't share. She tripped down the stairs and headed toward home.

"I'll walk with you."

"That is not necessary." She trained her eyes on the road ahead, not trusting herself to look at him. With his shingled haircut and too-short barn-door pants she should have found him anything but intriguing. And yet she did. "My *bruder* will be expectin' you to ride with him."

"Are you serious? Your *bruder* has got to be the worst driver I've ever had the misfortune to meet. I'm more than happy to have the excuse not to get in the car with him behind the wheel."

"*Ach!*" John Paul protested. "I'm a fine driver."

"Right," Zane Carson replied, stretching out the word until it was as long as a country lane. "If it's all the same to you . . ."

John Paul shrugged. "Beat yourself out."

Her *bruder* had taken his *rumspringa* a bit too seriously. He had started watching *Englisch* movies and trying to talk like those actors he saw there.

"Knock yourself out," Zane Carson corrected.

"Right." John Paul jingled his keys and slid into his crazy *Englisch* automobile.

Katie Rose resisted the urge to shake her head and instead reminded herself to say an extra prayer for him tonight. If his driving was indeed as bad as Zane Carson reported, then he would need the Lord watching over him for sure and for certain.

"So can I walk with you?"

"If'n you wish." She turned to make her way behind the *kinder*. What else could she say? The man had no other means to get home, and she was positive he couldn't manage the feat by himself. He had only been there three days.

He held out a small brown paper sack toward her. "Would you like an Astro Pop?"

She shook her head. "*Danki*. No."

"You're not on one of those low-carb diets, are you?"

She had no idea what he was talking about, so she just shook her head and made her steps a bit faster. She was determined to keep her students in sight until the turn-off toward home.

Zane Carson lengthened his strides to match hers, and Katie Rose knew she'd be out-walked in no time. "Why do I get the feeling you don't like me very much?"

"That's bunk, Zane Carson. I have no reason to have feelings for you one way or the other." But she did. As much as she hated to admit it, she did.

"Bunk?"

"Nonsense. Poppycock. Drivel."

He laughed. "I know what it *means*, I just didn't know anyone used that word any more."

His laugh stopped Katie Rose in her tracks. "Are you callin' me backward?"

He shrunk back, and she immediately regretted her harsh words. "Of course not. It's just not every day a person hears the word *bunk* used in that way. That's all."

Heat crept up her neck and flooded her face. It might have been a lie, but if asked, she could blame it on the wind, the sun, the exertion of trying to keep ahead of such a tall man. In truth, it was embarrassment that reddened her cheeks. Surely the Lord would allow her one little lie. She said a silent prayer for even thinking such a thing and kept on walking.

"Why would I think you're backward?"

She shrugged. "It's a common thought among the *Englisch* world." Katie Rose chanced a look at him through her lowered lashes, surprised to see color filling his handsome face as well. "Tell the truth, Zane Carson, did you not think us backward when you came here?" She studied his carefully schooled, if not a little flushed, features and tried not to drown in the rich chocolate of his eyes.

"I didn't know what to expect. I'd never really given the Amish much thought. Sorry." He grinned to take the sting from his words. "I'm a war correspondent. I'm normally in some third world country where *backward* has an entirely different meaning."

"Why aren't you there now?" She owed the Good Lord many prayers of forgiveness tonight.

He shrugged. "My editor thought I needed a change."

Katie Rose opened her mouth to ask him what it had been like to be off in the world, but she stopped herself. It didn't matter how Zane Carson lived. It wouldn't change her past. She wouldn't be able to find the reason that Samuel Beachy had left her just months before they announced to their families their plans to marry. He'd told her there had to be something more out there. Something he was missing. She just couldn't understand what. And trying now wasn't about to change the course of events. The Lord had different plans in mind for her, namely, teaching the children and serving Him and their district. That was what her life consisted of now. And she was happy with it that way. Very happy.

"Do you think I could come by tomorrow and see the school? I'd love to do a special story—"

Katie Rose started shaking her head before he even finished. "No."

"Why not?

"Because tomorrow is Saturday." She hid her smile, feeling wickedly superior that she had verbally one-upped the fancy writer from Chicago. Just one more item to add to her prayers tonight.

"Monday, then?"

"I do not think that is a good idea, Zane Carson."

"I'm not going to hurt them or corrupt them. Everybody out there wants to know what goes on here."

She stumbled then, and would have fallen headlong onto the asphalt road had he not snatched her upright. Her arm burned where the warmth from his fingers soaked through the thin cotton of her sleeve. Emotions coursed through her: indignation, embarrassment, anger, and something else she didn't want to name.

She pulled away from him, feeling an even-deeper red flood her cheeks. She straightened her dress and raised herself to her above-average height. "We are not animals to be put on display. If the world wants to know about us they can just wonder. It is no concern of anyone's how we choose to live."

Zane Carson blinked, then stared at her as if she had suddenly grown horns on her head. She resisted the urge to smooth a hand over her *kapp* to make sure all was in place.

"Is that what this is about? You think I'm here to exploit you?"

She crossed her arms in front of herself and pressed her lips together. It was one thing to harbor wicked thoughts and quite another to admit them . . . out loud . . . to an outsider.

"That's not my intent. I . . ." He stumbled over his thoughts. "I was invited here to do a job. Write a series of articles about life in a small Amish community. And that's what's I plan to do. I'm not here to make anyone look bad, or stupid, or anything."

He sounded so sincere, Katie Rose wanted to let her resolve crumble right there on the spot and tell him anything and everything he wanted to know. But she couldn't. She wouldn't. Instead, she picked up her steps again, leaving him to follow behind.

"This is where I turn," she said, indicating the red dirt drive that led to her brother's house. A white fence lined the property, and the sight had never been more welcome. Ahead she could still make out the boys, Samuel's bright red head among them as they made their way home.

She nodded down the road they'd been traveling. "About half a mile, you'll reach my *elders' haus. Gut dawk* to you, Zane Carson." She turned down the drive and didn't look back.

Zane watched her walk down the road, behind the children. As far as he knew he hadn't done a thing to warrant her antagonism toward him. But whenever he was around she acted like he was the Big Bad Wolf who had come to eat her up.

Maybe she was naturally suspicious, maybe she had been hurt by a man before, or maybe she didn't trust him because he was an outsider. He remembered the sisterly affection he'd witnessed between Katie Rose and Annie. She didn't have any trouble with *that* Englisher.

Maybe she just doesn't like you, Carson.

He should tell her that he had a fiancée waiting at home. Almost fiancée, he corrected himself. Maybe if she knew he was practically engaged to another she would trust him a little more— not stare at him like he was an ax murderer in Amish clothing.

He hadn't realized that the oldest and the father were neighbors. Yet out in the country like this, he knew "neighbor" was a loose term.

He hooked his thumbs through his suspenders and glanced down at his feet. He was going to have to do something about these pants. And while he was at it, get that suspicious light of mistrust out of Katie Rose's green eyes. How was he supposed to get a good look at the school if she wouldn't let him within three feet of her?

That was the only reason he cared. Truly, the only reason.

He smiled to himself and continued on his way to the Fishers'.

The chickens were fed, the cows milked, and he had helped Annie and Ruth pick the last of the tomatoes from the garden. Now it was time to put his plan to befriend Katie Rose Fisher into place.

Zane dusted off the knees of his ugly Amish pants and knocked on the door. He was surprised no one had already come out onto the porch, considering the ruckus the dogs made, barking at him as if he were a rabid vacuum cleaner salesman.

Yet nothing stirred inside the rambling, white house. There were no curtains on the windows, something he was beginning to think was part of the Amish culture, so he peeked through the glass. He made a mental note to ask about window coverings at the next opportunity. The inside looked quiet and dark. Dark he could attribute to the lack of electricity, but quiet? With six kids? That could only mean one thing—no one was home.

So much for his brilliant plan, but it wasn't like he could call first. Now he'd have to get John Paul to take him into town to pick up his computer and his cell phone from the charging station at the general store.

He sighed and made his way back down the steps. Oh well, the walk had been good for him. The fresh air, too. In fact, there was a lot about this trip that had been good for him. In the barely three days that he had been here, his shoulder had started to limber up. Evidently the Amish Farm Workout was proving to be better than organized, paramilitary physical therapy.

Zane rolled his shoulder to test the range and was pleased with the results. By the end of his three months in Oklahoma he'd be more than ready for whatever awaited him in Mexico.

4

Somehow—maybe by the grace of a higher power—he'd made it into town and back in the front seat of John Paul's rattletrap of a Ford.

Zane dropped his laptop bag on the bed and fished his phone out of his pocket. He was long overdue to call Monica. She'd probably think he'd forgotten all about her. Knowing her, she'd expect more attention during this trip since he was barely six hundred miles away, but assignment meant work, no matter the distance. He had to keep focused on the task at hand and not get distracted. The sooner he finished here, the sooner he'd be on his way across the border. After the wedding, of course.

He punched up his phone book, and scrolled through the contacts until he found her name.

She answered on the second ring. "Hi, darling."

He smiled at the sound of her cultured tones, hating that he compared them to the gentle German-country twang of Katie Rose. And Ruth and Mary Elizabeth. Annie was the only one who didn't sound like a cross between a good-natured hillbilly and a German scientist.

"Hi, yourself."

"I was hoping you'd call today."

"Sorry, it's been busy here, and there's no electricity at the house."

"Are you serious?"

"Very."

"I thought that was like an urban legend. So they really live that way, huh?"

"And of course without electricity, my laptop and phone died. We had to take them into town to charge. So I'll be incommunicado at least every other day, depending on the work schedule."

"I understand." This was one of the things he appreciated most about her.

"It could be worse," he added.

"Who's 'we'?" she asked. "You said 'we' had to take it into town."

"Oh, me and John Paul, the youngest Fisher. He has a car so he drove me into town." He purposefully left out the details of the horrific ride into Clover Ridge, probably because he felt so guilty over his walk home with Katie Rose. Or maybe because he sought her out this morning. He shook away the thought. He'd done nothing wrong. Not really.

"Wait. They don't have electricity, but they do have cars?"

"No," Zane scrambled for the words to describe Amish customs. "It's not that simple."

"But you said—"

"I know what I said, but it's too complicated to go into right now. I need to keep the charge on my phone as long as possible."

"That complicated?"

"You know it."

"All right, then. I need to go anyway. I have a spa appointment at four."

"Sounds wonderful," he said, giving Monica the answer she expected. He'd never been to a spa in his life.

"I love you," she said, her voice earnest, even as he imagined her grabbing her designer purse before heading out for an afternoon of pampering.

"Me, too," he said. The words didn't slip out like they normally did.

Monica seemed not to notice, blowing him a kiss before hanging up.

In silence, Zane stared at the wallpaper of his computer screen. After a moment he pocketed his phone and sighed.

He was tired. That was all. He had stayed up a little too late last night logging questions and answers about the Amish and writing down the anecdotes from the day. He was sure Jo would be pleased. Except for the part about no pictures. But he'd figure out a way around that. A twinge of something—*remorse maybe?*—pinged him at the thought.

Again, it could have been the fatigue. After the troubles from the day before, he had opted not to take something to help him sleep, and that had meant dreams. It was unfair to true sufferers of post-traumatic stress syndrome to call them nightmares or terrors. They were disturbing. Dreams so real he could smell the war surrounding him, feel the hot desert air on his face, the grit in his mouth and eyes. There wasn't anything overly horrific in these night visions he had, just work and war and death, same ol' same ol' of his job. But they didn't let him rest. It was beyond strange to him that when he was living it everyday, the dreams never came, but the minute he returned to the States, they returned. Haunting him at night. The people he couldn't save—the soldiers, children, innocent civilians.

Longing for a nap, he looked at the colorful quilt on his bed, and then checked his watch. He had about fifteen minutes before he would need to start the evening chores with John Paul. Fifteen glorious minutes of daytime sleep more restful than his efforts in the dark, but not nearly enough to make up for what he had missed.

He shook his head and hiked up his too-short pants. Tonight, he promised himself. Tonight he'd take a sleeping pill and go to bed early.

Sunday morning dawned bright and beautiful, another crisp day that Zane had learned would quickly turn into a warm afternoon. He caught Ruth in the hall of the ambling house reaching a hand up to her bonnet, ensuring it was in place.

"*Guder mariye*, Zane Carson," she said with a wan smile.

Zane had gotten used to everyone calling him by his first and last name, but the sound still brought a smile to his lips. "And to you too, Ruth Fisher."

"There is somethin' I need to speak to you about."

He nodded. "All right." He waited for her to begin, but she just smiled.

"Let's go to the kitchen, we will talk this out over a piece of pie."

If pie was involved, surely the topic couldn't be too serious. Zane nodded and followed her down the stairs.

He got out plates and cups for coffee as she cut and served the pie. Together they carried their early morning after-breakfast snack to the table.

Amish pie was wonderful if not a little odd, the flaky crust as thick as cardboard. John Paul had told him it was for convenience, to allow them to eat the pie without plates and forks as they carried out certain chores.

"Today is a church day, Zane Carson."

It was the first he had thought about attending church since his arrival. They read from the Bible every night, prayed before and after every meal, and stopped to pray silently several times during the day. Zane had even caught John Paul praying in the middle of the afternoon before milking the cows. Church seemed . . . redundant.

"We invited you here to learn our ways, but there are some things the Amish like to reserve for themselves. Church is at the top of that list."

"I understand." He couldn't tell her that Jo didn't pay him enough to get him into the church building. He didn't want to offend her, or even worse, have her kick the heretic out of the house. So he just nodded.

"Today's service is at the bishop's *haus*. Afterwards, we'll eat and have fellowship, but we'll be home in time to milk the cows."

"Did you say the bishop's *house*?"

"*Jah*." She laughed a little, and Zane liked the sound. She needed to laugh more, though her eyes looked tired and worn. "We have church in the homes of our members. Week after next it will be our turn. Lots of work will have to be done to 'redd-up' the house for worship."

Zane made a mental promise to help in any way he could. Not because he cared about the Amish means of worship, but he did care about the well-being of the woman seated across from him. "Where's the service next week?"

"Next week isn't a church Sunday for our district. We'll be travelin' to Bishop Stoltzfus's service to worship with them."

"So you have church every other Sunday."

"Sort of. We have church on every one of the Lord's Days.

One Sunday in our district and the next we go a-vistin'. After each service we eat and talk. Then that evenin' the host family holds a singin' for the teenagers."

"For the ones in *rumspringa* or the others?"

"You have been learnin' your *Deutsch*, Zane Carson." She patted him on the hand. "Best let John Paul tell you about the goin's-on at the singin' these days. It's a mite different than it was in my day."

With the gentle progress of the Amish, Zane sincerely doubted that. The conversation seemed to have taken a lot of Ruth's energy, but she pushed up from the table like a real trooper and took their plates to the sink. Before she could come back for their cups, Zane had them in hand.

"It is time to get ready for the service, Zane Carson. It was nice visitin' with you this mornin'."

"You too, Ruth."

He resisted the urge to follow her up the stairs and support her elbow as she navigated her way. He had a feeling Ruth wouldn't appreciate the help in the way it was intended. One thing was certain: Ruth Fisher was a fighter.

Katie Rose pulled the horses to a stop in front of the house and set the brake. "Whoa."

Zane stood on the porch, hammer in hand.

"Zane Carson!" Her mother called from beside her in the buggy. "Ho there, Zane."

She started to scramble down from the seat, but Katie Rose touched her arm to stay her. "You came home because you were tired. Don't go gettin' all riled up now." She hated the pinched look around her mother's mouth. She did look tired, but Katie Rose feared something else was bothering her *mudder*.

Halfway through the food service, her mother had started looking weary. It had taken nearly half an hour, but Katie Rose finally convinced her that no one would care if they returned home early. John Paul would stay for the singing, and Annie would want to go visiting with Gideon after they ate. Katie Rose asked Noni if she might be tired and ready to leave as well, but the old woman fanned herself, sitting in the shade drinking lemonade as she watched the children play. "I'll get some rest when I have my reward," was her reply. Once her father assured her that he could find his own way home, Katie Rose hopped in her *elder's* buggy and drove her mother home to rest.

But sometimes her mother was just so stubborn.

Katie Rose hopped down from the buggy, the springs and wheels squeaking as she hit the ground. "Zane Carson," she called, annoyed by how good his name sounded from her lips.

He shaded his eyes as he watched her come near. "I didn't expect you back so soon."

She glanced at the hammer in his hand. "It would appear so."

He smiled at her words, watching her with those brown eyes. She pressed one hand into her side. "It's the Lord's Day, Zane Carson. We only do what is required of us on the Lord's Day."

"I was just repairing this loose floorboard on the porch. Nothing more."

"If'n you want to fix it, you may do so tomorrow. Today is a day of rest." She dropped her voice so only he could hear. "Will you come and walk *Mamm* to the house? She's done too much today as well. I fear she might fall." She didn't add how fragile her mother was, how the weight loss and cancer drugs had made her bones and spirit brittle. Zane Carson was a smart man. He could see that for himself.

"Of course." He set the hammer down and dusted off his hands and knees.

"Ruth," he called. "Stay right where you are."

Katie Rose winced at the sternness in his tone. Maybe with all his fancy education Zane Carson wasn't as smart as she had given him credit for.

"You are a guest here, Zane Carson. You may not order me about like a new puppy."

"And I won't just as soon as you're not as weak as a newborn kitten." His sure strides carried him across the yard in half the time it would have taken her. In the blink of an eye he put his hands on her mother's waist and swung her to the ground.

Ruth frowned. "I am capable of liftin' myself down from a buggy."

"I'm sure you are, Ruth, but why expend the energy for something I can do for you when you need all the strength you have for healing?"

She was sure her *mamm* would harrumph and march stiff-legged toward the house, but there was something in Zane Carson's manner that seemed to calm her mother.

He offered *Mamm* his arm and linked them together before walking her toward the porch. When they got close, Katie Rose took her other elbow and together they escorted her into the house.

Katie Rose contemplated the man who'd come to visit. He was gruff and soft at the same time. He had a way with her mother, somehow making her see reason where no one else had, all the while giving her the space she needed to remain self-sufficient. Suddenly Katie Rose felt as if she had underestimated the fancy reporter from Chicago.

Or maybe she hadn't, and that was the problem.

It took some talking, but Zane finally persuaded Ruth to lie down for a nap. Only the threat that she'd be back in the hospital before sunset was enough to get her upstairs and in bed. Stubborn woman only did it so she could oversee supper that night.

She reminded him so very much of his own mother. Not in looks or temperament but in spirit. Thalia Carson had been that same kind of woman—sufficient, brave, positive. Bold in a womanly manner that made men do her bidding, then wonder what had happened to make them so readily comply.

He smiled to himself and made his way back downstairs. Katie Rose could see her safely in bed while he finished the porch.

The sun was bright when he pushed through the screen door. A beautiful day as he had ever seen. How long had it been since he'd enjoyed a Sunday afternoon? How long had it been since he'd enjoyed any afternoon? Maybe Monica was right. Maybe he did work too much. But he didn't know how else to be. Once he started a project he had to see it through to the end.

He retrieved the hammer and started back to work. Just a couple more good whacks and that should do it.

Katie Rose stormed out of the house, green eyes glaring. For the peace-loving Amish, she looked downright murderous. "I believe I mentioned that it is the Lord's Day."

"That you did." *Whack.*

"And the Amish don't work on the Lord's Day."

"I'm not Amish." *Whack.*

"But you're stayin' with us now. Tryin' on our lifestyle so you can write about it in your magazine." She plucked the hammer from his grasp mid-swing. "You'll do well to remember that."

It didn't matter anyway. He was finished, but something in him wasn't going to let the matter go easily. Zane straightened to his full height, once again dusting himself off before looking at her. He was considered tall by many, but the willowy woman challenging him was only a few inches shorter.

He crossed his arms and hid his smile. "Okay, if that's how you want to play this. How are you spending the afternoon, Katie Rose?"

"If you must know, I have papers to grade and a lesson plan for the third grade to get ready."

"And the reading test for the sixth graders?"

"*Jah*, that too."

"Well, missy, that sounds suspiciously like work."

She opened her mouth to speak, but closed it again instead. He tried not to be too pleased with himself for leaving her speechless.

"Tell me, what's allowed on Sundays?"

She took a deep breath, a thoughtful look on her face. Or was it annoyance?

"Milkin' the cows," she started. "Cookin' and cleanin' up afterward. Feedin' the animals. Readyin' for church service. Cleanin' up after that."

"What about a buggy ride?"

"*Jah*, I suppose a buggy ride would be allowed."

"Good. Then let's go." He took her arm, intent on steering her down the steps toward the Fishers' buggy still parked in front of the house.

She pulled back, as focused on not going down the porch steps as he was on drawing her down them. "Actually, I was just about to unhitch the wagon."

"Perfect timing, then."

She shook her head, the loose strings of her head covering waving with the motion. "The horses need to be watered and brushed down."

"If we give them a drink now, couldn't we brush them down after a slow and easy ride?"

She nodded, her brows knitted together.

Why was she so bent on not spending any time with him? Unless . . . he tilted his head, watching her. "Are you afraid of me?"

"Don't be silly." She turned her face away.

Her attitude could only mean one thing: she felt the same pull between them. But what good would it do either one of them to pursue such an attraction? In a couple of months he would head back to Chicago. He was getting married and going back on assignment—a *real* assignment. And she would be here, among her people, with her church and family.

He reached for her, guiding her gently along the porch. The chemistry they shared could pull them together, make them the best of friends. Even if that's all they would ever be.

At the bottom of the porch steps, he turned her to face him. "I don't want anything from you. You know that, right?"

She stared at the ground, not acknowledging his words one way or the other.

Zane hooked a finger under her chin and tilted her face up so he could see her eyes. "We can be friends, can't we?"

"Of course." Her voice was the barest whisper.

"And friends can go on walks and buggy rides." He still held her chin in his hand, her mouth at the perfect angle for kissing.

She nervously licked her lips as if she knew exactly what he was thinking. "I reckon."

He released her and took a step back lest he fall into the temptation of finding out if her lips tasted as sweet as they looked. Like pink cotton candy. It would be unfair—more than unfair—to take advantage of the moment. Even if she were an English girl, accustomed to such advances, he couldn't have kissed her. He was engaged—practically.

"Then let's go for a ride." He led the horses over to the water trough, wishing he had let the subject drop. After the moment that passed between them, he should have let her retreat into her corner and wait for another day, but something inside him wanted to spend time with her. More than he could understand. Even after the bristle and claws he'd gotten from her, he still wanted to be her friend.

She shook her head, smiling, the strings of her prayer cap dancing in the breeze. "Okay then, Zane Carson. We'll go for a buggy ride."

He smiled in spite of himself. "There's only one problem."

"*Jah?*"

"I can't drive the buggy."

Her smile was bright and infectious. "Come then, Zane Carson. I will show you how."

5

Fifteen minutes later, Zane was sitting in the driver's seat, behind the swaying rears of the horses.

"Just hold the reins loosely. The horses know what to do. If you pull too hard, you'll confuse them."

He loosened his hold, trying not to be so tense. "Like this?" He was sixteen again and getting his license for the first time.

"*Jah.*"

He chanced a quick peek at her sitting next to him. By the way her gaze flitted around, she seemed almost as nervous as he. Was that because of his lack of driving skills? Or due to their close encounter earlier?

He turned his eyes back to the road. Traveling by buggy was both good and bad. He enjoyed the gentle sway of the animals, the feel of the woman who sat so close to him, the breeze blowing through his hair, caressing his face. The afternoon held the slight chill of fall, but the bright sun warmed in retaliation.

Thankfully, they were in no hurry. He was sure the horses could gallop with the best of them, but there would always be the danger of flipping the buggy or laming one of the beasts. As for today it was nice to sit up high and enjoy the ride for the sake of riding.

"I must apologize for Friday," Katie Rose said, her voice as soft as the wind. "I . . . I . . ."

He wasn't sure what she was going to say, but whatever it was, it didn't need saying now. "No hard feelings."

She shook her head. "*Nay*, I shouldn't have treated you so—"

"Rudely?"

She shook her head. "You are not helpin' matters, Zane Carson."

"Am I supposed to?" He shot her a quick smile that she didn't return.

"This mornin' the bishop talked about forgiveness and understandin' others and the trials they have walked."

"Bishop Beachy?"

"*Jah*, we never know who might deliver the sermon. Whoever speaks is who God has chosen as His messenger for the day."

"How many bishops are there?"

"One. And two ministers, a preacher, and the deacon. Did you not have a service like this at your church?"

He shook his head. "I've never been to church."

"You are talkin' about an Amish service, *jah*?"

"Any church."

Katie Rose swung around in the seat to stare gape-mouthed at him. "Please tell me this is not true."

Zane shrugged. "Sorry." Never before had he felt like he'd missed out on anything by not attending church, but after Katie Rose's reaction he couldn't help but wonder.

She watched him, her brows knit together. "And how do you get the Lord's word, Zane Carson?"

"I don't."

She gave him that look. The one that all believers gave those suspect of not being among them. Zane was accustomed to the look. Normally he brushed it off and went about his way. But Katie Rose had him wondering about what he might be missing.

He mentally shook himself. He was just under the power of her jade-green eyes. He had taken the "when in Rome" creed a little too far. Just because she needed the Bible and its contents to make each day valid didn't mean everyone did.

"Do you not believe in God?"

He sucked in a breath. *Did he?*

She looked as if she would pray for him at any moment. "One look at a battlefield and even the most devout would doubt."

"One look at the beach, and it would all come back," she primly replied.

His head swiveled in her direction. "And when have you seen a beach?" He gestured toward the fields and trees around them. He might not be a geography scholar, but the last time he checked, Oklahoma was a landlocked state.

"Some friends and I went to Cabo San Lucas for a trip."

He straightened. "On your *rumpringa*?"

She nodded.

"To Mexico?"

She gave him the tiniest of smiles.

He continued to watch her. "If you won't allow your picture to be taken, how'd you get a passport?"

"There are ways around such matters, Zane Carson." The mystery in her voice set him back.

"Abram and Ruth let you go all the way to Mexico without a chaperone?"

"That is what *rumspringa* is all about. Seein' the world, experiencin' it. Samplin' what it has to offer before we make the commitment to God and church."

When he was younger, he'd wanted to be a part of something like that, something larger than himself, something more meaningful than his own wants and needs. But once he reached his teens he knew it was a hoax. The cooperative was close, but it was still made up of the people who formed it, and they weren't always what they seemed. Every organization he joined turned out the same. His college fraternity, the Army, everything. So he'd given up and concentrated instead on getting the most out of life.

"What has you frownin', Zane Carson?"

"Just thinking."

"And that makes you frown like the devil has ahold of your tail?"

He laughed, her silly question chasing away the dark thoughts. "My what?"

"Your tail. That never fails to make Samuel smile."

"Where is Samuel?"

At the mention of her nephew's name, Katie Rose straightened in her seat. "We should probably get back. I left him with Mary Elizabeth. But they are siblings, and I know he is missin' me."

"He loves you very much," Zane said, thinking of the small redhead that occasionally peeked out from the folds of Katie Rose's skirt. It was a wonder she came without him at all.

"I'm the only mother he's ever known."

"What'll happen when you get married and start a family of your own?"

A hint of melancholy crept into her eyes. "I am way past the marryin' age, Zane Carson."

He tried to hide his surprise, but knew she saw it regardless of his efforts. "You're what? Twenty-five. Twenty-six?"

She nodded. "*Jah*, I am long past the years to take a husband. I accept this. God didn't have a plan for me there, because He needs me to take care of the children."

"Samuel?"

"And the school children. That is my ministry for God."

He shifted in his seat. "Care to explain that?"

"The school is always in need of teachers. We teach our own, you know. But then once a teacher gets married, she leaves, and there has to be someone to take her place. I know this is where I am supposed to be, so I will remain with the students. It is God's plan for me."

Must be nice, Zane thought. To know with such certainty the purpose of life.

"Turn left right here," Katie Rose said.

"Turn left or turn right?"

She laughed at his joke. "Turn left. The road circles around, and we'll be back at my *elders' haus* in no time."

He did as she asked, wondering all the while if a person had to believe in God to know what He had planned for them.

───── ⚜ ─────

Monday, it seemed, was wash day. Everyone got up very early – even earlier than normal. Zane knew this because he could hear them downstairs as they raced around, gathering clothes and taking them outside to the gas-powered wringer washer.

He looked at the sky outside his curtain-less windows. He had discovered that the Amish considered curtains to be vain and prideful, but after seeing the washer the women had to use, he'd bet they didn't have curtains so they wouldn't have to clean them.

The bed next to his was empty, which meant John Paul was already up or had yet to return at all. What he did at all hours of the night was beyond Zane. His uncle hadn't imposed a strict curfew on Zane when he was a teen, but he could vouch that not much went on after midnight. If he could say that about Chicago, then he was certain there was nothing going on in small-town

Clover Ridge. And yet the young man left most every evening and returned sometime in the night. Sometimes sooner, often later.

Zane pushed himself out of the bed and checked his watch. Four a.m. With a shake of his head, he pulled on a shirt and made his way to the bathroom. He washed his face and hands, brushed his teeth and hair, then stumbled down the stairs.

Since the women were outside with the clunky old washing machine, the kitchen was empty. He grabbed himself a cup of coffee from the pot on the stove, thankful one of them had made his favorite vice before chores. No one should eat at this hour, he thought, and pushed himself out of the house and into the dark before dawn.

A few birds started their morning song. Fresh dew lay on the grass, and the sky was almost—*almost*—purple. A sure sign that sunrise was imminent.

"Here," Ruth called to Annie. "Get that load right there, and go back for the detergent. *Mach schnell, mach schnell.*" Ruth all but clapped her hands at the young woman.

Annie ran around doing Ruth's bidding. The exhaustion that plagued Ruth yesterday seemed to have vanished, leaving in its place a drill sergeant of a laundry commander.

Zane watched for a few more minutes before curiosity got the better of him. He sauntered barefoot across the yard, thankful for once that his pants were too short. At least they wouldn't get a wet hem.

"What are you two doing?"

"It's wash day," Annie panted, not bothering to look up from pulling clothes out of the wringer.

"I gathered that much."

Ruth ran a hand across her brow where sweat had formed despite the coolness of the morning. Fall had set in overnight, and today promised to be much cooler than the days past. His gaze flickered to Annie, who bit her lip and shot a worried glance toward Ruth.

"I'm fine, child." If the sparkle in her eyes was any indication, Ruth Fisher was indeed fine, but Zane couldn't help but be a little worried after yesterday's episode with exhaustion.

Annie propped her hands on her hips and blew an imaginary strand of hair out of her eyes. "Ruth wants to get finished before Katie Rose and Mary Elizabeth."

"I'm sorry. Get finished?"

"With the washing."

Zane took a sip of his coffee. "So you and Katie Rose do your laundry on the same day."

"Everyone does," Ruth said.

"Everyone who's Amish," Annie explained. "So, of course, they race."

Zane laughed. "Naturally."

"But Katie Rose and Mary Elizabeth always win," Ruth said.

Annie looked at Ruth. "And then Katie Rose goes over and helps Deacon Esh with his wash."

Of course she did. She was just that kind of person.

"He doesn't have anyone else to help him," Ruth explained. "He's an old man now, with no family to speak of."

Zane nodded. "What can I do to help?"

Ruth shook her head. "Laundry is a woman's work."

"But I'm here to learn all I can about your traditions and customs. My article is for both men and women."

Ruth relaxed her shoulders. "Then grab that basket, Zane Carson. You can hang whilst we wash and wring."

Zane did as he was told, carrying the basket of water-heavy clothes to the line. Neither of the women should have been able to lift that much weight. How in the world had they managed all the Mondays before?

He reached for the first shirt on the pile, a blue button-down with tiny hand stitches. And as he hung it on the line, memories from his childhood came flooding back. Standing in the Oregon air, hanging clothes alongside his mother. He could see her clear enough in his head that he could reach out and touch her round face, brush her wild blonde curls from her eyes, plant a kiss on her sun-pinkened cheek.

He shook the thought away. Being in Oklahoma had brought back so many memories of his youth. Things he hadn't thought about in years. Once the fire had taken his parents, his uncle came to get him. From that point on, he'd lived in Chicago, a world away from their small cooperative. Tim Carson had been Zane's only living relative, and fate had cruelly taken him too.

That tiny part of Zane that needed a family had long since been destroyed. No use wishing for something he couldn't have. Not that he even thought he wanted one. He hadn't allowed himself to think about the possibility of a family. Ever. He wouldn't know what to do with one.

Now he was practically engaged. Marriage usually meant family, but he and Monica had never talked about it. He made a mental note to bring it up the next time he called her. Or better yet, face-to-face when he was back in Chicago.

The thought of starting a family, then shipping out on assignment didn't seem fair. Her family had enough money to support them, but . . . well, that was out of the question. She said she understood his need to work. Would she understand this? She wasn't exactly the maternal type.

Katie Rose drifted into his thoughts. Pretty as you please, the striking image of Monica was replaced by the honey-haired vision who lived next door. Now *she* was maternal. One look at how she cared for Samuel and any fool could see that. Katie Rose cared for her brother's children as she would care her own, but according to her assessment, she would never have any. That's not what she believed God had planned for her.

He tried not to laugh at the idea as he reached for the next shirt, another blue one, almost the same shade as the first.

Katie Rose would make a wonderful mother. He knew the school would be sad to lose her as the instructor, but she was destined to be a mom. He saw it in the gentle brush of her fingers across Samuel's brow, the silence in her eyes as she mentally accounted for them at the school, her watchful gaze as she trailed them home. Still, she said she was too old for marriage.

"Tell me," he said, reaching for the next article of clothing and stretching for a clothespin. "Do women get married young around here?"

"*Jah*," Ruth said, nearly shouting over the roar of the machine engine. "Most girls join up when they're about twenty. It is nothin' unusual to have a marriage one year and a baby the next."

A baby at twenty-one. That seemed on the young side, but then so did motherhood at twenty-five. He knew women in their forties who were just getting around to starting their families. So what made Katie Rose so certain that a family wasn't part of God's plan for her?

He looked down the row of clothes he had just hung. Either Ruth and Annie liked to wash in color sequence or blue was a prominent color in the Amish world. He dragged the basket around the end of the pole and started down the other side. Amazing what he remembered from his childhood days. Using a common clothespin for two items came back as naturally as walking. He smiled, pleased with himself.

Next shirt up was green, then blue, followed by dark blue. "Tell me, Ruth. Do the Amish have something against red?"

"It's too flashy to practice humility."

He gave that some thought. He supposed red could be considered showy. And just in his short time with the Amish he understood their need to blend, to be as one. "And yellow?"

Ruth gave him a quiet smile. "We reserve the showy colors to decorate our flower beds. We wear the colors of serenity."

"So purple's okay?" he asked, holding up an eggplant-colored dress.

"Only certain shades," Ruth explained. "If the bishop finds it too bright or boastful, he'll send one of the ministers to have a talk with the person in question."

He blinked, trying to take that all in. It seemed controlling, almost cultish, but he hadn't really seen anything to make him believe the Amish were more bent toward a cult than a normal run-of-the-mill religion.

Annie must have heard something in his tone, as she approached and said, "It's important for the church members to stand united before God, show their trust in Him. Their obedience. It's not about color as much as it's about reverence. Being part of something bigger than oneself."

Ruth smiled. "Well put, my dear."

"*Danki.*"

"You understand now?" Ruth asked Zane.

"I'm going to have to think about that awhile."

The cooperative was about serving the greater good of the community. What the people grew, they shared with their friends and neighbors. There was a community garden, a community everything. But what they wore was of no consequence. Maybe because they didn't worship a god who expected anything from them in return. It was about living off the land and staying out from under "the man's" thumb.

This, it seemed, was something entirely different.

He made a mental note to talk to Annie about it. What better way to find out about the differences between the Amish and the English than talking to a convert?

⁓⦿⦿⁓

Once the clothes were hung, they went in to have breakfast. The sky had turned the most beautiful shade of lavender that faded to blue, promising a beautiful day.

"How will we know if we've won the laundry standoff?"

Annie smiled. "I haven't seen Katie Rose drive by yet, so I'd say we did it."

Zane couldn't stop his smile. Maybe because the news brought one to Ruth's face as well. Then he realized this had more to do with being capable than it did about being first. Ruth had to prove to herself, despite her treatments, despite her cancer, that she still had it. The woman had spunk, he had to hand it to her.

"Katie Rose drives by each day?"

"Only on Mondays when she goes to help Deacon Esh."

"Right." Zane snapped his fingers, in remembrance. "She helps him do his laundry, after she does her own, then she goes to teach school?" Amazing.

"After she cooks breakfast."

"And in the evening?"

"She takes care of the family," Ruth said with a shrug, but Zane could see the light of admiration in Annie's eyes. That was a lot of work for one person, but such effort was looked upon favorably in the district. As it should be. Hard work like that should never go unnoticed. Surely a woman who worked that hard for others would be a prime catch for an Amish man. So maybe her fate was more a personal choice than anything else. But why was she so against marriage? It didn't have anything to do with his story, but Zane made a mental note to find out the answer.

Zane was about to head down the stairs for afternoon chores when his cell phone rang. "Hello?"

"Tell me you have pictures to go with these notes."

"Good afternoon to you too, Jo. Yes, as a matter of fact, it is a lovely day."

"Don't play with me, Carson. These notes you sent over are spectacular. But I need the visual angle."

"About that . . ." Zane rubbed the back of his neck trying to ease the tension that had settled there. "They don't allow their picture to be taken."

"Of course they don't. That's why I sent you. If anyone can get the photos, it's you."

The image of the stern-faced Abram Fisher popped into his head. Abram was nothing if not fair. Pious and straight-walking. And Ruth who was so self-conscious of her post-chemo body, plus Annie, John Paul. Katie Rose. He had grown to care for them all since coming here, and Zane couldn't find it in himself to betray their trust.

His silence must have said it all. Or at least enough. "Listen, Zane. Juarez is a big job. Big job. If you can't handle the Amish . . ." She didn't elaborate. She didn't have to. If he couldn't complete his assignment with the Amish, then he'd lose the Mexico assignment to another reporter.

He heaved a sigh, resigned to follow through with his instructions. "I'll see what I can do."

"I'm sure you will."

Zane could hear the triumphant smile in her voice. Jo always liked to get her way. Now all he had to do was figure out how to complete his assignment without alienating the people around him.

$\sim\!\!\mathbb{Q}$ 6

Zane heard the car approach and moved even farther to the side of the road.

"Wanna ride?"

He looked up at John Paul's smiling face. Zane knew for a fact the young man had been out half the night, but he still looked as refreshed as if he'd slept plenty. He stopped and thought about asking where he'd been, but that surely wasn't part of his story. Instead he shook his head. "Nah. It's too pretty to be cooped up in a car."

John Paul looked crushed. "You'll get there faster."

"That's exactly the problem."

"I'll drive the speed limit."

Zane shook his head. "No, thanks. Driving too fast isn't your only problem. How did you get a license, by the way?"

John Paul just smiled. "Where are you headed?"

Zane nodded down the road. "The schoolhouse. Katie Rose said I could come by today and she would show me around, tell me about teaching all the grades in one room."

"If I drive, you won't miss the first bell."

"I can live with that."

John Paul laughed. "Suit yourself."

"You dad was looking for you this morning."

John Paul's easy smile faltered. "Was he mad I was late?"

"Late is not quite the word for not showing up at all." And *mad* was not quite the word he would have used to describe Abram Fisher's mood. More like silent seething.

The young man shrugged, but his mossy-green eyes clouded over.

"I take it *rumspringa* isn't a good enough excuse to miss milking the cows and feeding the chickens?"

John Paul shot him a look. "Have trouble this mornin', city boy?"

"I didn't try to milk the chickens, if that's what you're asking."

John Paul laughed. "Well, I guess I will go work on the tractor engine in the barn. *Dat* said it was burnin' oil. Let me know if you want a ride home." He held up a shiny black cell phone.

Zane's brows rose. "Where'd you get that?"

He smiled. "I have skills."

"I hope that's not why you're late."

"*Nay.*" But his smile held secrets. "See ya later, Zane Carson."

He gunned the engine, leaving Zane standing in a cloud of dust and rattletrap exhaust.

Zane was rounding the last bend when he heard the bell—an old-timey metal one with a string tied to the dangly thing inside. School had begun.

He quickened his steps, his mind going back to his years racing for the bell. He was homeschooled—or rather taught by his parents during his years at the cooperative. His uncle had dumped him in public school the minute they landed in Chicago. Culture shock was too mild of a word to describe Zane's reaction to the huge urban school. There were more people in his grade than lived in their entire settlement in Oregon. It was loud, noisy, and concrete. He hated it immediately. Only his budding love for girls had kept him coming back. The experience had been hard for him, but it made him stronger. He had learned to adapt, overcome, and find his niche. He credited the experience with allowing him to grow into the man he was today. A man who could jump on a plane at a moment's notice and travel halfway across the world to cover the latest breakout of war. Compared to facing a sea of middle school faces as insecure as he had been, sleeping in war-torn countries and living off whatever he could find was a piece of cake.

His conversation with Jo weedled its way to the front of his thoughts. Her orders shouldn't have been different from any of the others he'd received in his career. He was well-versed in overcoming the confines of his situation in order to bring in the story. Why should this time be any different?

He reached the schoolhouse steps.

"I thought you might not make it, Zane Carson."

Zane smiled at the greeting, letting the soft lilt of Katie Rose's voice wash over him. It was the people, he decided. These loving, caring people who worked side by side helping each other in an uncertain world. They struggled without war, modern conveniences, and outside help. Their fight was inspiring. And he wasn't sure if his own conscience would allow him to betray their wishes. Invading their privacy was enough. "I wouldn't miss this for anything."

She shook her head, and he resisted the urge to reach out and touch the strings of her untied cap. "I fear you will be sorely disappointed."

I wouldn't count on it. "I'll be the judge of that," he said and followed her into the schoolhouse.

He had thought he would encounter antique everything inside to match the outside, but apparently, even the Amish had trouble replenishing the old with the same. There were five rows of seating, two the old-fashioned wooden kind, but the next three rows were plastic chairs with small tabletops bolted on one side. There was a green chalkboard instead of a smart board, and another blackboard covered one wall, lesson plans for each grade written there.

Students of varying sizes sat at the desks. It was hard to guess ages and class levels, but it seemed that Katie Rose had reserved the newer desks for the smaller children. Everyone had turned in their seats, all eyes trained on him.

"I'll just . . . sit here." He found an old metal folding chair and pulled it to the back of the classroom. His job was to observe, not interfere, and he wanted to make his presence in the room as unobtrusive as possible.

Katie Rose smiled that Amish Mona Lisa smile of hers and motioned him forward. "Let me introduce you first. Otherwise we won't get any work done."

He made his way between the tiny desks to the front of the room. Had the desks been that small when he was in school?

"Scholars, this is Zane Carson. You may have heard your parents talk about my family's *Englisch* visitor. Well, here he is. Zane Carson wanted to come and visit the school today. So I need you to be extra good. And if'n you are, maybe this afternoon, we can talk him into sharin' a little about his life with us, *jah*?"

The children nodded enthusiastically.

Zane hid his laugh and tried not to breathe too deeply. This was as close to Katie Rose as he had been in a long time. The desire to soak in the special lilac and ginger scent that belonged to her was almost more than he could bear.

He was almost dizzy from lack of oxygen when she said, "You can go back to your seat now."

"Oh. Right." Zane walked to the back of the classroom, hoping his face wasn't too red and wondering if this idea of being friends with Katie Rose was a good idea.

She could feel his eyes on her as she moved around the room. Allowing him to come today was not the smartest idea she had ever agreed to. She had felt so guilty over her harsh treatment of him, but with him watching her, she could barely keep a thought in her head.

Jacob Kauffman had to remind her about the reading test she'd scheduled for the sixth grade. She gave him a few extra points for honesty. Since he was the only twelve-year-old she had, he could have easily skated right through the day without the test, and no one would have been the wiser.

From the morning bell to the lunch bell seemed like an eternity. She was certain Zane Carson had received a top-notch education from his fancy *Englisch* school. And although she was raised not to judge, she knew that others hadn't had the same upbringing. Had he found his visit informative or backward? She hoped he didn't think she was a simpleton. She might not have a fancy diploma or years of education to her name, but what she had served her well. Too much school was a bad thing, but she didn't want to come up lacking in the eyes of Zane Carson.

She said a small prayer and asked forgiveness for her prideful thoughts. The Lord was good, but she had to get ahold of the devil to keep him out of her mind's wanderings. What the *Englischer* thought of her was really no matter. By the beginning of the new year he'd be back in fancy Chicago, and she'd still be teaching the Amish children of Clover Ridge. It was as simple as that.

"All right, children, it's time to put away your books and get out your lunches. It's a beautiful day, so let's go outside and enjoy what the Lord has provided for us, *jah?*"

Amid the choruses of "*jahs*" Katie Rose put away her own papers and wondered just how long one school day could be.

⸙

Katie Rose tried to hide her surprise when Zane Carson wandered up and dropped down beside her under the elm tree. It was a beautiful day for being outside, but it wouldn't be long before the weather changed. Oklahoma weather could be so unpredictable, one day it could be eighty degrees and the next one forty. It was *gut* to get outside and enjoy the blessings of a warm sunny day before the winter set in.

"Good lesson, teach."

She tried not to smile at the compliment. It was a sin to be prideful, and she'd best remember it. Instead, she made a show out of looking for Samuel. He'd made a play for independence this year, following behind his brothers and emulating their actions. She was proud of him, but worried all the same. A part of her mourned the little boy stuck to the back of her skirts. Her baby was growing up.

"He's fine," Zane said, and Katie Rose knew he was right. When they got home tonight, Samuel would be back in her skirts once again, his play at "big boy" ending when there weren't so many people around. But for now she'd let him enjoy his role in the family.

She pulled her lunch box into her lap, not so much from hunger, but for something to do with her hands. Her fingers itched to reach out and touch the wheat-colored strands of Zane Carson's hair, pushing back in place what the wind had ruffled. He might be used to such familiarity with sophisticated *Englisch* girls, but she wasn't used to the feelings a'tall.

"Did you not bring anything to eat, Zane Carson?" She opened the small plastic container of chicken salad and the baggie filled with crackers.

"I never even thought about it."

"I should have told you."

He shook his head. "No big deal. Your mother and Annie cooked a huge breakfast, and I had a piece of pie before I ate that."

"I'll share." She offered him a cracker covered with the chicken salad.

"Really. I'm fine."

She couldn't let him starve for the noonday meal. He wasn't accustomed to their ways. She should have warned him that everyone packed a lunch for school.

"Take it, Zane Carson." She used her best teacher-to-student voice. It must have worked because a heartbeat later he accepted the cracker from her. His fingers brushed against hers, and an unfamiliar feeling shot up her arm, like the time she picked up a battery with wet fingers. Not entirely unpleasant, but shocking in its surprise.

"*Danki*," he said, then popped the entire cracker into his mouth.

"Are you learnin' your *Deutsch*, Zane Carson?"

"Why do you do that?"

"Do what?" She gave him another cracker, this time careful not to touch him at all.

"Always call me by my first and last name?"

She shrugged, stalling for time to properly answer his question. The Commandments warned against lying, but she couldn't tell him that calling him anything other than his full name seemed too intimate, that his Christian name on her tongue felt like a sin.

"It is just our way, I suppose." She tried not to notice how the wind ruffled his hair. Or how brown his eyes were, deep and bottomless, dark like rich chocolate.

He was an *Englischer*. Not like them.

Why the Lord sent him here to tempt her, only He knew. But it was time for her to be strong. Keep her focus. Maybe God was just testing her faith like He did with Abraham. Or maybe He was making sure she knew her life's calling and embraced it like she should.

Jah, that's what it had to be. She passed Zane half of the apple she'd sliced that morning and stood, automatically dusting the bits of grass from her skirt. "All right, children. Five more minutes."

Customary groans rose from the kids, but she only smiled. She well remembered the days when she galloped and played outside, enjoying the feel of sunshine on her face. Just because being around Zane Carson made her as anxious as a teenager at her first singing didn't mean she had to take it out on the kids. She sank back to the ground and grabbed a bite of the apple for herself.

Maybe she'd let them have ten minutes.

Ten more minutes.

Because that's all she could stand.

"Katie Rose, I thought Zane was going to tell us about his life?"

"What say you, Zane Carson? Would you be willin' to come up and answer a few questions from the *kinder*?"

Zane opened his mouth, unsure of how he should answer. By English standards he led an exciting life, but did the children need to hear about his life in a war zone? Twenty-five pairs of eyes stared at him, imploring him to talk and give them a break from boring lessons.

"I'll do the best I can." He stood and stretched his legs, then slowly made his way to the front of the schoolhouse.

Zane rubbed his hands together to expel some uncharacteristic nervousness. "So who wants to go first? How about you?" He pointed to one of the boys in the middle of the room. The young fellow was sitting next to Gabriel Fisher's son, Simon.

"Why are you dressed like us?"

Easy enough. "I came here to learn how it feels to be Amish. So Mr. Fisher—"

"Abram!" one of the kids shouted.

Katie Rose frowned.

"Yes, Abram gave me some clothes like you wear to help me get a jump on things. Next question."

"Are you a farmer?"

"I suppose that I am right now, but normally I'm a reporter."

A little girl with blonde braids raised her hand. "My *dat* writes a column for *Die Botschaft*."

He turned to Katie Rose for explanation.

"It is our weekly newspaper. Old Order Amish, that is. Most people in these parts take it."

He made a mental note to find a copy. "That's *gut*." He smiled at the young contributor, and the class laughed at his attempt at *Deutsch*.

"Children," Katie Rose's voice was mild in its warning, but still had the desired effect. The kids quieted immediately.

Zane answered questions for another half hour. The children were charming with their inquiries about his car, movies, and television. Not one of them asked about the dangers of covering wars all over the globe, though one little boy asked him if he'd ever seen a kangaroo.

"Only in the zoo," he answered, much to the child's disappointment.

"Well, that's not sayin' much. I've seen one in the zoo."

The class burst into laughter. Even Katie Rose had a smile twitching on her lips. Zane wished he could bottle it and save it for later. Instead, he savored the moment.

Zane returned to his seat at the back of the room while Katie Rose delivered homework assignments. "Spellin' test for the second grade tomorrow first thing."

The smaller kids groaned.

"And math for all grades."

This time everyone groaned until she said the magic words. "School dismissed."

And Zane realized that he still hadn't thought of a way to photograph the Amish.

"Can I walk you home?"

Katie Rose nearly jumped at the sound of his voice. She had thought she was finally alone and able to deal with the warmth that the fancy *Englisch* reporter sent to her middle.

"Zane Carson. I thought you'd be halfway there by now."

He shrugged, and she noticed how broad his shoulders were. Commanding, solid. The kind of man a woman could depend on to work by her side and raise a family, build a home.

She shook away the thoughts. If God were to send a man for her, it surely wouldn't be the *Englischer* standing opposite her desk. Standing so close she could smell the fresh scent of his shirt, the commercial shampoo he used in his hair, and something special that belonged to him and him alone.

"I thought it might be nice to walk together."

She raised a questioning eyebrow. It would be more than nice. It would be pure temptation, a delightful way to get home.

Her hesitation, it seemed, was enough to send him into explanation. "I thought we'd agreed to be friends," he said. "I've already told you that I mean no harm to you or anyone in your family. I'm here to help."

The question was: *Who would help her if she started to care for the blond-haired man from the big city?*

Ridiculous. She had control over her feelings. There was no need to be concerned. God was on her side. He would help her fight the feelings that Zane Carson sent zinging through her. Obviously it wasn't God who was testing her, but the devil himself.

"Of course." She smiled as if his grin didn't melt her heart with its charm. She swung her bag across her shoulder and preceded him to the door. He stood too close as she pulled it shut and locked it behind them. She felt every steady breath, heard every beat of his heart. "We have to lock the school against vandals," she said, her voice squeaky.

"Vandals? Are you serious?"

"*Jah*, I'm afraid so. Most of Clover Ridge is happy to share the town with us, but there are a few who do not understand our ways. They think they can bully us into changin'."

He nodded. The wind ruffled through his hair, the sun burnishing the strands to near copper. "I understand. I grew up in a cooperative in Oregon, and a lot of people there didn't like what we stood for."

"A cooperative?"

"A commune. A hippie compound."

She frowned. "What is a hippie?"

He laughed, but she could tell that he wasn't laughing at her.

"Hippies are a lot like the Amish, but with modern clothes and without the Bible."

"And this is where you were raised?"

"For most of my childhood." He tripped down the steps, and Katie Rose took a big gulp of Zane-free air.

"What did you do with the rest of it?" she asked, following him down the stairs.

"My parents died in a fire when I was ten. My uncle—my father's brother—came to Oregon and took me back to Chicago."

"And you were close to your uncle?"

"I'd never seen him before that day. He wasn't the easiest guy to get to know."

"That is a sad tale, Zane Carson." She held her voice steady as they started for home.

He shrugged. "I learned a lot from the experience. How to adapt, how to survive. It's carried me well though my life. Though it was quite a shock to go from commune living to inner city Chicago."

Katie Rose was careful not to let their shoulders touch as they walked side by side. "So it was like your own *rumspringa*."

He smiled. "I guess you could say that. Tell me about your 'run around' time."

"There is not much to tell."

"What did you do? What was the one thing that you longed for?"

Even as she enjoyed her time in the world, her only heart's desire had been what she would get when she joined the church fold: Samuel Beachy as her wedded husband. That was all she had ever wished for—even when she wore pigtails and a pinafore.

Samuel was everything she had wanted and more. A godly man, the son of the bishop, he was from a good Amish family. He was handsome and charming, destined to be a fine member in the community until . . .

"Movies," she said. "I really enjoyed going to the movies. Eating popcorn and watching the pictures move in front of me like they were so close I could almost touch them." She had enjoyed the movies, but it wasn't enough to keep her from being Samuel Beachy's wife. Even when she set out to experience the outside world, she knew she would return. There were kids who lost their raisin' as they went out, drinking alcohol and going to parties. Most returned; some didn't. Like her Samuel.

If Zane Carson thought she was hiding something, he didn't let on. Instead he just nodded. "Movies are the best. It's the one thing I miss the most when I'm on assignment."

"Do you really write about wars, Zane Carson?"

"I really do."

Katie Rose couldn't help the shudder that rocked through her. So much destruction, so much heartache. "How do you do it? Watch those people suffer for no reason?"

"It's what I do."

That was no kind of answer.

He pressed his lips together, then shook his head as if he didn't have the words to answer. "I can't change the world. And I don't leave my emotions behind. I've cried at some of the things I've seen. But there's something about being out there, something that makes me feel . . . alive."

"I don't understand, Zane Carson."

He let out a sigh. "I don't understand it myself. I just know that's what I was born to do."

"Then why are you here, instead of where the war may be?"

He waited so long Katie Rose wondered if he was planning to answer at all.

"I was shot."

Her heart stuttered in her chest, and her stomach roiled. The mere mention that he'd been hurt and could have died sent tremors through her.

"Are you okay?" He reached out to touch her cheek, but stopped, balling his hand into a fist before dropping it back to his side.

"*Jah*," she whispered. Then louder, "*Nay*. You were shot? You could have died."

He shrugged as if it was of no concern. "But I didn't."

"And then you came back? To America?"

"About six months ago."

"And after you leave here?" She asked the question, though for sure and for certain she didn't want to know the answer.

"I'll go back to Chicago for a while, and then to Juarez, Mexico."

Even the Amish knew of the troubles on the US border with Mexico. Her breath caught in her throat. The mere thought of him being in harm's way was enough to bring tears to her eyes. She turned away so he couldn't see and said the only thing she could. "I will pray for you, Zane Carson."

"Thank you," was all he said in return.

~⊙ ⊙~

"Zane Carson!"

He looked up from where he walked the fence with John Paul, checking for any holes and weak spots that would allow the livestock to escape. So far they hadn't found anything, but something was scaring the horses, keeping them on the run for hours on end. The poor beasts were coming into the barn each evening, lathered and exhausted.

John Paul thought perhaps a coyote might be responsible.

Zane shaded his eyes and watched as Abram approached. Saturday was upon them once again. All in all, the last week had been as good as the first. Four days of deep, untroubled sleep achieved without pills. Four days of hard, yet satisfying work. Of home-cooked meals and the best coffee he'd ever tasted. Four days since he had last seen Katie Rose.

He didn't know why he'd told her about being shot, other than she asked and it was the truth. But his words had caused her pain for some reason. Maybe she, too, felt the pull between them. So Zane did the only thing he could do. He avoided her. He stayed away on Wednesday when she came by to take Annie to town to get some new fabric for a dress. And again on Thursday when she stopped to check the outcome of Ruth's latest doctor appointment.

Thankfully, Ruth Fisher was a fighter. Her checkup went well. It wouldn't be long before she'd be declared cancer free. Zane knew all the Fishers were counting down to that day.

"Abram," he called in return.

"Get the horses readied, we need to go visitin'. Hitch 'em to the wagon. There's work to be done."

Among his list of accomplishments this trip, Zane had learned to hitch the horses to the buggy with expert skill. He didn't know why the skill pleased him so, but it did. Maybe because John Paul had tried his hand at being English and drove like a blind NASCAR racer while Zane had taken to the change like a baby to his mother's milk.

"*Jah*," he said, lifting his hat from his head and wiping his fore-head on his sleeve. He knew better than to protest about the inter-rupted chores. The first reason, there were always chores. They walked the fences continually searching for weak spots, holes that could damage the horses and cattle, and tracks for wild animals like the coyote they suspected was running their stock.

And secondly, he'd learned that it wasn't a good idea to argue with Abram. He was the undisputed leader of the household. It was his way always—though Zane was certain Ruth and Annie could talk him into doing almost anything they wanted as long as they did so over a piece of pie.

"Come on, John Paul, you come, too."

"Where are we goin'?" John Paul asked his father as they crossed the pasture toward him. Together, they all turned to walk toward the barn.

"We need to go check on old Ezekiel Esh."

"He's the deacon," John Paul explained. "Very old."

"So I gathered."

Zane whistled for the horses. They trotted up, their coats glossy in the afternoon sun.

He loved the beasts. They were magnificent, strong, and proud. Every time he got near them he thought it a shame that man had invented the automobile.

Once the horses and wagon were ready to go, Abram loaded some tools and lumber into the back. John Paul jumped in, and they started off toward the Esh place.

Half an hour later when they pulled into the dirt drive that led to the deacon's house, Zane remembered passing it on the way to town.

It was in need of work, a lot of work.

"Ezekiel Esh doesn't have kin around here to help. His last boy moved off to Missouri a year ago," Abram explained. "His wife's been gone for a while and his daughters moved a long time ago."

"He only had one son?"

"He had three total, but one died when he was small, and the other died in a roofin' accident awhile back." Abram pulled the wagon to a stop in front of the barn. It was almost as dilapidated as the house.

How sad that Esh was alone in this world, with barely anybody there to help him care for his house.

A niggling thought tickled the back of his mind. At the rate he was going, life would turn out the same, and that's exactly why he had decided to marry Monica. No man should be alone in life.

And yet he was.

Monica. He hadn't thought about her in days. Hadn't called or e-mailed her in even longer. Since last week. He was a bad fiancé. A fact he made a mental note to correct as soon as they returned home.

"Why doesn't he move close to members of his family?"

John Paul laughed as he swung down from the wagon. "That just proves you haven't met the man."

Abram climbed the porch steps and beat on the door. If Zane didn't know better he'd think the elder Fisher to be angry. Abram pounded again, even louder. "Ezekiel Esh, we've come to fix your roof."

The old man opened the door, face to face with his neighbor. "What?" he bellowed.

"We've come to fix your roof," Abram repeated, his voice still as loud as ever.

"*Danki, danki,*" the deacon yelled in return. Zane realized the man was remarkably hard of hearing.

"Why doesn't he get himself a hearing aid?" Zane asked John Paul.

The young man shrugged. "He's Amish."

Zane opened his mouth to ask what that had to do with anything when John Paul interrupted. "If the good Lord wants a man deaf, who is he to go against the Almighty's wishes?"

"The same thing could be said about your mom's cancer."

"*Jah*, that it could. But she and *Dat* prayed about it, and the Lord told her to fight."

Zane was glad that He had. For if Ruth Fisher hadn't decided to battle the cancer, then he never would have come to Oklahoma.

All things for a reason, Katie Rose would have said. As easily as that, she entered his thoughts once again. He pushed her out of his mind and got down to work.

The men had just unloaded the wagon when a buggy carrying Katie Rose pulled up.

From his thoughts to reality.

Katie Rose Fisher hopped down from the buggy, then pulled a cloth-covered basket from behind the seat. She looked as fresh as ever in a royal-blue dress that only made her eyes look greener. The black of her apron and cape made a handsome contrast over the dress. Despite the dark colors, she reminded him of a daisy, crisp and full of sunshine. Her hair was the same as always, parted down the middle and pulled back from her face into a tight bun at the nape of her neck. Zane wondered how long her hair was. He'd never seen it down, but the urge to move close to her, pull it from its confines, and see just how long it was ricocheted through him.

He adjusted his suspenders to give his hands something to do. He'd let out the black elastic to keep them from hiking his pants up and make them ever shorter, but now all that happened was they slipped from his shoulders with clockwork regularity.

"*Guder mariye, dochder,*" Abram called. "What brings you here this fine morn?"

She smiled prettily for her father, but her eyes never once moved toward Zane. It was as if he didn't exist. "Mary Elizabeth and I just came to check on the deacon. Have him some bread here."

"And some pickles?" Esh called. It seemed his hearing improved greatly when there was food involved.

"And some pickles." Mary Elizabeth laughed as she pulled the cardboard box from behind her seat. "*Guder mariye* to you, Zane Carson." She smiled a greeting to go along with her words.

He nodded in return, noticing that only then did Katie Rose's gaze flit in his direction.

He watched the women walk toward the house, Katie Rose nodding toward her host before she stepped over the threshold.

John Paul clapped him on the shoulder. "Time to work, city boy. You know how to roof a house?"

Zane watched Katie Rose disappear inside, then turned back to the younger man. "As a matter of fact, I do."

✧ ✧ ✧

"I think he likes you," Mary Elizabeth said.

The blush rose in Katie Rose's cheeks. She hid her face in the refrigerator under the pretense of cleaning it out, hoping that Mary Elizabeth wouldn't notice. "You're just being plain silly," she said.

"He was watchin' you the whole time we were outside."

"That doesn't prove a thing. Now make some lemonade. The men will be mighty thirsty when they are done."

"What?" Ezekiel yelled from his perch at the table.

"I said the men will need some lemonade when they're done." Katie Rose dearly loved the old man. He and her grandfather had been close friends back before *Grossdaadi* had gone on to see the Lord. Katie Rose felt an even greater responsibility to see after the old deacon than even the *Ordnung* demanded. Every Saturday she and Mary Elizabeth brought over the extra bread they had baked that week, along with other foods, and cleaning supplies.

"What about the *Englischer*?" The man had the uncanny knack of hearing the very thing a body didn't want him to hear.

Mary Elizabeth opened her mouth to say something, but Katie Rose shot her a quelling look. The young girl closed her mouth with a secretive smile.

"It's good for him to come and help, *jah*?" It wasn't a lie, but even so, Katie Rose felt a smidgen guilty. No sense getting the church elder riled up over Mary Elizabeth's foolish girlhood dreams, though. Even if he had been looking at her, Katie Rose knew it wouldn't be like *that*. He was of the world, an outsider. She had seen the town's women come into the general store with their man-made fingernails and cosmetic-painted faces. Beauty in the outside world and in the community held two different definitions, and she knew she could not compete with all that man had devised to make a woman more desirable.

Good thing such matters weren't important to her. She squelched down any opposition to this philosophy and poured the lemonade into four plastic cups. She had been duly surprised to see her *dat*, her *bruder*, and their *Englisch* guest already at the Esh house.

It surely wasn't *gut* the joy she felt at seeing him once again. She hadn't seen him since that Tuesday when he had visited the school. She knew she had no cause to be disappointed by his absence. She had still missed him all the same, his questions about their way of life, his different take on things. Yet he seemed to understand the importance of their rules and the life they led. Maybe it was all those years growing up in . . . what did he call it again? A cooperative? She supposed that the church district could be called a cooperative. That was what they did. They all worked together for the common good of the community. Everyone pulled together for something greater than themselves.

She wanted to ask him more questions about his growing-up years, what he meant by "without God." How could an entire community be without God? That just didn't seem possible.

But she knew that getting to know Zane Carson would not give her a true understanding of why Samuel had left. Why the lifestyle they grew up in could no longer satisfy him.

"He seems to be a *gut bu*."

Boy wasn't quite the word that came to Katie Rose's mind when she thought of their *Englisch* visitor, but she supposed to Ezekiel Esh, most people seemed young.

Katie Rose nodded since it seemed a response was demanded of her. "He seems to be a hard worker."

"More than the average *Englischer, jah*?"

What was the old man hinting at?

"I suppose."

"And not hard on the eyes a'tall." Mary Elizabeth said the words as lightheartedly as if she were talking about sewing fabric.

Katie Rose frowned at her niece. There was no need going 'round adding fuel to fires that weren't going to burn.

"He has a lady friend back in Chicago," the deacon said.

Katie Rose tried not to whip around, but she did anyway, making herself dizzy headed in the process.

"Where'd you hear that?"

"I reckon Abram told me . . . or maybe it was Annie or young Gabe."

Or John Paul, Katie Rose thought. Her brother had been appointed as Zane Carson's companion of sorts. She suspected that her father was trying to keep both men on a short leash, tethering them together to keep them from getting into trouble. The wisdom of the decision had not yet been seen.

"Said he was goin' to marry her once he prints his story in that fancy magazine of his."

Katie Rose tried not to let her disappointment or surprise show. Of course Zane Carson had a girl back home. He was handsome to a fault, hardworking, and . . . well, nice. Zane Carson was considerate of others, caring to those around him. Whether it was the years he spent with his uncle or the ones with the hippies, someone had taught him the Golden Rule—treat others as you would have them treat you.

"Aw-ah." Mary Elizabeth groaned, her disappointment clear.

Ezekiel pointed his knotty cane at her. "Surely you didn't have your sights set on him as a potential suitor. You are way too young, Missy Mary."

Mary Elizabeth blushed. "Of course not. But I was hopin'—"

Katie Rose elbowed her into silence.

Her niece shot her a look, then continued. "He seems like such a *gut* man."

Ezekiel started shaking his head before she was even halfway finished. "I can't believe the bishop would agree to let another outsider in—even if he wanted to join up. Which no one has even thought about. *Ach*, t'would be a mess, it would. You girls best leave that young man alone and worry which Amish man's heart you can capture."

Katie Rose opened her mouth to protest, but closed it instead. More and more these days it hurt to say the truth out loud: that if she was meant to have an Amish man, she would have found him by now.

Or that she had found her Amish man, but hadn't been able to compete with the lure of the *Englisch* world.

The men made short work of the roof repair. As far as Zane was concerned, the old man's house needed a new roof, and he mentioned the idea to Abram.

"*Jah*," he said, "but it will have to wait till spring."

Zane dipped his chin in agreement. The days had been unseasonably warm, but if he'd understood the talk at the general store, a cold snap would be coming soon. Surely the repairs they made today could withstand the mild Oklahoma winters. Then once spring came back around they would . . .

Zane's thoughts came to a sudden halt. Once spring came he'd be in Mexico. *And* he'd be married. He couldn't imagine Monica traveling to Amish country Oklahoma to help an old man with his caved-in roof. Her idea of helping the needy was donating last year's clothing to the Salvation Army. That didn't make her a bad person. She'd just been raised differently. When someone needed something, she'd write a check, take the tax deduction, and jot a checkmark next to "good deeds."

This cohesiveness that the Amish displayed was part of their raising as well. They didn't keep score. They did what needed to be done because it was the right thing to do. What made Katie Rose so different than the rest, he had yet to figure out.

7

Katie Rose took another step down the dirt road. It was a fine day for fishing, that was all. The birds were still singing their summer song. The trees had started their turn from green to shades of red and gold. Soon fall would be in full swing. Sometime next month, the courting couples of the district would state their intentions, and wedding season would be upon them.

And soon, it'd be too cold for fishing. In fact, this might be her last chance to fill up the freezer with bass and tasty *katfisch*, which the boys so loved. So while they had been harvesting the last of the pumpkins and squash, she'd decided to get out her rod and reel and head over to old Ezekiel Esh's pond. With any luck she might have enough *fisch* to spare for the deacon's freezer as well. But that might take an extra hour or two, maybe more.

That's when the idea struck to invite Zane Carson along. What a fun and beneficial pastime to introduce him to. It wasn't so terribly out of the way to walk over to her *elders' haus* and ask the *Englischer* if he wanted to join her.

Who was she fooling? She enjoyed the man's company, and she should admit it in her thoughts, even if she would never say the words for others to hear.

She took a deep breath. There was no harm in spending time with a person she liked. Besides, he had come here to learn about their lifestyle. Fishing to put food on the table was just one more facet for him to discover and write about in his fancy magazine.

She turned down the dirt drive that led to her parents' house, relieved and happy to see Zane Carson hammering on the front porch, as Noni sat in a nearby rocker and oversaw the project.

"Good mornin', Zane Carson." She waved and tried to hide her smile at the sight of him.

He shaded his eyes, his expression unreadable, though she thought she saw the flash of his dimples before he turned back to his work. "Good morning, yourself."

Katie Rose's steps slowed. She was traveling at a snail's pace by the time she reached the porch. "*Guder mariye*, Noni."

Her *grossmammi* just nodded her head. The old woman didn't speak much, but Katie Rose had learned from experience that the little she did say was wise and true.

"Did you come to help your family get ready for the church service?" Zane asked.

She would have if she had remembered that the service was to be held at her parents' *haus* the following day. She swallowed a sigh. She would need to say an extra prayer for allowing Zane Carson to fill her thoughts to the point that she had forgotten her duties to her church and family.

"Of course." She laughed. "And afterwards, I thought I might do a bit of fishin'."

"Fishing, huh?"

She nodded, aware that Noni's sharp green eyes didn't miss her anxious swallow or the shaking in her hands. *What was wrong with her?* She was acting like a teenager on her way to her first singing. "Would you like to come along?"

"Sure," Zane Carson said. "Let me know when you're ready to leave. If I'm done with the porch, I'd like to tag along. If that's okay."

It was more than okay, but Katie Rose just nodded her head, the untied strings of her prayer *kapp* tickling her neck. "*Jah*, I will, Zane Carson."

A great deal of work went into getting ready for the Sunday church service. All of the furniture in the main room of the house had to be moved aside and wooden benches would be brought in. There was cleaning to do, baking and lemonade making, just about every thing a body could think of. So much so that it was late afternoon before the house was ready, and Katie Rose felt as if she had done her part and was free to go fishing.

But there wasn't enough daylight left to fish and cook. She bit her lip, still longing for the time to spend with the *Englischer* and knowing that her responsibility lay with cooking for her brother and his rambunctious brood.

"You've had that look on your face all afternoon. Spill it."

Katie Rose's head jerked to attention. Annie Hamilton, her brother's newly converted *Englisch* fiancée, stared at her intently. Her violet-colored eyes were unusual and intense in their study of her.

The women were alone in the kitchen, the men out making sure there was enough hay and water to care for the district's horses, and Ruth had long since gone upstairs for her afternoon nap, the church-readying activities quickly taking their toll.

"I do not know what you are talkin' about."

"At the risk of sounding too much like your brother, it is a sin to lie, Katie Rose Fisher."

Katie Rose smiled, then her face crumbled. "I . . ." she started, but wasn't sure what words she should use, nor even how much she should say. *I'm unworthy, I'm a bad daughter. I need forgiveness.*

"The *Englischer*, huh?"

She blinked. "How . . ."

Annie shot her a look.

"Is it that obvious?" The air whooshed from her lungs like a deflated balloon. It felt *gut* to say it out loud, but at the same time, she wanted to call back the words.

"I've seen that look before."

"*Nay*, it's not like I love him or anythin'." Katie Rose ignored the look on her future sister-in-law's face. "He's just nice to be around."

"He is handsome," Annie agreed.

"*Jah*, there's that." It was the devil's temptation. And she'd do well to remember that.

"He seems to have grown accustomed to Plain living," Annie added.

"He was raised by hippies is all."

Annie laughed. "The hippies aren't out there pitching hay down from the loft."

Katie Rose couldn't allow herself fanciful thoughts. He was good looking, and he had adjusted well, but that didn't mean anything past the three months that he had agreed to visit.

"Get that look outta your eyes, Annie Hamilton. He's not about to join up with the Plain folk."

Annie shrugged. "Stranger things have happened."

"Look how hard it's been for you—and you have a reason to be here."

"That's true."

They both nodded, and Katie Rose knew that, like her, Annie was thinking back to the late spring snowstorm and Gideon's rescue.

"It's not likely the bishop would allow for another outsider to join the church," Katie Rose said.

"Even to save the heart of the girl his son once loved?"

Katie Rose shook her head. The bishop didn't care about such things. "Samuel Beachy didn't break my heart."

"That's not the way I hear Gabriel tell it."

"Hear Gabriel tell what?"

Both women shot to their feet as if they'd been scalded with fire.

"Zane Carson," Katie Rose admonished at the sight of him. "You scared the life outta me."

"Sorry. I didn't mean to."

Just how much had he heard of their conversation? Enough to know they were talking about him? Enough to hear the unwelcomed sigh in her voice whenever she said his name?

Annie moved toward the fridge without waiting for his answer. "Are the folks ready for a drink?"

She began pouring cold lemonade into plastic cups as Zane Carson sat down across from Katie Rose.

"You still planning to go fishing?"

She shook her head. It had been a foolish idea. She should have never considered it. But her heart seemed to get silly around marriage time. Well, around *this* marriage time. The best thing to do for the remainder of Zane Carson's visit was stay as far away from him as possible. "*Nay*. There's not enough daylight left for fishin' and cookin'."

"Of course, there is," Annie interrupted. "Mary Elizabeth can cook tonight."

Katie Rose wanted to fold her arms on the table and hide. "What do you have against Gabe today, Annie?"

It was no secret that Gabe had grudgingly accepted Annie into their lives, but to punish him by subjecting him to Mary Elizabeth's attempts in the kitchen was not to be taken lightly.

"Pee-shaw," Annie said with a smile. "Her cooking isn't all that bad. Plus, it'd be good to have some fish to feed the teenagers tomorrow night. Maybe I could talk Gideon into setting up the fryer." Just like that Annie was off and running with ideas.

And Katie Rose was free to go fishing—with Zane Carson right behind.

She gathered up her supplies while Zane fetched a pole from the barn, then they set off toward her favorite fishing hole, the one at the backside of Ezekiel Esh's place. It was a perfect pond. Spring fed, with cool banks and the perfect shade tree off to one side. Long ago someone had rolled a felled trunk close to the tree. Katie Rose loved nothing more than an afternoon of sitting on the log with a line in the reedy water.

She dropped her tackle box then, stood on the bank staring out over the peaceful pond.

Zane Carson stepped beside her. "Relax and have a good time." His voice so close made her jump like a skittish pony.

She whirled around and wiped her hands down her oldest everyday apron. "I am havin' a good time."

He shot her a look that said he didn't believe her.

"I just don't want you to get the wrong idea about today."

He crossed his arms and watched her shift from one foot to the other. "Wrong idea about what?"

"Me. Invitin' you to come fishin'."

"There's not much else I can get from it other than you wanted somebody to bait your hook."

Katie Rose planted her hands on her hips, her anxiety gone in one fell swoop. "I'll have you to know I am not afraid of baitin' my own hooks, but I use lures instead. For no other reason than they catch the best *katfisch* in the county."

"Uh-huh." He held up one of her lures. "I've never seen anything like this before."

She plucked it from his fingers. "That's because they're one of a kind. That one is my favorite."

He picked another and held it up. It was a hook with the tiny, bright yellow frog on the end. A hot pink feather was attached to one side.

"How do you know they're one of a kind?"

"Because I made them myself."

An interested light kindled in his deep brown eyes. "Really?"

"For sure and for certain," she said, but self-doubts floated to the surface. "What's wrong with them?"

"Nothing, they're great. I think you could make a fortune selling these. If they work."

"Oh, they work all right." She placed the sticky purple octopus to the end of her line and threw it into the water. In no time at all, she pulled a large catfish to the bank.

Zane laughed as he watched her take it off the hook and string it on the live line. She drove the stake into the ground, then washed her hands in the pond water.

He tried to imagine Monica standing on the muddy bank in green rubber boots with a fishing pole in one hand, but came up short. That was unfair. He sure couldn't make it work in the other direction either—Katie Rose, in a sequined gown, at the latest fund-raiser. No, wait. That one did work. Her hair pulled up in a ringlet hairdo with makeup and a ball gown. But he didn't like the image. He took in the shape of her face, the glow in her eyes. Yes, he preferred the one in front of him now.

Like it mattered.

Katie Rose threw her line back into the water and sat down on the towel she'd brought.

Zane leaned back against the tree, but the accuracy of her lures came to the forefront of his thoughts. "Were they expensive to make?"

She cocked her head. "Sorry. What?"

"The lures. Was it expensive to make them?"

"*Nay.* The feathers are cheap. Coln Anderson at the general store orders them in a big bag. The frogs and such came out of the gumball machine in front of the gas station."

Zane couldn't stop his laugh. "You realize you could charge ten dollars a pop for these."

Katie Rose shook her head. "Plain folk are not about takin' advantage of people."

"It's not about taking advantage; it's about marketing and fair trade. At an eighty-percent profit rate, you could make a bundle."

She was shaking her head before he even finished. "We do not work for profit, only for what we need."

"And your mother's treatments?"

She sighed. "It would help a lot. To put the money back in the church."

"You ought to give it some thought. Even if you just sold them around here, it'd be a great addition to the family business."

"Family business?"

"The pickles."

Katie Rose nodded and pulled at the fish on her line. "I suppose it would."

Zane was glad to feel the tug on his own line. Not that he was afraid she'd out fish him, but to give him something to do besides stare at her.

Once both fish were on the live line and their lures dropped back into the water, she asked, "If'n I decided to start sellin' my lures, would you help me?"

"Sure. I mean, for as long as I'm here." He hadn't thought about leaving in days, hadn't made any plans for his return. Strange, but Chicago seemed a lifetime away from this day, this bank, this company.

His admission must have upset her for she got really quiet after that, staring out at the water, a pinched look wrinkling her otherwise smooth brow. "I hear tell you have a special someone waiting for you in Chicago." Her voice was quiet and unreadable.

Was she feeling the same pull as he?

He sat up, pole forgotten, then picked up a small stone for something to do and tossed it into the pond. Ripples formed and swam to the shore one after another. The disturbance wasn't good for fishing success, but he had to move. Had to do something. "Yeah," he finally said.

"What is she like?"

A few weeks ago, marrying Monica seemed like the most natural thing in the world. And now . . . ? "She's got dark hair, and she's small like Annie. But her eyes are blue."

"But what is she *like*?"

Zane had to think about it a second. "She runs a magazine that her father owns. It's about fashion and makeup and girl things, so she's very aware of how she looks when we go out. She's always dressed up and made up and . . ." He'd been about to say perfect. But was there such a thing? "She does a lot of charity work, benefits and that sort of thing."

"What kind of church does she go to?"

"I don't believe she does." How could he have known someone as long as he had known Monica without knowing her religious affiliation?

Katie Rose finally turned to look at him, her jade-colored eyes questioning in their disbelief. "She doesn't go to church?"

"Not everyone has such a strong church background as you do, Katie Rose."

"I do not understand that."

Zane shrugged. "I grew up without believing in God." Saying the words out loud in such a peaceful place seemed like an abomination. Well, they would have if he believed in such things.

"You said that the cooperative was a lot like here but without God. You meant—"

"Without God."

Katie Rose was quiet for a moment. Thoughtful. Then she turned toward him, ignoring the slight pull on her line. "How do you do it? How do you live without God?"

Zane shrugged. That was one he'd never been asked before. "You just . . . do."

Katie Rose wasn't about to let it end there. "Who do you pray to?"

"I don't pray."

"Not ever?" Her line went slack. The fish must have lost interest and moved on, but Katie Rose dug in for the fight, such as it was. "And when somethin' bad happens, and you wish that it was different, who do you ask for the change?"

"I dunno."

"Is that not a prayer?"

"I suppose." Zane shrugged again. "I never really thought about it."

"You should. It's impossible to live without God. He's in your every footstep. Every beat that your heart makes. In the wind and the trees."

In that moment Zane wanted to believe. He wanted to bask in the poetry of her words. Bow to a higher power. The earnest light in her green eyes made him want what she had, a faith beyond measure.

He cleared his throat, uncomfortable with the turn of the conversation. "Didn't your parents ever teach you about the three things you should never talk about?"

She shook her head.

"Religion, Politics, and—"

"And what?"

He coughed, hoping she didn't notice the flush of red creeping into his neck. "Two's enough for now."

"We do not speak of politics, Zane Carson. But God? He's our way of life."

Katie Rose's words echoed through his mind for the rest of the evening. During the prayer at suppertime, when he was the only one at the table who didn't bow his head before or after the meal, and again during the Bible reading when everyone looked to Abram with eager eyes and open hearts as he read Scripture.

Zane had lived his entire life without God. But what if what Katie Rose said was true, that it wasn't possible to live without God? Was He always there? Surely for those who believed He was. But was God there for the nonbelievers? How could that possibly be?

Morning came with an increase in the normal flurry of activity. Aside from the milking, egg gathering, chicken feeding, cooking frenzy that normally occupied the Fisher household each morning, this Sunday held even more. It was the Fisher's Sunday to host the church service, which meant the regular chores had to be completed extra early. That way the rest of the morning could be spent on final preparations for hosting nearly two hundred people for singing, worship, and eating. The singing for the teenagers would be held in the barn that evening, so it had to be especially clean.

Zane went about that morning doing his part to ensure that the service went off as smoothly as possible. Annie, it seemed, was unusually nervous. John Paul had told him that it was the first service she would be allowed to attend. She would state her intentions of joining the Amish church district, and the members would vote.

Or maybe her anxiety came because church would be held in the house she had helped run since Ruth had taken ill. She shouldn't have worried because Mary Elizabeth and Katie Rose had come early to help, with Hester Stoltzfus and Beth Troyer arriving soon after.

Zane couldn't help but watch Katie Rose whenever she was near. Her grace and smile were mesmerizing as she moved through the kitchen. Her words of yesterday haunted him even more. Could she be right about God? That it was impossible to live without Him because He was everywhere? And if she were, what did it mean to him? He couldn't wrap his mind around the idea, couldn't see it in its entirety, so he stuffed his thoughts back down. They'd keep for later, for a time when he could take them out and examine them carefully.

Zane had wanted to disappear as soon as the buggies started to arrive, but Ruth and Abram wouldn't hear of it. Though he wasn't allowed in the church service, they asked him to remain in the yard greeting the members, talking, and getting to know the people of the district better until it was time to begin.

The bishop, ministers, and deacon went inside the house first.

"They'll go upstairs and decide what they're goin' to preach

about today, and who's goin' to do most of the preachin'," John
Paul told him.

Zane nodded to Ezekiel Esh. The old man seemed to be moving a little slower than usual. The day had turned out a little colder
than the one before, and tomorrow morning, the first frost of the
season was supposed to arrive. *The cold must be getting to him.* He
turned to John Paul. "They do this every Sunday?"

John Paul nodded. "*Jah.* Each Sunday we have church."

"Right." He'd forgotten. The church district only held church
every other Sunday. On the off days, they visited with surrounding
districts, traveling to see friends and loved ones.

Another half hour later, Zane found himself alone in the yard.
Well, alone if he didn't count the dogs, the cats, and the crazy number of buggies parked over to one side. He was still scratching his
head over the orderly way they entered the church. Men first, then
the women, followed by the younger boys who had not yet joined,
and finally the young girls.

Suddenly he wished to be a part of them. For the first time in
his life, he felt as if he were missing something important. He tried
to shake off the thought, but the feeling lingered. He'd lived his
entire life without religion, and he'd been just fine.

But have you lived your entire life without God?

A shudder crept over Zane's spine. That was a question he did
not have the answer for, wasn't sure if he ever would.

※◎ ◎※

Three hours later the church members filed back out into the cool,
sunny afternoon. Zane tried not to crane his neck to get sight of
Katie Rose as the women started coming out of the house. He was
about as successful as he had been not listening in on the church
service.

He had kept to the yard, playing with the dogs and otherwise enjoying a lazy mid-morning, doing a whole lot of nothing. But he wasn't able to understand a word that was said or sung. As far as he could tell, the words were German, not the rhythmic Pennsylvania Dutch he'd grown accustomed to hearing.

Now that church was out, his heart gave a hard thump at the thought of seeing Katie Rose once more, of sitting next to her as they ate, and talking some more. Maybe she could tell him a little more about her God. And maybe he could gain a little more understanding.

As he filled his plate with pickles and cheese, sliced apples and bread, he noticed the men on one side of the yard and the women on the other. He'd love to break ranks and sneak over and sit by her for a little while. It wasn't like he was Amish, only pretending to be for a few weeks.

John Paul snagged his elbow as he started toward the women's side.

"The men sit over here." He nodded toward the rest of the men, young and old alike, dotted across one half of the yard. Most were talking and laughing, but there were a few, Zane noticed, who gazed at the women like lovesick puppies.

He sure hoped he didn't look like that. No way. He just enjoyed Katie Rose's company. It wasn't like he was in love with her.

He gave her one last glance, then allowed John Paul to lead him away.

⊷⊶ ⊷⊶

Katie Rose pried her gaze off the *Englischer* and focused instead on the food before her. The men had gone through the food line, and the women had their turn, filling plates for themselves as well as some of the younger children. Katie Rose had thought one day she would be filling a plate for her and her children while their father sat with the men and talked farming and horses.

Instead she loaded up a plate to share with Samuel. Strange how God's plan for her was to be the one thing that she wasn't. But she was happy with her life. Really, she was.

As she made herself comfortable in a bit of weak autumn sunlight, Samuel crawled into her lap. Katie Rose looked up to find Mary Beachy staring at her husband, John. She'd heard that Mary was going to have another baby. Sometime in early spring. This child would be number four. That sinful monster, Envy, rose up within her. She was happy for Mary and John. Really. But she had always thought some of that very same happiness would belong to her.

She sighed and bowed her head, saying her thanks for the food and for the beautiful day and asking forgiveness for her selfish thoughts. The good Lord knew what He was doing. She had to trust and believe, but so far she hadn't kept her half of that agreement.

She looked up from her prayer to find Zane Carson staring at her again. Was it her own fanciful thoughts that had her imagining that his look was similar to the one John gave his wife? For sure and for certain, it must be. And yet . . . if she were mistaken, and if he truly was looking at her in that way, why did he have to be an outsider?

Samuel Beachy had looked at her like that before he left, but she wasn't about to let herself dwell on that either. She gazed at the little boy lolling in her lap, and bent forward to plant a small kiss on the top of his carrot-red hair. She had her Samuel now. She really should be thankful for all the things she had and not the secret longings she'd kept hidden for so long.

Thoughts like that would only leave her with a broken heart.

It was after three before the last of the churchgoers left. A clique or two of teenagers still hung around, eager to get to tonight's singing. Katie Rose smiled remembering the times she had waited for Samuel Beachy to come pick her up for the Sunday singing.

She folded up another of the tables and balanced one side on the ground until John Paul came over to lift it and take it into the barn. Tonight's festivities would be fun and loud, couples discovering each other and hoping to make a place in the community for themselves. The couples destined to be married this year had already stated their intentions, but next year's couples were as of yet unspoken. Tonight a few of those pairs might state intentions to each other, promises they would keep a secret for the entire time of their courtship. That was the Amish way.

But it was just as fun to watch for pairings of the boys and girls. Many of those happened after they left her classroom, but the following year when the students who had graduated returned for their German lessons, the pairing began. Katie Rose could almost see them in advance. How ironic that she had not been able to see the truth about Samuel Beachy when it was right before her eyes, and yet she could tell the intentions of others.

John Paul took the weight of the next table and nodded toward the barn. Caleb and Lilly stood there, talking quietly while everyone else drank the rest of the lemonade and chased the kittens around.

"There's a match if'n I ever saw one."

Katie Rose shook her head. "Maybe as far as Caleb was concerned, but Lilly wants to stretch her legs a bit more before folding them down to join up with the church."

He shook his head with a jaunty wink. "I'll bet you a strawberry rhubarb pie they'll end up married this time next year."

Katie Rose let him take the table, then propped her hands on her hips, aware that as she did so she probably looked remarkably like their mother. "First of all, John Paul Fisher, it is a sin to place wagers, and second of all, where are you going to get a pie?" She raised her brows at him and tapped her foot waiting on the answer.

John Paul smiled in his crooked way that got him nearly everything he could want from life. The boy was too charming by far. "I don't think the bishop or the deacon could find fault with a friendly little wager, sister dear, and I won't need one, seein' as I'm right. They'll be married soon enough. If not this year, then surely the next."

"They're too young," she said. "For this year or the next." Caleb, the bishop's youngest son had just turned sixteen in the summer. And Lilly Grace Miller was only now out of Katie Rose's classroom.

Still, she could tell the young man had his choice of a wife already picked out and that lucky girl was Lilly. If Lilly were truly lucky, Samuel Beachy's younger brother would find his *rumspringa* complete when the time came to bow before the church, and he wouldn't go traipsing off to see more of the world.

She pushed down that uncharitable thought. Now was not the time to bring up ghosts from the past. It was a beautiful day, a singing was about to begin, and there was work to be done.

＊＊＊

Katie Rose stood on her parents' porch and gazed up at the stars that decorated the night sky. She had stayed after the service to help get ready for the singing. Her mother had been through her last cancer treatment weeks ago, but the medications and radiation had taken a toll on her overall health. They only had a few more weeks to go before *Mamm* would be declared cancer free, and the time couldn't pass quickly enough for Katie Rose. Not that she minded the extra work. Amish life was full of needs for family and community, but she looked forward to the day when her mother would start to feel like herself again. The light had gone out in her mother's eyes, and Katie Rose knew that every day she fought with the needs of her body versus the needs of her family. Her body was winning, but no one could convince her to take it easy. She wasn't about to let her family down, let anyone do without because she was not feeling as well as could be. No, Ruth Fisher continued on like nothing had ever happened.

A perfect example would be today's church service. Several families had offered to host the service in order to let her parents have a break from the responsibilities, but Ruth wouldn't even talk about it. When someone brought it up, she ignored them and went to the kitchen to bake another loaf of bread for the occasion.

Finally everyone just stopped talking and started helping instead.

Now that it was nearly done, Katie Rose breathed a sigh of relief. Their duty was over—until it was Gabe's turn to hold the service—but with the Lord's help, her mother would be long past her mending before his time came around.

She glanced toward the barn, the light coming through the crack between the doors showing no signs of going out anytime soon. Strange music floated on the cool, gentle breeze, as if someone had brought in some type of battery-powered radio. She supposed she should go out there and stop them, but since most of those still left were living in their run-around years, she decided against it. Better they figure out their path now than weeks before their time to join the church.

As she stared out into the night, letting her thoughts skip from topic to topic as it would, two figures rounded the corner of the barn and started toward her.

"Are you sure you don't want to go?" John Paul asked.

That could only mean the other shadowy silhouette belonged to . . .

"There's no way I'm riding in that car with you ever again."

"Suit yourself." John Paul clapped Zane Carson on the back and headed across to the field behind the phone shanty where *Dat* made her *bruder* keep his car.

As far as she was concerned, John Paul was taking his *rumspringa* a bit too seriously. He hadn't even made out like he was seeking the company of a young girl with hopes that she would one day be his wife. Instead he left the house at all hours of the night, going who knows where and doing who knows what for hours on end. *Rumspringa* was one thing, but Katie Rose had a feeling that had her mother not been ill, her father would have not let John Paul's *rumspringa* be so . . . liberal. Especially since her sister, Megan, had left to see the world, much like Samuel Beachy. And like Samuel, Megan Fisher had yet to return. Katie Rose had been unable to find her missing sister to tell her of their mother's illness. Not that it would bring her back—no one had spoken to Meg in years. Yet despite the heartache she had caused, Katie Rose hoped her sister was faring well in the *Englisch* world.

She watched her brother cross the paved county road toward his car, and said a tiny prayer as he hopped in and sped away. Then she turned back to find Zane Carson approaching her through the night.

Part of Katie Rose wanted to tuck tail and head back into the warmth of the house. Her father could take care of the young people left singing in the barn, but nothing called for her return home. By now Gabe had put the children to bed, all but Mary Elizabeth. Secretly, Katie Rose was glad when these opportunities arose.

As much as she loved taking care of her brother and his children, she wondered if perhaps her presence in his household had kept them both from reaching for the lives that should have been theirs. Or at least his. Katie Rose knew that Gabe had loved Rebecca with all of his heart. Everything not given to God was offered up to his wife and family. When she died, a part of Gabe died with her. Unlike Gideon, Gabriel hid his grief, called her fateful childbirth God's will, and moved on. But only part way. Instead of remarrying, like most Amish men, he simply relied on Katie Rose to care for his family.

She had waited too long. Zane Carson now stood at the foot of the porch, gazing up at her face.

"Hi, there."

She hoped that the night shadows hid her expression from him. She didn't want him to see how happy she was that he'd come to find her. "Good night to you, Zane Carson."

He hooked his fingers through his suspenders and rocked back on his heels. "Come walk with me, Katie Rose."

She shook her head.

"Why not?"

"An Amish gentleman is never so bold as to ask a lady to walk with him after dark."

"In case you haven't noticed, I'm not Amish."

Ach, she had noticed all right. That was most of the problem. Too much time spent with him, and she was for sure and for certain when he left town he'd take a big hunk of her heart with him. It was better by far to leave it this way.

"Where'd you get those pants, Zane Carson?"

He looked down at his too-short pants as if seeing them for the first time. "I believe they are a gift from your father. A lesson in humility."

She couldn't stop herself and laughed at his joke, her defenses crumbling around her. Amish were never good at that anyway. They were not fighters. How could she be expected to keep these feelings at bay? She had warned herself against those deep brown eyes, against that dimpled smile, but his sense of humor and good spirit? She had no fortifications for that.

"Are you going to walk with me or not?"

"And if I say *nay*?"

"Then I might call you a chicken."

Katie Rose smiled into the night. "And if that doesn't work?"

"Then I'll ask again, even nicer this time."

"And if the answer is still *nay*?"

"Then I might resort to begging."

She stopped and stared at him through the darkness of the night.

"Are you going to make me beg, Katie Rose?"

She shook her head. When had his tone changed from funny banter to funeral serious? She should tell him no. All the common sense she had told her to say *nay*, then gather up a flashlight and run home as fast as she could. "I will not let you beg. Nor will I walk with you. It is time I went home, Zane Carson."

"Then I'll walk you there."

She shook her head.

"Surely that's an Amish enough virtue, to not let a lady walk home in the dark unprotected."

He would protect her, she knew that without a doubt, but who was going to protect her heart from him and those deep brown eyes? She sighed. "All right, then."

She went back into the house and told her father good night. Her mother had long since gone to bed, the extra effort of hosting the church service taking most of her energy.

Katie Rose's heart thumped loudly in her chest as she made her way back out onto the porch. Zane was still standing where she'd left him, like an anxious suitor awaiting his love. But he was *Englisch* not Amish. She had heard tales of *Englisch* men and their lack of morals, their disregard for the holy, their wild desires when it came to matters of the flesh.

She shivered, then pulled her shawl a little closer around her. She should have brought a coat. And she should have never agreed to walk home with Zane Carson.

He didn't say a word as they headed for the road, moonlight and the stars shining almost as brightly as the light he carried.

"There are so many more stars here than in Chicago," he said, gazing up at the sky.

Katie Rose kept her arms wrapped around her, but tilted her face upward to the darkened sky. "How can that be, Zane Carson? The sky only changes at the bottom of the world."

He lifted one shoulder in half a shrug. "City lights, I guess. Block out the light from the stars. Or maybe the stars are there, but the lights distract everybody from noticing."

She couldn't imagine living in a big city like that. Her visits to Tulsa were enough to make her head spin.

They walked a few more minutes, slower than average so they could study the stars. Katie Rose wished she knew what he was thinking. What did he see when he looked at the heavens?

"Are you cold?" He nodded toward her arms still folded around her.

"A little," she admitted. The night had a definite chill in the air. Fall was well on its way.

"If I had a coat, I'd lend it to you."

She nodded, secretly glad he didn't. It would smell like him, and she didn't think she could stand walking home wrapped in his scent. Just having him beside her was chore enough.

"Why didn't you ever get married, Katie Rose?"

She gave a halfhearted shrug. No one had ever asked her that before. "It just never came up."

"Because of Samuel Beachy?"

She turned to look at him, but his face was in shadow, his expression hidden by the night. "Who told you about Samuel?"

"John Paul may have mentioned it a time or two."

Katie Rose shook her head. "It is a sin to speak ill of others, but John Paul is almost as chatty as Beth Troyer."

"Now I know who to talk to when I need information."

She smiled. "You don't want to hear my tale."

"Actually, I do."

She watched the rise and fall of his broad shoulders, before she answered. "John Paul told Mary Elizabeth that you are gettin' married when you return to Chicago."

"He is a chatterbox."

"I think *rumspringa* has loosened his tongue."

Zane Carson laughed.

They walked in silence, the only sound around them the rustle of leaves in the trees as the ever-present Oklahoma wind blew through the night.

"Are you?" she asked again.

"Yes."

Suddenly her mind was filled with questions. Did he love his *Englisch* girl with the love of the romance books she'd read during her own *rumspringa?* Did she love him back?

"Your turn. Why did you never get married, and what does it have to do with Samuel Beachy?"

"What does it matter? It was long ago."

"It matters."

She shook her head. "Why do you want to know, Zane Carson?"

"Because I do."

"That's not really an answer."

"It's the best you're going to get. So just tell me."

She took a steadying breath to gain courage and stall for time. "*Jah*, it's because of Samuel, I suppose."

"Did he break your heart?"

"Not all Amish couples marry for love, you know."

"I do now."

She smiled into the darkness. "But . . ." she stopped, unwilling to say the words out loud. Ridiculous, she admonished herself. It wasn't like everyone in the district didn't know. "But I loved Samuel Beachy with all of my heart."

He paused. "So what happened?"

"A few weeks before we were to be baptized into the church, Samuel came to me in the middle of the night and said that he needed to go out and experience the world."

"He didn't do that during his *rumspringa*?"

"His father is the bishop, you know."

Zane Carson nodded.

"Bishops are chosen for life. Bishop Beachy took . . . takes his position with the church very seriously. He keeps his children close to him. Even durin' their run-around time."

"But that's not how it's supposed to work. Is it?"

"Everyone is different, Zane Carson. Even the Amish interpret the *Ordnung* with different eyes. That's why we have church elders to lead us through. For the bishop to have a son who ran crazy all over the district and beyond was more than he thought he should let his church see."

"I can understand that."

"But what taste of freedom Samuel did get, he discovered he liked . . . very much."

"More than you?"

She smiled, despite a stab of sadness. "I suppose so, Zane Carson. Samuel Beachy left the district and has never been back since."

"Does he ever write or call? Scratch that last part. Does he ever write?"

"If he does, the bishop has not said. As far as he is concerned, his son is dead to the world and all those in it."

"That's harsh."

"He wasn't baptized so he wouldn't be shunned by the church. But the shame of havin' such as wayward spirit in a child was too much for Bishop Beachy to bear. He never so much as speaks his name. Not since the day Samuel left us."

"But other men . . . I mean, to an upstanding Amish man you'd be quite a catch. You're pretty, good with children, and a great cook."

She was thankful for the darkness that hid her blush over his kind words. "*Danki*," she said, when she really wanted to twirl about in a circle and bask in the knowledge that Zane Carson thought she was pretty. That was ridiculous. Plain folk didn't set much store in looks, and it was not a good idea to let such compliments go to her head. Or her heart. She steeled herself and continued. "At first I had some offers. But I turned them down."

"Why?"

"I thought Samuel would get it out of his system and come back. But then a year passed and another. Then my Samuel . . . *Gabe's* Samuel was born. Rebecca died and my brother was on his own with six children to care for. He needed me, and I guess I needed him just as much. Once I moved in with my *bruder*, the offers just stopped comin'."

"And Samuel never returned."

"*Jah*. But the Lord has a plan for us all. Mine is to provide for my family, my niece and nephews, and to teach the children of our district."

He made a noise somewhere between a snort and a laugh.

She tilted her head. "You don't believe the Lord has plans for us?"

"I don't know."

"Then why do you scoff?"

"I don't know." His voice was close to a whisper, almost a sigh.

"So you believe that humans are just floatin' around with no one to guide them home?"

"Maybe."

"That's not what you believe. I can hear it in your voice."

She saw him dip his chin in a jerky sort of nod. For someone with such strong beliefs he surely had a time trying to express them.

"I just have . . . trouble with God, you know?"

"*Nay*, I'm sorry; I don't."

He took a heaving breath, and she supposed the dark gave him the courage to finally speak his thoughts out loud. "I don't understand how a man can live His life without thought of consequence, then ask forgiveness one day and, *bam!* All's forgiven, and he's going to heaven."

"*Jah*, that is understandable. But it is true. Amish also believe in living everyday with his sacrifice in mind. Treat others with love and respect, even if you have trouble. Help your neighbor. And do all you can for each other."

Despite the cold and the feelings he stirred in her, Katie Rose was sorry to see Gabriel's driveway just ahead.

"Almost there," Zane Carson said, nodding toward the dirt drive that led toward home.

She held back her sigh. She wanted to talk more, more about his *Englisch* love, the beauty of the night, God. Especially God. She had a feeling Zane Carson needed to find his way to the Almighty more than he let on. Maybe even more than he knew himself.

Instead, they turned silently down the narrow road and made their way toward the warm lights of the house.

"*Danki*, Zane Carson," Katie Rose said as they drew nearer. She didn't want this time to end. Didn't want to leave him to walk back to her parents' *haus* by himself. Didn't want to say good night.

Her thoughts otherwise occupied, she didn't see the tree root and caught the gnarled wood with the toe of her lace-up black boots. She would have gone sprawling had she not been scooped up by Zane Carson.

He wrapped his warm, strong hands around her arms and pulled her close to him.

Katie Rose's breath left her in a quick rush. Her entire body was pressed up against the *Englischer*, the hard planes of his torso sending heat flooding through her system.

She couldn't remember ever being this close to a man. Not even Samuel Beachy, and if she had, she certainly never felt like this. Warm. Hot. Cold. Breathless. All at the same time.

"Kate, I—"

She couldn't read the light in his eyes, but thought perhaps he felt it too, this strange and wonderful current that ran between them, that pulled them closer and closer together. If she raised her face to his, he just might kiss her. Oh, how she wanted that kiss. Just one taste of the forbidden, and she would go into the house and never ask again.

His nostrils flared, his hands tightened on her arms, and he drew her even closer, though she hadn't known that was possible.

His head lowered an inch, then another. Katie Rose waited breathlessly for his kiss.

"Katie Rose? You comin' in?"

She tore herself from Zane's grasp, thankful and disappointed all at once.

"Of course, *bruder*." Was that her voice? That high-pitched squeaky sound, like a mouse?

She turned away from Zane. It was better this way. She had no future with a man like him, an *Englischer*. Kissing him would only leave her with more heartbreak when the time came for him to go. And she'd had enough heartbreak for a lifetime.

"Good night, Zane." She turned without looking at him and followed Gabe into the house.

8

Zane pounded down his pillow and flopped onto his other side. Amish beds were not known for comfort, but he couldn't blame his sleeplessness on the lumpy mattress. Or the fact that John Paul was still not back. If he had known that he was going to flop around instead of go right to sleep, he could have taken a sleeping pill. He hadn't had to take one in days, the hard work of the daylight hours chasing away the nightmares with sheer physical exhaustion.

He stared at the bed opposite his, still neatly made up. John Paul didn't even make a pretense about his catting around. There was no telling what he was out doing. Drinking, drugs, running around with English girls, while Zane lay here in the dark and fretted over Katie Rose. And God. Don't forget God. As soon as he managed to push one concern from his thoughts, the other popped up in its place.

Katie Rose. She was so warm and so innocent. She didn't even know how beautiful she was, which increased her beauty. But it was more than that. The light in her eyes was steady and true. She worked hard every day taking care of children that weren't hers by birth, teaching the scholars of the district, cooking, cleaning, and fretting over her family. He had promised himself that he wouldn't touch her, wouldn't do so much as hold her hand. He was leaving in a couple more months. He was getting married. Going to Mexico. He had no business toying with her emotions. He had to steer clear. And he had almost succeeded too. Until she fell against him and all of his good sense fled. In that moment, he'd forgotten all the vows he'd made to himself. Forgotten that he wasn't from her world. Forgotten everything except how warm and sweet she felt against him, and how much he wanted to lean down for a taste of those sweet, pink lips.

He flopped onto his back and stared at the darkened ceiling. They were so lucky that Gabriel had picked that time to come out onto the porch and check on his sister.

Or maybe it wasn't luck at all, but the plan of a divine power.

Zane wasn't sure how much of that he truly believed. Why would God care if he kissed Katie Rose? What reason would God have for planning out the tiniest details of their lives? Didn't He have better things to do?

But what really filled his mind were the words that Katie Rose had spoken to him. How a man can be forgiven.

He shook the thoughts away. He'd lived this long without God and His divine plans. He could survive a few more years.

The thought persisted. He really wanted to talk to Katie Rose more about it, but he'd probably scared her off with his Neanderthal advances. She hadn't even looked at him as she made her way into the house, more than happy to get away from him. He'd need to apologize to her as soon as he could. Maybe even tomorrow. But it was wash day, and he needed to get up early in order to help Ruth and Annie. After the work they had put in for the church service, they would especially need his assistance.

Katie Rose would be up washing clothes tomorrow, too. And just like that she filled his thoughts once more.

He was pounding his pillow into submission yet again when the door to the bedroom creaked open. He watched as John Paul snuck in, sat down on his bed, and unlaced his boots. Zane's eyes had long ago grown accustomed to the darkness. He could see John Paul as clearly as if it were the middle of the day.

John Paul placed his boots next to his bed, then stripped off his shirt, folding it neatly and tucking it away inside a box under his bed. Completely out of sight.

"That's quite a hiding place you got there."

John Paul jumped and whirled around, somehow managing to stifle his yelp of surprise. "Zane Carson, you scared years from my life. What are you doin' awake?"

"Couldn't sleep." No sense going into why. That part was no one's business but Zane's. "A better question would be: Where have you been and why are you hiding clothes under your bed? Wash day is tomorrow, you know."

John Paul collapsed onto his bed and propped his elbows onto his knees, his hands dangling in the space in between. "You have to promise not to tell. *Mamm* and *Dat* wouldn't like it much, if they found out."

"I thought anything goes in *rumspringa*."

He shrugged. "Mostly, but this they wouldn't like."

How bad could it be? Zane wasn't sure he wanted to know the answer to that question. "Tell me."

John Paul took a deep breath. "I have a job."

Zane tried not to laugh. Honestly he did. "There's living life on the edge, buddy."

"It's not funny."

Zane sobered up immediately. "What is it, then?"

"I got the job to help pay for the medical bills. When I told *Dat* what I was goin' to do he said, *nay*, that this was the time for makin' sure about joinin' the church."

"And you got a job regardless."

"I hide my work clothes under my bed so the girls won't find them. Each Friday when I get paid, I slip the money into the pickle fund."

"And they never notice? That has to be hundreds of dollars."

John Paul smiled somewhere between a cocky teenage grin and a grimace of pain. "Annie's not an accountant. She's a rich *Englischer* from Dallas. She doesn't keep up with such things. Plus, I know she's been linin' the fund. We can't sell *that* many pickles."

"Good point."

"So you won't tell?"

He shook his head. It wasn't often that someone exceeded his expectations, but John Paul had done just that. Of course, if Abram found out that Zane knew about this, he'd probably toss him out on his keister. All the more reason to keep his mouth shut.

If only he could push God and Katie Rose from his mind as easily as that.

❧ ❧

One day slipped easily into the next. Before Zane knew it, the weather had turned cold and winter was upon them. An Oklahoma winter was very different from Chicago's. Not quite as cold, the air more humid. On the days the cold rivaled that of Chicago, it seemed as if it might blow straight into his bones. Chores still had to be done. Chickens fed, cows milked, hay pulled down and spread for the horses.

If it hadn't been for the heavy wool coat John Paul had supplied to him the week before Thanksgiving, he might have seriously considered going back home without finishing out his required three months. Chicago might be colder, but he had heated indoor air and winter clothes. He supposed that a person would eventually get used to the weather, the sudden and sometimes drastic drop in the temperatures. But as far as Oklahoma weather was concerned, he was a greenhorn.

Another bright spot was Katie Rose. He hadn't seen her much since he'd almost kissed her that Sunday after church, but she'd been on his mind every day. He recalled the longing he'd heard in her voice as she told him about not expecting to have a family of her own. How God had a plan for her to take care of Gabe's family.

What garbage. She was kind and nurturing and as loving as they came. If God truly had a plan for her it was to find some handsome guy to marry and raise a bunch of kids and live happily ever after here in Amish land.

Now why did his stomach drop at the thought?

Just because he found her warm and refreshing didn't mean anything beyond that. They were from two different worlds and that's how it would forever remain.

Maybe he was just getting a taste of figurative cold feet to go with his literal ones.

Yes, that sounded logical.

Thankfully his cold ankles were a thing of the past. Katie Rose had taken pity on him and found another castoff pair of barn door pants for him to wear. He glanced down. At least these covered the laces in his boots, and unless he sat down, his sock color was a mystery to all those around him.

She also let out the hem in his first pants. So now he had two pairs to get him through to wash day.

John Paul tossed a set of waffle weave underwear to him. "Come on, city boy."

Zane caught them, one eyebrow raised. If the late nights working to bring in extra money for his mother's hospital bills was taking its toll on the young man, it was yet to be seen. "Come on where?"

"Thanksgiving is in two days. Let's go bag us a turkey."

He frowned. "Like at the store?"

"Like huntin'."

Of all the time he'd spent in Oregon in the cooperative with his parents, Zane had never gone hunting. He'd milked goats and weeded the garden, harvested food, and otherwise helped with the day-to-day chores much like the Amish children that he'd encountered. But since most of the members were vegan, hunting was out of the question.

"What happened to peace and love and all that?" he asked.

"It is not a sin to kill for food. It is a way of life. We hunt to put food on our tables," John Paul added as Zane stripped out of his clothes and donned the insulated underwear before getting dressed again.

"So that's an acceptable form of violence?"

John Paul frowned, an unusual expression for the happy teen. "You are tryin' to make this too complicated. We hunt for food; we do not kill for sport."

Zane supposed that made sense, but there was one thing he'd learned since living among the Amish—there were a lot of gray areas that were hard to understand. He could see why they expected Annie to learn their ways before she committed herself to the church. The whole concept was just out of his grasp.

They walked down the stairs together, John Paul leading the way.

Zane slowed, and turned to John Paul. "So what happened to Halloween?" There hadn't been any trick-or-treaters, no black and orange pumpkins set about. The entire day had gone unnoticed weeks ago.

John Paul shook his head. "We do not participate in such nonsense."

Halloween was pagan at its core, but the rest was just in fun. He was about to say so, but took in the serious expression on John Paul's face. In that moment, he looked so much like his father that Zane thought better of voicing his opinion. What did it matter to him?

They got to the bottom of the stairs, and the women were nowhere to be seen, yet the smell of baking pies and cooling bread filled the downstairs portion of the house. The aroma only added to the warmth given off by the stove.

The men grabbed their coats and hats off the pegs, then John Paul fetched the rifle behind the door, and together they walked out into the brisk afternoon sunshine.

The blast hit Zane like a bucket of water to the face. And he thought the wind blew hard in Chicago. Or maybe it wasn't the persistence of the current, just the surprise that the Oklahoma wind could possibly rival that of the city named after its breeziness.

Zane pulled on the leather work gloves he'd picked up at the general store on their last trip into town. "That gun hasn't been there the whole time."

"*Dat* keeps it in the barn. It's *gut* to own a gun, but not *gut* to let it own you."

Wise words.

After all the war-torn countries he'd been to, all the devastation he'd seen . . . well, an idiom like that made a lot of sense. How would the world look if more people adopted that mentality?

It would have to be all of them, the cynic inside him whispered, but he could see the philosophy worked here in Clover Ridge. It might not be the entire world, but it was a start. He'd make a note of that tonight when he sat down to write. That had become his habit. John Paul sneaked out for work, and Zane took out his notebook and pen and recorded the day's events and thoughts. It would take him awhile once he got back to Chicago to record all his notes on to his computer, but he thought it'd be easier this way. Instead of having to constantly risk life and limb jumping in the car with John Paul to drive into town to charge his laptop.

The last time had been . . . well, it must have been almost three weeks ago. Until recently, his primary concern had been his computer and being able to record his thoughts and findings. Strange how his plans had shifted by necessity and that pen and paper had taken its place.

Even stranger, his cell phone went dead long before that. Instead, he had used the phone shanty across from the house to call Monica, but the last time he'd spoken to her had been a couple of days ago. Surely not longer than that.

Instead of using his computer, each evening he'd taken to writing in a journal, recording his thoughts for the day. With any luck he'd have enough to print several articles. Or a maybe even a book.

Like most writers he felt he had a book somewhere inside, a novel to rock the ages. He imagined a work of fiction, maybe something about a daring photojournalist who captured all the ladies hearts as he gunned down his story with a surprising single-mindedness. Like James Bond—with a camera.

But after spending time with the Amish, that idea seemed naïve at best.

He and John Paul headed into the forest behind the back garden that Ruth and Annie used to fill the table.

He slid a glance at John Paul. "We're just going to walk in there and . . . hunt?"

"Somethin' like that." John Paul led the way into the woods, a curious mix of evergreens and live oaks. A carpet of dead leaves, reddened pine needles, and fallen twigs snapped beneath their feet as they walked deeper and deeper into the forest.

Finally, they came to a small clearing. John Paul eased to the far side, where a small tree had long ago found its resting place. He sat on the trunk, propped up the gun next to him with its safety firmly in place, and started emptying his pockets. A thermos of hot coffee, extra shells, and a funny little box that looked as if it were made of cedar tumbled out.

Well, at least there was coffee. Zane sat down beside him and stretched his legs out in front of him.

They sat for a few minutes, listening to the wind careen through the tops of the trees. Zane had never been hunting a day in his life. He knew the importance of keeping quiet, but he couldn't imagine sitting being fruitful in this endeavor. He enjoyed the breather from the hard but productive Amish life, but after twenty minutes or so he turned to John Paul.

"Is this normal to just . . . sit . . . like this?" He kept his voice low.

"You ever been huntin'?" John Paul whispered.

"I grew up with vegans and a citified uncle."

"What's a vegan?"

Zane stifled his laugh. "It's a person who only eats and uses plant-based goods. They don't wear leather shoes or eat eggs. Just veggies and tofu."

A frown puckered John Paul's brow. "What's tofu?"

Zane grimaced. "You don't want to know."

They settled in and waited. Every now and then, John Paul would rattle the cedar box back and forth. It turned out it was a turkey call and that shaking it would produce a sound just like a gobble.

Hunting, Zane decided, was a little like fishing and required a lot of patience to get the prize. But when fishing, he'd had Katie

Rose for company, which in and of itself was fun—and warmer. A *lot* warmer.

John Paul nodded with the merest movement of his head. "Look there."

Zane cut his eyes in that direction. It took a second or two to see what he was referring to: a brown rabbit hesitantly hopping their way.

John Paul inched toward his rifle.

"You're going to shoot it?" Zane's words were barely louder than the wind.

"*Jah*, he'd make for some fine eatin'."

"I thought we were hunting for turkeys."

"True enough. But a good hunter takes what shot he can. And that'll be one less forager the womenfolk will have to worry about next spring."

Carefully, John Paul took aim, and with a quick single shot, took down the rabbit.

Zane watched the young man skin and clean the animal. It was easy to forget where the food came from when all a person had to do was walk into the nearest grocery store. A touch of remorse twisted in his gut, but it battled an equally strong sense of pride, of accomplishment. They would eat tonight because he and John Paul had gone hunting.

John Paul wrapped the meat in a plastic bag and put it in the cooler he'd brought along. The outside temperature was probably cool enough to keep the meat fresh until they got home, but this way sure beat having to lug around the carcass.

John Paul passed him the gun and returned to his seat on the log. "Next shot is yours."

Zane held the weapon in his gloved hands, conflicting emotions searing him. It seemed like yesterday he had felt the intense burn in his shoulder, felt the blood wet his clothes, and drip down his arm as someone wrapped a belt for a tourniquet around his bicep.

It wasn't *this* gun that hurt him, but one in the hands of the wrong person. He cleared his throat. "Is one rabbit enough to feed everyone for supper tonight?"

"*Nay*, not if you want to fry it up. You'll need three or four to have a good mess of rabbit, but one is enough to make a goodly sized pot of rabbit and dumplings."

"Like chicken and dumplings?"

"*Jah.*"

"Is that a traditional Amish dish?"

John Paul shrugged. "I think it is somethin' Noni dreamed up."

Zane nodded, once again in awe of the resourcefulness of the Amish people.

Their hunting trip lasted most of the afternoon. It was nearly dark before they found their turkey, as if the birds knew Thanksgiving was upon them and that showing their faces was not a good idea.

John Paul actually bagged the bird, but that didn't make Zane feel any less about his role in the hunt. Or maybe it was the four rabbits he bagged that made him feel like king of the world.

"The Lord has smiled upon us today."

Zane had never heard John Paul speak of grace before, and he was humbled. They had been . . . blessed. Strange, but something so violent as a rifle could kill a man or put food on his table. Blessed. That was the only way to look at it. They had gone out into the forest and not only found the treasure they originally intended, but enough for two more meals as well.

Zane smiled at John Paul. "And there is enough bounty to share." The wrinkled face of Ezekiel Esh came to mind. Alone and without any family, Zane felt a kinship to the man. He could see himself in Ezekiel, a man who had lost all of his family. Getting shot had done that, showed him his solitary life and where it would lead. So he had asked Monica to marry him. Zane hadn't known the old man then, but he knew the possibilities of a life lived alone.

The difference, of course, was Ezekiel had married and had a family. Still, he was alone. Well, mostly. He might live alone, but he had a whole community of like-minded people to care for him.

He glanced at John Paul again. "Mind if we take one of the rabbits to the deacon?"

John Paul smiled as if he knew what Zane had been thinking, as if he were proud that the *Englischer* finally "got" it. "How about we take two of them to Katie Rose? She can make somethin' for them and somethin' for the deacon as well."

Perfect.

They gathered their kill and started back the way they came, winding around and through the mismatched trees and toward the house. John Paul veered off to the left, and they eventually found themselves behind Gabriel's house. The wash was still pinned to the line, the colder temperatures lengthening the drying time.

John Paul nodded toward the back door. "Go on. It is your meat."

His meat. He shouldn't be so prideful over something so simple. Maybe that was why the Amish warned against pride.

Zane took the cooler to the small back stoop and knocked.

A few minutes passed before he knocked again, and Katie Rose jerked the door open almost as soon as his knuckles touched the wood.

"Zane Carson." Her voice sounded breathy, as if she'd been running a marathon.

"Katie Rose." His didn't sound much better.

He hadn't seen her in weeks, but she'd never been far from his thoughts. Suddenly he felt as shy as a schoolboy with a crush on the teacher.

Pull yourself together, man.

"John Paul and I went hunting for turkey this morning, and we found a few rabbits as well. We thought you and Gabe might like a couple. And the deacon."

He opened the cooler and took out two of the rabbits.

He couldn't read her expression. She looked . . . stunned. What did that mean for him? Stunned as in *I can't believe you killed an innocent animal?* Or stunned as in *I can't believe you're such a big strong he-man and brought me food for the table?*

Maybe the last one was pushing it a bit, but that's how he wanted her to feel. He'd stepped outside of his box today, and he was proud of himself. He wanted her to feel the same way about him.

Her shoulders relaxed, and she gave him a small smile, though it promptly disappeared. "*Danki*, Zane Carson," she said. "Your gift is most appreciated."

Warmth flowed through him, as if the sun was shining straight out of his heart. "You're very welcome." He bowed, not knowing what else to do, and then turned to leave.

He got as far as the bottom of the steps before she called out to him. "I will see you on Thanksgiving, Zane Carson."

And the sun shone even brighter.

Thanksgiving Day dawned bright and sunny, but cold. Frost covered everything in sight, making the world look strewn with diamonds.

Despite the holiday, Zane and John Paul went out to take care of the morning milking as soon as they got up. Breakfast was a simple affair of thick-crusted pie, dried fruits, nuts, and a hunk of sharp cheddar cheese. Back home that would have been an odd combination, and Zane might have refused, but somehow today it seemed more natural than toast and eggs. Pickle-making had been put on hold for the holiday, and Zane's job for the day was to stay out of the way. Every time he stepped near the kitchen the women sent him disapproving looks that no man should have to suffer. As much as he wanted to help, he decided to use the time to get a few of his notes organized. So he spent the morning upstairs, going through the pages he'd collected so far.

He shook his head at the changes he'd been through in nearly two months. He had learned so much about the Amish culture, so much that at times he felt as if he actually belonged here. Other times he wondered how anyone could keep up with the ins and outs of the *Ordnung*.

He had learned that the list of rules changed from district to district. While Bishop Beachy had decided that his members should be allowed to ride bikes and have phone shanties on their property, the neighboring district was not allowed these luxuries.

One thing seemed certain: they all believed in Jesus as their Savior. Zane thought back to his walk home with Katie Rose, how peacefully adamant she had been about her faith. A piece of him wanted a little of that for himself, to believe that a higher power cared enough to guide his daily life, cared enough to give him what he needed.

But you do believe.

The voice was there in his head, and for the first time in his life Zane knew that he did believe in God. He had just never really thought about it. Never gone to church, never had anyone question his faith. Not even in the Middle East where wars were fought over religion every day.

The thought made him sad. Why was it that people couldn't get along? Why wasn't believing enough?

Yet without the wars, he wouldn't have a job. That's what he did, he covered wars, showed their horrors and brought in a hefty paycheck to do so.

A twinge of guilt settled in his heart, but he pushed it away. He loved living life on the edge. His job made him feel alive, made his heart beat faster. He needed it to know that he was truly alive.

He looked down at the drawing he held in his hands. When he'd first arrived, Abram had made it perfectly clear: no pictures. He had hoped by now to have changed the patriarch's mind. Despite all of Jo's determined coercing, Abram had not relented. So he'd taken up drawing instead. He couldn't see the difference between one and the other, but there was something about pencil and paper that captured more emotion than he could with camera and film.

There was the one of Annie standing at the stove, only the side of her face showing, her hair escaping in short little tendrils unlike the other women who had never had a haircut. There was one of John Paul low on the milking stool. And his favorite, the one of Katie Rose in front of the class teaching the minds of tomorrow. He had taken a page from the Amish dolls and not given anyone a face. Somehow that made the pictures distinctive, so much so that he wanted to keep them for himself. He hadn't told anyone about them. Not even Monica. It would be easier just to not turn them in with the few generic photographs he'd taken of the barn and the house. These drawings he'd made of these people he'd grown to care for were too special to let slip through his fingers.

❧ ❧

Katie Rose watched her breath dissipate into the sunshine. Thanksgiving Day, and she had so much to be thankful for.

How many times was she going to say that to remind herself?

She did have a lot to be thankful for, but as the holidays set in, she found herself often wishing for . . . more.

Was this truly God's plan for her, and if it was, why did He let her have these feelings? A sense that she didn't have the life she was destined to have encroached on her mind. Unhappy as a teacher, she felt unworthy for the blessings God had bestowed on her. She bowed her head and said a quick prayer asking for forgiveness. She had so much more than a lot of folks, and for the most part, she was happy. She was.

"Katie Rose? Are you comin'?"

She opened her eyes to realize she had been sitting in the buggy all alone. Mary Elizabeth had taken the box containing pies and the dish of scalloped potatoes into the house. Gabriel had helped all the boys down, and now he and Samuel were waiting on her to finish up and precede them inside.

"*Jah*, I . . ." There wasn't anything to explain. It wasn't unusual to stop and pray. That was why women wore prayer *kapps*. There was nothing wrong with that, but she felt the heat rise in her cheeks. They had to be bright pink, but with any luck she could blame it on the cold if she were asked. A white lie, but surely forgivable.

Gabriel helped her down from the buggy and together the threesome made their way into the house. To the outsider they surely appeared like a family: husband and wife and child. Surely they did. Maybe Katie Rose had let Gabriel's need color her own decisions.

Or had it been her own need for a place to escape all the sad looks and pity? She had put on a brave face and pretended like all was well. That she was more than satisfied to help her *bruder* in his time of need, when all she had been doing was hiding her feelings and pretending like she wasn't hurt. She had pushed those feelings deep inside and not let them see the light of day. And that's where she would keep them. It was too late to mourn now. She had made her choice, and she would have to live with it.

"My goodness, Katie Rose"—Annie broke away from the

kitchen and crossed the room to give her a tight sisterly hug—"You look—"

"It's from the cold," she blurted before Annie could finish.

"I was going to say angry."

She shook her head, her lips pressed together to keep all of her secrets from tumbling out. Since she had been here, Annie had been like a sister to her, had almost taken the place of her blood sister, Megan. Megan had clearly been their father's favorite, and her leaving had nearly broken his heart.

Katie Rose released Annie and ignored her frown of concern. She couldn't admit out loud that just the thought of their *Englischer* visitor sent bright color rushing to her cheeks. Of its own accord, her gaze scanned the room and found Zane, sitting on the couch, one ankle crossed over the opposite knee. He had a coffee cup in one hand and a smile on his face.

Her stomach gave an uncomfortable lurch.

Annie followed her gaze. "So that's how it is?"

Katie Rose shook her head. "*Nay.*"

"Well, something's put that mournful look in your eyes."

Katie Rose squeezed Annie's hand. Today she should be especially thankful that the Lord had sent Annie to them. "Maybe we can talk after we eat."

Annie's sharp, lavender-colored eyes softened with affection. "You can count on it."

9

As usual the house was filled with love and noise. Aside from Christmas, Thanksgiving was Katie Rose's favorite holiday for fellowship, even topping Easter. The Easter holiday tended to be more quiet and subdued, a time to reflect on the sacrifices God had made for His believers. Thanksgiving was about taking stock of blessings, eating heartily, and reminding oneself of the things for which they were thankful.

They were just about to sit down and eat when a knock came at the door.

Looks were exchanged all around the room. Who could it be on a day like today? Yet Katie Rose knew. It had just slipped her mind once she'd gotten so caught up with her feelings—*nay*, thoughts—about Zane Carson.

She stood up, ready to tell her family that she had invited a guest for supper, when Zane beat her to her feet. He rubbed his hands down the front of his barn door trousers and looked sheepishly from one to the other of them. "I hope it's okay. I invited Ezekiel Esh to supper."

A chorus of *jahs* went up around the room. Katie Rose hid her smile. She and Zane had invited the same guest. Katie Rose had asked the deacon to come and sup with them when she had taken him a pot of rabbit stew. She had been worried about him. She knew she couldn't be the only one in a district full of caring souls, but she had to make sure the man knew that his closest neighbor was thinking about him as the holidays approached.

That Zane Carson had been thinking the same way as she . . .

He looked around the room. "I suppose I should have said something before now, but I totally forgot. I'm sorry."

Katie Rose knew her family. What they had they would share with others. After everything that the church had provided for them, to be allowed to feed a church elder on this holiday would be an honor indeed.

"Nonsense," *Mamm* answered smartly. "We'd be most glad to have the deacon with us today."

Her father nodded. "*Jah*. It is *gut* to have someone for fellowship."

"And there's plenty of food," Annie added.

Katie's gaze swept across the heavily laden table. Roasted turkey that Zane Carson and John Paul had brought in, pecan dressing, bean casserole, cheese potatoes, ham, cornbread, yeast rolls, and more chutney than she could shake a stick at. They had more than plenty, thanks to the Lord. And they'd been blessed enough to be eating on this feast for days.

Katie Rose crossed to the door and opened it.

Ezekiel stood on the porch, his gnarled fingers curled around his cane. He knocked against the door frame on his way in the house. "I was beginnin' to think I'd have to sup on the porch." His eyes twinkled in jest.

"That'd do no good for our standin' with the Lord," Abram shot back, and the room once again filled with laughter.

John Paul went to fetch Noni, then family and guests prepared to sit down and feast.

Once everyone was seated around the table, Abram bowed his head and the others followed suit. How had she managed to end up straight across from Zane Carson?

She glanced down the table at the bowed heads. Annie Hamilton. Annie had seated them. She was responsible for them sitting so close together. Katie Rose wasn't sure if that was a good thing or bad, but her heart gave a hard thump at the thought of watching him all through the meal. He was handsome, she grudgingly admitted. A fine man to show off God's handiwork. Strong jaw, now covered with a rusty-colored beard. He'd cut the beard close to his face, trim and neat looking she supposed, but to an Amish man, the longer the beard, the more devout he appeared. Zane had been clean shaven when he'd arrived at the farm, but he had grown his face hair, for warmth no doubt.

His head was bowed as if he were praying with them too. Well, with her family. She had been gazing around the table and thinking about the physical attributes of their guest, not thanking the Lord for the blessings He had bestowed on them. Quickly, Katie Rose bowed her head and promised to say extra prayers before she went to bed.

And if she got the chance she just might ask Zane Carson what he's thankful for this year.

***

After supper and pie and more tea and some coffee and more pie, Zane decided he'd never been so full in his life. Even on the inside. He'd bowed his head during the silent prayer, not really knowing what to say to this being he had decided was alive and listening. God. But somehow he'd found words inside him, words of thanks and gratitude for the things that he had in his life. He couldn't contribute them all to God. He'd worked hard to get where he was. Paid his own way through school. Worked nearly every day to pay rent and tuition. He'd sacrificed a great deal of his personal life to show the doubters that he was worthy, that he had the moxie to take care of himself, even though he was alone in the world. Even though the odds were stacked against him from the very start.

Like every other night since Zane had come to Oklahoma, Abram pulled the worn Bible from its place on the mantel. He settled himself into the rocking chair while everyone else gathered 'round. The fire crackled merrily in the grate, giving off a warm, golden glow that seemed to reflect the contentment that had grown within him.

Zane glanced around the room, one face to another, marveling in the friends that he had found, the sense of family and belonging that he hadn't known was missing until now.

Then Abram began to read. "Give thanks to the LORD for He is good; His faithful love endures forever. Let Israel say, 'His faithful love endures forever.' Let the house of Aaron say, 'His faithful love endures forever.' Let those who fear the LORD say, 'His faithful love endures forever.'"

Zane felt safe . . . warm, loved. Blessed. The thought came gently, easing its way into his mind. What if he didn't leave? What if he stayed? The possibilities filled his very being. Working the land each year, caring for livestock, marrying a sweet Amish girl and raising a passel of green-eyed kids as sweet and gentle as their mother.

He looked up and caught Katie Rose's gaze. She blushed as if she knew what he was thinking. He smiled and looked away, the intensity of the moment nearly frightening.

The sentimentality of the holiday must be getting to him. He couldn't stay. He had a perfectly fine life in Chicago. He was happy. He loved travelling, he loved Monica. Yeah, he loved her. Of course he did. Why else would he be marrying her?

He stifled a nervous chuckle. What a hoot that he had even considered the idea. Moving to Amish country. Converting.

"Zane? Are you all right?"

He snapped out of his thoughts, jerking to attention. Katie Rose sat across from him gazing at him, concern in her eyes.

"Yeah, yeah, I'm fine."

He must have been sitting there awhile, warring with himself. Everyone else was gone. Even Annie was nowhere to be seen. "Where is everybody?"

"Packin' up the buggies and gettin' ready to go home."

"Annie?"

A rose-colored blush filled her cheeks. "I think she's sayin' good night to Gideon."

He supposed that their good night included a scorching kiss. He tried to forget the fact that Katie Rose was within an arm's length and such a kiss could be just a heartbeat away. He couldn't reach for her for so many reasons. True enough he longed to taste her lips, but she was different from the women he'd known. If they were anywhere else, and she wasn't Amish, then he'd kiss her until the heat from their bodies set fire to everything around them. But they weren't any place else, and she was Amish. And sheltered. And beautiful. Special. So very special that he couldn't take advantage and cross the line between friendship and more. No matter how badly he wanted to.

"I guess I should go on up to bed." He regretted the words as soon as he said them. She didn't seem to notice anything out of place or maybe she didn't realize the intimacy he felt at saying those words to her—and the effect they had on him. "I mean, daylight comes pretty early." He stretched and tried to cover his expression.

She lowered her lashes, hiding her eyes from him. An English girl reacting the same way would have been coy and trite, but for Katie Rose, it seemed sweet and unassuming. He had it worse for her than he had thought.

He turned and started up the stairs toward the room he shared with John Paul, getting away from Katie Rose before he did something stupid and wasn't able to take it back. "Good night, Kate."

"Good night, Zane Carson."

10

Friday dawned with overcast skies that sagged heavy with snow. In Chicago, such clouds meant inches upon inches of the white stuff, but no one else seemed concerned with the weather. Abram said it was early for snow, but not impossible. And even if it did snow, John Paul had added, it would melt before the day was through. That was good enough for Zane. These men knew the weather, had watched the skies for too long for him to doubt their word.

The outside chores went on as usual, but the inside chores shifted as the women started to "redd up" for Christmas. Excitement spiced the air. This would be Ruth's first Christmas since her diagnosis, and as far as anyone was concerned she had licked it good. But Zane could see the hesitation in her eyes whenever her next doctor's appointment was brought up. He didn't say anything to her, let her keep that bit of doubt to herself. Negative words held less power when not spoken aloud.

"How will the doctor contact you with the test results?" Zane asked as they all sat around the dinner table the night before Ruth's last appointment. At least that was the consensus of hope—that this would be the last appointment. That the doctor would declare her cancer free and the family could breathe a sigh of relief at the power of miracles and modern science. But for now everyone was subdued and quiet. Even John Paul seemed preoccupied and usually silent.

"He will call the phone in the shanty out front."

There was no way of knowing when the doctor might call. Too much work still needed to be done for someone to stand by the shanty and wait on a call, but the idea of missing that call was ludicrous.

When Zane said as much, Annie replied, "The bishop allows us to have voice mail so customers can leave messages for pickle orders. It wouldn't be a problem to check for the message when we go to see about orders."

Zane couldn't imagine having to wait day after day not knowing the results of the test. "You can give them my cell phone number. I can take it into town tomorrow and have Anderson charge it." That would give him a chance to go by the school and check in with Katie Rose, too. He hadn't seen her in a couple of days, and he missed her. Plain and simple.

"That is mighty kind of you, Zane," Abram said as Ruth nodded.

John Paul brightened up for the first time the entire evening. "I can take you in my car."

Zane opened his mouth to politely refuse, as he would much rather take three times as long to get into town than risk life and limb in John Paul's old Ford. "Aren't you taking them to the doctor?"

Abram shook his head. "*Nay,* Ruth Ann's got Bill Foster, the Mennonite driver, to take her tomorrow."

Zane couldn't help but notice that Abram didn't talk about going himself. He didn't look anyone in the face, and he especially avoided looking down the table to where his wife sat, her own head bowed, gaze dropped.

Something was going on between them, and Zane couldn't help but worry about their sadness. Cancer was a nasty bedfellow. He knew firsthand as he had watched his uncle slip away. But Ruth had more hope than Tim Carson ever had. She had God on her side.

Zane just hoped He was paying attention to her marriage as well.

The morning of Ruth's appointment dawned bright, but cold in the way that Zane was slowly becoming accustomed to. Winter in Oklahoma was a curious mix of sunshine and wind. A person couldn't judge the temperature by looking at the sky. He'd heard the men talking about crippling ice storms and blizzards so bad visibility was nonexistent. Of course, extreme weather wasn't nearly as hard on the Amish as it was on their English neighbors.

Despite the fact that the morning and afternoon that were to follow would be momentous in the family dynamic, chores went on as usual. Zane and John Paul went about their usual routine of feeding and milking.

Zane had learned early on that wintertime brought about a break in the work. Amish farmers and their wives—their entire families—spent the spring and summer and half the fall trying to get ready for the winter. Food was planted, grown, harvested, and canned. It was a constant and busy life, but there was also something inherently satisfying about self-sufficiency. Something good and wholesome. How the Amish kept down their prideful feelings about such things was a mystery to Zane, for he felt nothing but pride at the end of the day.

Katie Rose would tell him to pray about it. He smiled just thinking of her.

"It is good you have something to smile about, Zane Carson." John Paul pressed his lips together, worry lines etched into his young face.

"I was thinking about . . ." He shook his head. "What time will the driver be here?"

"Soon, I 'spect."

They stood at the door of the barn watching Ruth and Abram as they waited, sitting on the porch, the sun shining on their faces. Neither acknowledged the other, and Zane's worries of the night before resurfaced. He'd grown to care for the couple. They had taken him in, fed and clothed him, as it were. They were kind and caring people who deserved everything life had to offer them.

He remembered Katie Rose telling him that Amish couples didn't normally marry for love, but he figured that after so many years together, Ruth and Abram would at least be friends. He looked at their children, and somehow he had a feeling that Ruth and Abram cared for one another. It was obvious that Gideon loved Annie, and Zane had heard about his grief over his first wife's death. They had told him how much Gabriel had loved his wife, Rebecca, so much so that he never married after her death, and Katie Rose herself had admitted that she had loved Samuel Beachy to the point of waiting for him for years. Yes, the Fishers believed in marriages based in love as well as faith. And yet Ruth and Abram sat side by side like strangers at a bus stop on what was perhaps one of the most important days of their lives.

"Are you still goin' to town?" John Paul's question pulled Zane out of his thoughts.

He nodded. "I thought I'd wait until your mother left. See if your father wants to go with me in the buggy."

"I don't have to be at work today. I can take you if you change your mind. I promise to drive safely."

Zane smiled. "I've kind of gotten used to buggy travel. Besides it's a beautiful day. Now if it were snowing . . ." he recalled John Paul screeching around corners and himself hanging on for dear life. "Scratch that."

For once in what seemed like days, John Paul chuckled. The tension eased, and Zane had the warm feeling that everything was going to be just fine.

Katie Rose couldn't stop the joy she felt when she saw her father's buggy pull up outside the schoolhouse. It wasn't the buggy that caused her such joy, but the man driving it. Zane had come to see her. She smoothed down her apron and adjusted her prayer *kapp*. Why? She had no idea. The day's worries had left her feeling a bit disheveled. It wasn't at all because she was happy to see him, and for certain not because she wanted him to think her beautiful. *Englisch* beauty was much more complicated than what the Amish saw. She didn't stand a chance against the woman he was to marry.

"All right, *kinder*, keep lookin' over your parts. Matthew, go over it with them, and I'll be right back."

She forced herself to cross the room slowly, stopping at the door and taking in a heaving breath before opening it. "Good mornin', Zane Carson. What brings you by today?"

It had been days since she had seen him last, but that hadn't stopped her from making sure she looked her very best on the off chance that she did encounter him. He was, after all, living with her *elders*. He was also writing a story for his fancy magazine, and she wouldn't want to give him a bad impression about how the Plain folk lived their lives. At least that's what she told herself every morning when she stood in front of her closet painstakingly choosing the dress she wanted to wear that day. It was shameful indeed, and she had asked the Lord's forgiveness for such vanity. Yet everyday it reared its head and demanded her attention.

He smiled and the entire world seemed a brighter place. "I came into town to charge my cell phone."

She nodded, thinking back to the little phones that *Englischers* carried with them. The bishop had been trying to decide whether or not to let them use one for their pickle business and instead had decided upon a phone shanty in the field across from the house. But Katie Rose had heard tell of districts who weren't even Beachy Amish and were allowed to carry the shiny little phones.

"I offered it to your mother so she'd know right away when the doctors called with her test results."

"That's mighty kind of you, Zane Carson."

He smiled again, and she noticed how straight and white his teeth were. Except for the bottom two. They overlapped a little, reminding her of being a child and crossing her fingers for luck.

"You know, that's the exact same thing your father said."

Katie Rose laughed.

"Have you eaten lunch?

She shook her head. "We've been practicin' for the Christmas program next week."

He held up a sack from one of the diners in town. "I stopped by and picked us up a couple of cheeseburgers."

The thought of sharing lunch with him was more thrilling

than it should have been. But Zane was good company, like a burst of color in a world where things were growing weary.

She'd have to ask forgiveness for that as well. There were some colors that weren't allowed in the Amish world—too bright, too bold, too vain. For right now, she'd just enjoy his company and beseech the Lord later.

She opened the door a little wider aware only then that the students had stopped practicing. They were watching her and the *Englischer* with an unabashed curiosity.

"Children, put your scripts way. It is time for lunch."

Choruses of *Can we go outside?* rose from all corners of the room. It was hard in the winter to keep the children both healthy and well exercised, but today was a fine day to let them run in the cold winter sunshine.

"Of course. Everyone get your lunch boxes and follow Simon out the door."

"I thought I was line leader today," Mary Byler asked in her sweet, tiny voice.

Zane Carson had rattled Katie Rose until she forgot even the simplest of her duties. "Right you are, Mary. My apologies to you. Everyone line up behind Mary. We'll stay out for half an hour, then we all have math tests to complete."

There were mixed groans all over the room. Half an hour was not enough time and surely not worth cutting short for a math exam. Maybe she would let them stay out a bit longer. As long as their cheeks didn't get too pink. She wanted to spend as much time with the *Englischer* as she could.

She didn't have to tell the children again. They donned their coats as fast as they could and lined up behind little Mary, everyone with lunch box in hand.

In no time at all, she and Zane were seated under the big oak in front of the schoolhouse. The smell coming from the bag was more than tempting. Only occasionally did they stop at the diner to eat. More often than not, eating at a restaurant was a luxury the Gabriel Fisher family had no time to indulge in.

Zane sat cross-legged in front of her, doling out the food. "Fries?" He held up the steaming potatoes in their tiny, white paper sack.

Katie Rose's mouth watered and she nodded. "*Jah.*"

"A cheeseburger for me. And one for you"—he handed her the wrapped sandwich—"And one for Samuel." He pulled another smaller cheeseburger from the sack.

Katie Rose bit her lip, staring at the feast in front of them.

"What's wrong?" He stopped unwrapping his own sandwich and turned those chocolate brown eyes on her.

"It's just that the other boys will feel left out."

Zane pressed his lips together and nodded. "And I was so proud of myself for remembering to bring one for Samuel."

"Oh, I'm grateful, Zane Carson. Please do not think otherwise."

He smiled. "I don't."

"It's just . . ." She wasn't sure how to tell him what was wrong. He'd brought her food, and French fried potatoes and even remembered to bring enough to feed little Samuel.

"I've got an idea. You brought lunch right?"

She nodded. "I have a thermos of stew and some sourdough bread."

"Perfect. How about we share the burgers with the boys, and then you can share your stew with me. Sound like a plan?"

She smiled. "That sounds wonderful."

The two youngest boys, Samuel included, shared a half of one of the fancy cheeseburgers. Zane split the other in two pieces and everyone got at least a half. French fries were passed around, and everyone seemed content.

"This is mighty kind of you, Zane Carson."

He shrugged those broad shoulders of his as if it had been no hardship at all to accommodate the entire Fisher clan. He was a good man this Zane Carson.

"I haven't had one of these in so long." He closed his eyes, the complete enjoyment showing clearly on his face.

Katie Rose had to admit, the cheeseburger was very delicious. She glanced at him. "Do you miss your life back home, being here?"

He held up the little bit left of his sandwich. "This I do. When I go out on assignment, this is the first thing I get when I return. Well, right after a hot shower."

She smiled thinking about Zane returning from wherever the assignment was and ordering a cheeseburger. Then she remembered that he had been shot on his last trip. The smile froze on her lips. The thought of him injured, bleeding, possibly near death sent chills through her. War was such a waste of time, such a waste of life.

"What else do you miss?" she asked, needing to change the subject for her own sake.

"Tacos."

"I have eaten tacos. They are delicious as well."

He squinted at her, the sunlight through the trees chasing shadows across his face. "What kind of tacos?"

"There are different kinds?" Why did *Englisch* food have to be so complicated?

"Did you get the kind from a restaurant, or did you make them at home?"

"From a restaurant in Tulsa. We went there a couple of years ago to take Samuel to the doctor."

"Aw, then you've not really had tacos."

She frowned. "I haven't?"

"Nope. Because you haven't had *my* tacos."

"You can cook?" She didn't mean for her words to ring so loudly with disbelief, but she could not picture Zane Carson behind a stove.

He shrugged that one shoulder again making her wonder if his injury caused the unbalanced action. "I dabble some. Tacos are the one thing I learned to make when I was growing up. My uncle taught me." He shook his head as if he couldn't believe he'd picked now to bring that memory to life. His voice held a misty quality like he was miles away inside his head. "Every Tuesday night we made tacos together. Like a real family."

"I don't understand. What do you mean like a real family? Was he not your uncle?"

"He was."

"Then he was family."

Zane nodded. "Yes, but we didn't do a lot together. He was always at work, and . . . I dunno. We just didn't spend a lot of time together. Not like your family."

"That makes me sad for you, Zane Carson. You have missed much in your life." So badly she wanted to reach out a hand and smooth it down his face, run her fingertips across his lips and ease the pain she saw in his eyes.

"I survived."

"*Jah*. But have you lived?"

───※ ℮℮ ℮℮ ※───

Katie Rose's words followed him all the way back into town. He couldn't fathom why. Of course he had lived. He had traipsed through the jungles of Africa, walked amid the pyramids of Egypt, hiked through the mountains of Afghanistan. If that wasn't living, he didn't know what was.

The biggest mystery was why her words bothered him in the first place. It wasn't as if he'd asked her opinion. He wasn't worried about his future plans and outcomes. He had it all figured out. This job was just a means to an end.

He pulled the buggy up to the hitching post in front of the general store. The idea to run back by the school and visit again with Katie Rose after his errand was oh-so tempting. Twice was bad enough. He could play the first time off as research for his article, but twice in one day could be easily misconstrued. No, he'd better retrieve his cell phone and get back to the house.

He gave one of the horses a pat on the neck, then fed each of them one of the carrots he'd put in his pocket before the trip. Carrots were a lot cheaper than fossil fuels. Maybe there was a story in that too: *The Carbon Footprint of the Amish*. It would be a very short book.

He laughed at himself for going soft, then pulled open the door of the old-timey store. *Enchanted.* The word popped into his mind again as he stepped through the doors, planked floors underneath the soles of his boots, lazy fans turning overhead. Today it offered warmth by the potbellied stove and hot chocolate at the soda fountain.

Zane waved to the patrons who greeted him, tipped his hat to the owner, Coln Anderson, then went to warm his hands by the stove.

"Are you certain it will be here by Christmas?"

He didn't hear Coln's response to the shopper as the word *Christmas* pinged through his head. How could he have forgotten about Christmas? Maybe because it wasn't a big deal to him. Never had been.

But it should be.

There was that voice again. *Why?* he wanted to shout in return, but it was a bit frightening to argue with oneself. Instead, he looked around, for the first time seeing the decorations of red and green all over the store. That was what really bothered him about Christmas—the commercialism. Retailers profited greatly this time of year by getting people to buy things they couldn't afford for a list of people they rarely saw. And for what?

As his eyes darted about the store, he noticed no Santa Claus faces. There were a few snowflakes and a couple of snowmen, but what struck him was the huge star hanging in the back of the store over a nativity scene carved out of wood.

Zane left the warmth of the stove and, as if mesmerized, walked toward the star. The stable, manger, and all the characters seemed to be hand carved out of a bleached wood, giving them the appearance of aged ivory. He picked up the statue of Mary, turning the carving over in his hands and examining every detail. Her robe flowed from her body, her head tilted at a peaceful angle. But she had no face. None of them did. No eyes on the animals, no mouths, just a blank surface where features should have been. Somehow this oversight made them all the more beautiful.

How had he not noticed these this morning?

"Did you come to get your phone?"

Zane jumped, then put the Mary in her spot behind the manger. "Yeah, I did."

Coln nodded toward the statues. "They're beautiful, huh?"

Zane nodded.

"There's a man in Missouri who carves them for the Amish folk."

"It must take forever to make a whole set."

"He can only finish a few each year, but this is the first Christmas the bishop has allowed them in his homes."

Zane looked at the depiction of the birth of Jesus. How could anyone deny its beauty and art? "I don't understand."

"Bishop Beachy was worried that it would cause pride and envy among his followers."

"I want one." The words slipped from his mouth without any warning. "In fact, I want two." One for Ruth and Abram and one for him. For the art of it, he told himself. Something that beautiful was just too good to pass by.

Coln shook his head. "I know I can get one for you, but the other might be a little tricky. Could I send it to you?"

"Of course." Even if it came in time for next Christmas it would be a wonderful gift for . . . Monica. He'd be married to Monica next year.

They had never talked about religion; the matter had never come up. But with the revelations he'd had on this trip, it would be a good idea to have that conversation soon. Not that it changed things. Still, he wanted to know how she felt before they walked down the aisle.

Coln went behind the counter and unplugged Zane's cell phone. "Come back up front and I'll ring that up for you."

Zane nodded. "I will, but I need to shop some more."

Christmas was only a couple of weeks away. He'd be spending the Christian holiday with the Fishers, and he couldn't imagine not having any gifts for them on Christmas morning. He had never before bought Christmas presents, and the idea of giving gifts on the holiday was strangely thrilling. He felt like the Grinch when his heart grew two sizes.

He mentally started making a list in his head. He needed something for all of Gabe's boys, Mary Elizabeth, Annie, and Gideon. And one more.

He put his cell phone in his pocket, and a smile on his face as he started looking around for the perfect gift for Katie Rose.

Zane went through the remainder of the day like he had a secret. In a way, he supposed that was true, but this joy over buying gifts for his host was unexpected.

He pulled the wagon into the drive, hopped down, and immediately walked the horses toward the barn. The house looked quiet so he could only suppose that Abram was still out, and that Annie had gone to spend the afternoon with Gideon.

Zane smiled and unhitched the horses. Today had been a beautiful day. He could only hope that Ruth's day had been as wondrous. It would be a while before they knew the test results, but he had hoped she would find some bright spot in today and that the worry lines between her eyes would be softened.

He got the horses some water, brushed them down, and poured some fresh oats in their trough. By the time he was finished, he heard the purr of an engine. Ruth was home.

He shaded his eyes as he stepped from the dark interior of the barn. A car door slammed and then another.

"Bill Foster," he called, raising his other hand in greeting.

Bill waved in return. "Well, if it ain't Zane Carson. I almost didn't recognize you, boy."

Zane smiled. He supposed he did look different than he had just over two months ago. "I'll take that as a compliment." He shook the man's hand, then turned to Ruth. "I'm glad you're home, Ruth. Now, I won't have to worry about you riding around with this maniac."

Ruth smiled, but the action was weak, her eyes watery.

Zane knew what he needed to do. He looked to Bill. "Can you stay for supper tonight?"

"Abram will be disappointed if he doesn't get to see you." Ruth's voice was stronger than her expression.

But Bill was already shaking his head. "Not tonight, I'm afraid. It's my oldest daughter's birthday, and we're all goin' out to eat. Gotta save room for that." He patted his slightly rounded, middle-age paunch.

"Then I believe pickles are in order."

Zane helped Ruth inside and gathered up some pickles for the driver, walking him to his car with a case full of mason jars.

"Money for gas?" Zane asked as Bill got into the car and cranked the engine.

"You know what to do with that," the Mennonite said as he put the car in gear.

Zane nodded with a smile. "I sure do."

He watched Bill pull out of the drive, then turned to go back into the house to check on Ruth. To the casual observer, she looked fine, strong even. Shoulders set, chin lifted. But Zane had been living with the woman and her family for months and he could see that she was struggling. One good wind could knock her over.

She had her back to him as he entered. She was standing at the stove, as if about to cook, or make tea, or something, but she wasn't moving. Just standing there as if she could fool him.

"Ruth."

He said her name, and her shoulders stiffened, then fell. She buried her face in her hands, sobs taking over her body.

Zane shot to her side, turning her around and wrapping her in his arms. He knew it wasn't the Amish thing to do, hold a woman who wasn't his wife. This was one time he was very glad to be English. Ruth needed all the comfort she could get.

He didn't count the minutes that he stood there holding her, offering her the strength of his body to soothe her spirit. He only knew that she had given him so much—offered her home to him, fed and clothed him, given him a place to sleep with warm blankets. It was his turn to pay her back, even only a little.

Finally her sobs subsided. She pulled away from him, suddenly self-conscious of the fact that she was in another man's arms. She sniffed, a choked laugh escaping from her lips as she wiped at her tears. "Goodness me. Look at me, carryin' on like that. Where are my manners?"

"Ruth." She didn't have to pretend with him.

She turned back toward the stove and reached for the kettle that was always close. "Would you like a cup of tea?"

"Ruth." He stilled her hands. "Sit down. I'll make the tea."

She took a shuddering breath, and for a moment, Zane thought she might protest. Instead she gave him a grateful, if not tear-soaked, smile and eased down into a chair at the table.

Zane filled the kettle with water and set it to boil in the stove, then retrieved the tea bags and mugs.

"You know your way around the kitchen, Zane Carson."

He shrugged. "It comes with the territory."

"Territory?"

"Being a bachelor. Constantly on the road."

He looked at the propane-powered gas stove. "I've cooked on worse. Much worse."

"The stove was a gift from Gideon to Annie."

"And they're supposed to get married next year?"

"That is our custom. To get married in the fall when the harvest is complete, and the chores are lighter."

"Do you want to talk about it?"

"Gideon and his Annie?"

Zane shook his head. "Your appointment."

"I would rather talk about anything else."

The whistle of the kettle punctuated her words.

Zane added a tea bag to each mug and filled them with the hot water. He added honey, then carried them to the table.

He sat one down in front of Ruth, then took the chair opposite her.

"*Danki*," she said, blowing over the top of the mug to cool the scalding liquid.

They sat that way for a minute or two, steamy mugs and silence before Ruth spoke and shattered the quiet with her solemn words.

"I'm scared, Zane Carson."

He didn't ask her about what. "I think that's only normal."

She shook her head. "I'm not afraid about the cancer. I've prayed about that."

"What else is there?" To Zane, Ruth had it all—a loving family, a nice house, a network of caring friends.

Tears filled her eyes. "Will you pray with me now?"

A stab of apprehension shot through Zane. He'd never prayed for anything in his life. He had only in the last few days decided that there was even a God to pray to.

"In Matthew, the Bible says that when two pray together then the truth it shall become. Please, Zane Carson. Pray with me." Ruth reached across the table and clasped his hand into her own. Her knuckles turned white under the force of her grip.

How could he say no?

"I don't know how," he admitted.

Ruth smiled through her tears. "You just bow your head and talk to God. Thank Him for the blessings and ask Him for answers."

"That's all there is to it?" That sounded simple enough. Almost too simple. Still, apprehension raced through him.

"*Jah*." Ruth nodded. "But afterward you have to make sure to leave your heart open so that you can hear His answer."

He reached out his other hand and held both of hers in his as they bowed their heads.

Zane had seen the Amish pray enough times before and after dinner to know their prayers were silent. He wasn't exactly sure how God could hear his thoughts. But then, if God were truly the Creator, it seemed only natural that He would know everything.

God? he asked hesitantly, then with more confidence. *God. This is Zane Carson, down in Oklahoma. I'm here with Ruth Fisher, God. And she's hurting. She's just had her cancer scans, and we're waiting on her test results. She's scared, God, but I don't know of what. Whatever it is, she needs peace. I'm praying for that. I want her to have peace, God. Peace to stop crying and to be patient until her test results come in. But I don't think that's all that's bothering her, and I don't think she's going to tell me what it is. I know that You can give her peace for her worries, even if I can't name them.*

And God? I don't know why Abram didn't go with Ruth to the doctor today, but I think maybe that is bothering her as well. God, whatever has come between them, I ask that You heal it for her.

What else had Ruth said? Blessings. Thank God for the blessings.

I never really thought about it before, but I have a great deal of blessings in my life. One was being able to come here and be with the Fishers. I never believed in You before. That's not right. I'd never thought about it before. But now I have, and I am grateful for the opportunity to learn about You. And that I live in a free country where I can believe in You without persecution. I am thankful that I had the upbringing that I did. For it allowed me to experience life differently and be open to You when I had the opportunity . . .

Zane realized that the blessings were too many to count. He was thankful for Monica, his uncle, all of the Fishers, his job, the things he'd learned in his life, and the fact that he'd been shot. Strange as it sounded, without the injury he would never have had the opportunity to come here and learn about God. A blessing, definitely. Heavenly intervention? Only He knew.

Zane realized why the Fishers prayed so often. No matter how many times he prayed, there would always be something he forgot to add to his list of thanks and blessings.

Thank You, God, for all that and more. "Amen," he murmured.

He looked up to find Ruth watching him, a curious look on her face.

She squeezed his hands once more, then pulled hers into her lap. "You're a good man, Zane Carson."

"*Danki.*"

"It is no wonder why Katie Rose's eyes light up whenever you are around."

Did they? He hadn't noticed, maybe because he was too busy trying to pretend like seeing her didn't have any effect on him. "I don't think I'm comfortable talking about this."

"Sometimes what the Lord has planned for us, and what we think we want, are not the same."

Definitely not comfortable. No doubt about it. Time to change the subject.

Zane pulled his newly charged cell phone from the clip-on holder at the waistband of his pants and slid it across the table to Ruth. "You gave the doctor this number, right?"

She nodded.

"I set it on vibrate. That means you'll have to carry it around close in order to hear it. Do you have a pocket you can put it in?"

She shook her head.

He shouldn't be surprised. It seemed the Amish had something against pockets. Or maybe they preferred the simplicity of design in their pants and skirts. He unsnapped the holder and slid it across to Ruth.

"This part clips to your clothes. When it rings, it will sort of buzz. If it's next to your body, you'll be able to feel it. Just touch this button here to answer it. Touch it again to hang up. Got it?"

She nodded.

"If anyone else calls just ignore it. Okay?"

She nodded again, and Zane was afraid she was dangerously near tears. "*Danki*, Zane Carson."

"You're welcome, Ruth Fisher," he teased with a smile. He didn't want her to cry again. They both had so much to be thankful for. "Everything's going to be just fine. You know that, right?" He believed that. As he had prayed, a warm, peaceful feeling had washed over him. God, he had decided, was trying to tell him that everything would be okay for Ruth and whatever was bothering her.

He stood. "The Lord helps those who help themselves." Where had that come from? He must have heard it from Gabriel or Gideon. Maybe even Abram or Ruth herself. Had to be. "And you've done all you can do for yourself, Ruth. The rest is up to God."

Ruth smiled. "I will remember that, Zane Carson."

11

Bold. That was the only word Katie Rose could think of to explain her actions. She had gotten bold. Too bold. But she wanted to make sure Zane attended the Christmas pageant. She told herself it was because he needed to hear God's message, that he needed to foster his beliefs and turn his life over to God. Amish didn't go around trying to convert, and she labored under no pretense that he would give up his *Englisch* life as a reporter and take up the mantle of Plain living.

As true as all of that was, it wasn't the real reason. She wanted Zane Carson to come to the pageant because she wanted to see him again. She wanted him to look upon the eager faces of the children and watch their hard work. She wanted to show him her purpose in life. She wanted him to know that even though love had abandoned her, she still had a worthy calling.

And for all the talk of the sins of pride, she knew that she would have to pray extra hard for forgiveness from her thoughts.

Katie Rose raised her hand and knocked on the door of her parents' *haus* then let herself in. She only knocked once in case her *mudder* was resting. *Mamm* seemed even more tired of late, and Katie Rose knew that waiting for the test results had been the hardest part of this journey by far. But Katie Rose knew—she *knew*—with as much certainty that she knew the sky was blue and the grass green, that her mother would make it through this. The house was quiet. No sign of her mother or Annie. Her mother was probably upstairs lying down, and Annie was surely at Gideon's. Noni was likely in her room, knitting or resting herself. There was no sign of her *bruder*, her *vatter*, or Zane.

Katie Rose went back outside as the buggy pulled to a stop. She took a deep gulp of the cool air and willed her heart to cease its juvenile thumping. Zane Carson was sitting in the driver's seat. He was wearing a black coat that most likely had belonged to one of her brothers at one time or another and a black brimmed hat. He looked so much like a proper Amish man, her mouth went dry, and her heart gave a hard pound. She pulled her coat a little closer around her as he hopped down. She wasn't cold, but she needed something to do besides run to him and fling herself into his arms.

The thought was so brazen, that she gasped. What was the matter with her? She needed to get control of herself and quick. It was one thing to be intrigued with their *Englisch* visitor, but quite another to act upon it. With him looking so much like one of them, she was hard-pressed to remember her place.

"Hi." He waved one arm, then gathered up the horses' reins and walked them toward the barn.

Katie Rose waved back, hoping the pure joy bursting from her heart wasn't spread clear as day across her face. It was one thing to feel this way about the handsome *Englischer* and quite another to let him know. It would do no good to reveal her feelings. It would probably make it even harder when the time came for Zane to go back to his world.

A painful lump clogged her throat. He'd be going home in a

little over two weeks. The thought was so sad. He would be sorely missed when he was gone.

She blinked away unexpected tears as he came back out of the barn and approached her. She tried not to soak it in, the easy way he walked, each sure and confident footstep leading him toward her, the smooth grace that only he possessed.

"I didn't expect to see you today."

She tempered her smile at the pleased tone of his words. "I wanted to give you this." She handed him the invitation to the Christmas pageant. It wasn't truly an invitation, but a drawing the children made letting him know they wanted him to attend. Each child had written something and signed their name. Only because the children had so wanted him to be there, did Katie Rose feel comfortable delivering the paper to him. Otherwise, the action would have been too forward. Well, she hoped that the action was tempered since it came from the children.

He smiled as he opened the envelope, pulling out the paper and carefully unfolding it. She bit her lip as he scanned the paper, turning it this way and that to take in all the signatures and neatly printed messages.

"I'm honored. Of course, I'll be there." His smile grew even brighter, as if he truly meant his words, and Katie Rose smiled in return.

"The children will be so pleased." *And me too*, she silently added.

A heart beat thumped between them.

"It'll be my first Amish Christmas pageant. Do I need to do anything special? Bring anything special?"

"Only yourself."

"I can do that." He smiled again, and Katie Rose felt a little chunk of her heart fall away. She needed to figure out how to stay away from him before he ended up with it all.

Ruth had almost forgotten the shiny little phone she had clipped to the underside of her skirt. Almost. When it started buzzing, it scared her nearly out of her skin. She thought she had a bee trapped in her clothing.

Her heart thumped painfully in her chest as she unhooked the device. What if it was the doctor? What kind of news would it be? She didn't think she could handle any bad news, not after all the heartache the treatment had caused. Not after it altered her beyond recognition. Not after the amount of money it had cost them.

The phone continued to buzz as she said a little prayer to the Lord above. She almost prayed that it wasn't the doctor on the phone, but instead asked the Lord for the news that they wanted. News that she was indeed cancer free. That all of the heartache, pain, and money hadn't been in vain.

Monica the little screen read, and Ruth breathed a bit easier as she replaced the phone. Still her hands shook. Zane had told her not to worry if anyone else called. Yet, she just about ignored his wishes and went to find him. As far as she knew, Zane had no other family members, so Monica could only be his intended.

She'd just have to remember to tell him later that Monica had called his little black phone.

The Saturday before the pageant, Zane loaded up the wagon and rode over to see Ezekiel Esh. Abram had asked him to check on the man, and Zane willingly accepted the duty. He wanted to believe it was only because he liked the old man, but he was hoping to run into Katie Rose. There were no more fishing trips, no more rabbits to take to her, no more invitations to extend. Yet he still wanted an excuse to see her. Unable to find one, this was his best opportunity, and he readily seized it.

He would be able to see the deacon as well, to make sure he didn't need for anything. Esh had long since given up his livestock except for the few chickens he kept for eggs. Even the milk cow had gone on her way as Esh could neither sit down on the stool or squeeze hard enough to release the milk.

Zane didn't have much to do except make sure there was enough feed for the chickens, plenty of firewood close to the house, sufficient kerosene to fuel his lanterns, and to offer a bit of company.

Once his tasks were completed and he was getting ready to drive the buggy back to the Fisher's, Esh pounded his cane on the hard planks of the floor, the sound as loud as a gunshot. "I expect you to come fetch me for the pageant."

Zane blinked in response, then found his voice. "Abram said that John Paul was coming to get you."

"He might have at that. But I'll not be gettin' in that fancy *Englisch* car of his."

Zane had to hide his smile. John Paul's car was a disaster at best. He couldn't blame Esh for not wanting to ride in it, but fancy was not a word Zane would ever use to describe the old Ford.

Ezekiel raised his cane and pointed it at Zane. "I want to ride with you."

"Yes, sir."

"*Ach*, there's no need for that. We only bestow those called by the Lord with titles."

"But aren't you . . ." he let his voice trail off. "Yes, deacon." He was unable to stop his smile from stretching across his face. "I'll be by to get you."

"Better come about an hour before. I want to make sure I get a good place to sit."

Zane wasn't clear as to why Ezekiel Esh was so worried about a chair. Only a handful of people were afforded seats, the old deacon being one of them. There was also a chair for Ruth and one for a very pregnant woman who looked as if her baby could arrive at any moment. Silently Zane prayed that it was her full-skirted dress that made her look so very big and that the baby wasn't due for a few more weeks. Out of all his travels, everything he'd seen and done, delivering a baby was not among his accomplishments, and he'd like to keep it that way, thank-you-very-much.

More and more people filed into the tiny schoolhouse until he was certain that not one more person could squeeze in. He leaned down and shared his observation with Ezekiel, who sat in a chair directly in front of him.

"Repeat that, son," Esh yelled at him in return.

Zane hid his smile. There was just something about the old man, something so genuine. All of the Amish he'd met were sincere, but like any group of peoples there were always those who weren't as honest and true to the cause. Esh certainly wasn't one of them.

He leaned down closer to the old man and repeated his comment.

The deacon nodded and banged his cane against the floor. "*Jah*, a good turnout it is."

Along with Katie Rose's desk, the ones belonging to the children had been moved to the perimeter of the room. The children stood nervously in front of the blackboard awaiting the time to begin. Parents and relatives smiled and waved at their offspring much like any *Englischer* program, with the exception of the rabid mom taking pictures and multiple dads with video cameras.

The room fell silent as Katie Rose walked to the front of the crowd. She smiled sweetly, and Zane was certain she had never looked prettier. He knew if he told her so, she would blush that perfect shade of pink that made him want to run for his camera and save the moment for eternity. What it couldn't capture was the goodness of her heart—the way she cared for those around her, the children at the school, her mother, Gabe's brood.

"*Danki*," she said, her gaze travelling around the room. "Thank you, everyone, for comin'."

Zane was glad she switched to English, though he had a feeling he'd understand only about half of tonight's performance. That wasn't the point. He'd come because Katie Rose had asked him to, and he couldn't tell her no, couldn't bear to see a frown on her lovely face.

"The children have a special program planned for you tonight. But first we will pray."

Matthew, Gabriel's oldest boy, stepped to the front of the group and said in his clear, though squeaky, pubescent voice, "Bow your heads."

There was a slight whisper of noise as the group bowed their heads, silently praying for the children and the program they were about to perform.

Zane automatically lowered his head, closed his eyes, and asked God to be with the children, to keep them from being nervous and allow themselves to make mistakes without frustration. He prayed that the evening should go well for all involved.

"*Aemen*," Matthew finished, then stepped back into his place in line.

A small group of girls moved forward, and the evening was underway.

He couldn't help but wonder if the pageant was spoken in English for his benefit, but decided that was extremely arrogant. Katie Rose had told him that most of the children only heard

Pennsylvania Dutch spoken at home. English was learned after they started school and German was studied after the eighth grade. Surely they spoke English in the pageant in order to practice their skills with the language.

The first set of girls performed a sketch about making Christmas cookies. Another group acted out a three-person skit about soup they didn't think had enough salt. It ended up that all the women added salt without tasting the soup and thereby added too much. A good lesson in minding one's own affairs.

Some scholars sang songs. One little boy sang a beautiful song in German. Though Zane didn't understand a word of the language, he still had to wipe the tears from his eyes. The young boy was so tiny, barely waist high, with smooth blond hair and an angelic voice. The timbre of his voice alone was enough to move even the hardest of hearts.

Katie Rose stepped forward. "Now we will have a Bible readin' from Luke."

Zane expected a boy to step forward, Bible in hand to read.

Instead, a little girl about seven or eight stepped forward and recited, "In those days a decree went out from Caesar Augustus that the whole empire should be registered."

She stepped back into the formation of children, and another child stepped forward, this time a little boy about the same age. "The first registration took place while Quirinius was governing Syria."

Gabriel's son Simon came forward, shifting from one foot to the other. "So everyone went to be registered, each to his own town."

One by one, the children came forward, each reciting a verse.

"And Joseph also went up from the town of Nazareth in Galilee, to Judea, to the city of David, which is called Bethlehem, because he was of the house and the family line of David."

"To be registered along with Mary, who was engaged to him and was pregnant."

"While they were there, the time came for her to give birth."

"Then she gave birth to her firstborn son, and she wrapped Him snugly in cloth and laid Him in a feeding trough because there was no room for them at the lodging place."

"In the same region, shepherds were staying out in the fields and keeping watch at night over their flock.

"Then an angel of the Lord stood before them, and the glory of the Lord shone around them, and they were terrified."

"But the angel said to them, 'Don't be afraid, for look, I proclaim to you good news of great joy that will be for all people.'"

"'Today a Savior, who is Messiah the Lord, was born for you in the city of David.'"

"'This will be the sign for you: You will find a baby wrapped snugly in cloth and lying in a feeding trough.'"

"Suddenly there was a multitude of the heavenly host with the angel, praising God and saying . . .'"

"'Glory to God in the highest heaven, and peace on earth to people He favors.'"

"When the angels had left them and returned to heaven, the shepherds said to one another, 'Let's go straight to Bethlehem and see what has happened, which the Lord has made known to us.'"

"They hurried off and found both Mary and Joseph, and the baby who was lying in the feeding trough."

"After seeing them, they reported the message they were told about this child, and all who heard it were amazed at what the shepherds said to them."

"But Mary was treasuring up all these things in her heart and meditating on them."

"The shepherds returned, glorifying and praising God for all they had seen and heard, just as they had been told."

Zane exhaled, realizing, only in that moment, that sometime while the children were speaking he held his breath.

Then Matthew gave his brother Samuel a gentle push. The sweet, red-haired child grinned at everyone and yelled, *"aemen,"* with as much enthusiasm as Zane was sure the angel of the Lord had used when talking to the shepherds.

Everyone laughed at Samuel's zeal, and he ran to Katie Rose and promptly buried his face in her skirts.

After the pageant, everyone milled around, looking at the artwork posted on the walls of the school. Cookies, punch, and hot chocolate were served as the members of the district talked among themselves and with the beautiful teacher. Zane wanted an opportunity to talk to her himself. He wanted to tell her how glad he was for the invitation, how much the message meant to him.

He couldn't say he'd never heard the story. Surely somewhere in his agnostic life he had heard about Mary, Joseph, and the manger, but he'd never taken the time to examine the situation, to sit and listen while someone told the story, read it straight from the source.

He got chills at the thought of a woman forced to travel so close to her time to give birth. He thought about the woman who'd sat in the front row during the pageant. He couldn't imagine her on the back of a donkey, or walking all the way from Nazareth to Bethlehem. He didn't know how far it was, but if it were farther than across the street, it was too far. Mary couldn't get a room at the lodging house. How crazy was that? How selfish that no one would help a pregnant woman to the point that she had to sleep with the animals, give birth in a barn, and then lay her child in a feeding trough instead of a crib. If that happened today, Child Welfare Services would be all over it. That it happened at all was morbidly amazing to Zane. Didn't these people know who the baby was?

They didn't. They couldn't. Only the shepherds who had been visited by the angels knew the child was the Savior.

How wonderful. How amazing. How—

"I'm ready to go now." Esh banged his cane on the planked floor for good measure. "You can stare at the pretty young teacher later."

Zane jumped, not realizing he'd been staring. No one would believe he'd been that caught up in the story of Christmas that he hadn't realized he was staring at Katie Rose. He hardly believed that himself.

She looked up and caught his eye, her cheeks blooming into that rose-in-winter pink that made her look even more angelic.

Zane gave a small wave, mouthed "thank you," then helped Esh to his feet. He'd get the old man home, and then he would figure out when Jesus stopped being just a Bible story and became the Son of God.

⁕

The day after the pageant dawned cold and bright, a beautiful, typical day in an Oklahoma winter. For Ruth the pageant was the first outing other than church since she had finished her treatments. Too much travelling—too much of anything—left her exhausted and drained. But the pageant meant so much to her, so much to her family, that she had rested extra the day before, lying down with Zane Carson's cell phone near in hopes of resting, but ready in case the doctor called. Her sleep had gone undisturbed, and she felt better than she had in months. Maybe it was life as usual that made her heart light.

And the pageant! Hearing the children last night reading from the Bible and singing songs of God and His love, and hearing the Christmas story again had uplifted her too. She had heard it every year of her life at Christmastime, but that made the story no less powerful. She thanked God for the message, His Son, and all things good and holy. She especially thanked God that Zane Carson had received the story too.

She had heard through family gossip that Zane Carson hadn't been raised in church, hadn't had the privilege of hearing God's Word each day like she had. The thought saddened her more than she could say. There was a pain in his eyes, a sadness she was certain he didn't know was there. Yet there was nothing more healing than God's Word.

It was so much easier to see what other people needed than to accept these things for herself.

Ach, last night was *gut*, for sure and for certain. She had missed the activity of her day-to-day life. Amish women worked as hard as the men, gardening, canning, cooking, and baking. But since she had been sick, the majority of these chores had fallen to Annie. Gideon's intended was more than willing to do her share and even more, but Ruth hated relying on her. It was one thing to teach and quite another to be unable to do the work herself.

Ruth's easy mood vanished the minute she looked at herself in the mirror. It wasn't vanity that chased away her joy, but the fear of disobedience. Just looking at her bald head, devoid of the hair that she had groomed her entire lifetime, filled her with sadness like none she had ever felt before. Even when Megan had left. Ruth had always worn her hair long and covered at the request of God, and now it was gone.

She understood why the women she had seen at the hospital had covered their heads with handkerchiefs. But a scrap of cloth covered with drawings of pink ribbons would be considered vain by the bishop and somehow prideful. Those other women wore their pink like a badge of honor. Her heart gave a hard pound of recognition when she saw the ribbons that signified breast cancer and being a survivor. A part of her wanted to display a ribbon on her dress, pin it to her apron, or even get one of those pink rubber bracelets to show what she had been through. Why she looked the way she did. Why after being so carefully obedient her entire life that she appeared to have lost her faith. Instead she had to hide her badges. The little pink ribbon the nurse had given her when she started treatments was pinned to the underside of her dress. No one knew it was there. Not even Abram. Only she and God knew her secret. She tied the bonnet under her chin and tried to find the peace she had so fleetingly felt earlier.

She had done what God had asked of her. What she thought the Lord had wanted from her, but in the side effects she could find no peace. She couldn't uphold her end of the marriage. She could no longer cook and clean for her husband, not like a proper Amish wife. She required frequent rests and naps in order to make it through even one day. She didn't know if she would ever be the same again, or if the treatment would leave her dependent on others for the rest of her life.

Ruth didn't know how she would handle that. She was used to being strong, dependable, capable. Now she felt as helpless and as weak as a newborn fawn.

Annie was already in the kitchen when Ruth arrived downstairs. If she knew her energetic son at all, John Paul had already coerced Zane Carson out of the bed and into the barn. Abram had risen before her, as was his custom of late, not even bothering to wake her before he headed out to his chores.

They used to get up together, make their way downstairs and sit at the table and talk, enjoying the few quiet moments of their morning before the day took off into whatever direction the Lord pulled them. At night they'd meet back up in their room, sharing thoughts of the day, questions, ideas, troubles, and triumphs before bending their knees to thank God for the day's blessings.

That was just one more change her cancer had brought about, one more thing to be saddened about. She could barely look at her husband these days, so ashamed she was of her body. It was no longer whole, no longer the way the Lord had made it. She and Abram had made the decision together, but the repercussions of that decision she had to bear alone.

"I've made you some coffee," Annie said, pouring her a cup and setting it down at the table. "Biscuits should be out in a few minutes."

"You didn't have to do that." Yet Ruth was glad that she did. Annie made the best coffee, and her biscuits were coming along quite nicely.

Ruth eased herself into one of the kitchen chairs, resting her bones from the trip downstairs. It was downright shameful that her body could barely take the journey each morning and night. She had played with the idea of moving into Noni's quarters and avoiding the stairs altogether, but the thought so saddened her that she quickly let it go. She and Abram were so distanced that she couldn't imagine furthering the rift by not lying beside him each night. Her heart ached at the thought of not being able to hear him breathe as she fell asleep. Of not being able to roll into his warmth in the morning before sunrise. To know he was there in body, strong and steady, even if his heart was drifting.

Annie pulled the bacon out of the refrigerator and started laying strips in a big black frying pan. "The boys ought to be back in a few minutes."

Ruth hadn't rested her fill, but couldn't sit still any longer. Oh, Annie made fine bacon, but Ruth couldn't sit by and let her do all of the cooking by herself. There were too many mouths to feed. Too much responsibility. "Let me." She pushed herself to her feet, fully intending to take the meat away from Annie and cook the bacon herself.

"What are you doing?" Annie asked as she reached for the bacon.

"I'm going to help you."

"You most certainly are not." She turned so that her body shielded the meat from Ruth's grasp. "You had a late night with the Christmas pageant. You need to rest."

"Annie, I—"

"Don't start, Ruth. We are soon to be family, and families work together to help each other."

"But I—"

"No buts." She placed a gentle hand on Ruth's shoulder and pushed her back down in the seat. "We are working together."

Ruth shook her head with a frown. "Me sittin', and you workin' is not workin' together."

Annie smiled. "I'm counting on you helping me later."

"*Jah*? What do you mean?"

Annie blushed. "I hope that one day, after Gideon and I are married of course, that you'll come help me with the baby. Or help me get ready for the baby. Then I can sit with my feet up, and you can make the biscuits."

The thought of Gideon getting such a second chance at love and life filled Ruth with the brightest feeling she'd had in a long time. If she hadn't known better, she'd've thought she swallowed sunshine.

She took a sip of her coffee to hide the tears that sprang to her eyes. Thankfully Annie had turned away to pull the biscuits out of the oven. Then the bacon required her attention and Ruth was able to swallow down her emotions without the young girl being able to know they were even there.

That afternoon, as she and Annie sorted through her stash of fabric looking for the perfect cloth to make Mary Elizabeth a new dress for Christmas, Zane Carson's phone buzzed once again. This time Ruth recognized the purr against her side and didn't jump out of her skin. But her hands were still shaking as she retrieved the device and looked at the tiny screen the way Zane had showed her. 918 . . . Tulsa. The doctor was calling.

She shook her head. "I can't do this."

Annie laid a hand on Ruth's trembling fingers. "What's the matter, Ruth?"

"It's the cancer doctor." She hated the tears that sprang into her eyes. She didn't want to answer. Couldn't answer. What if the news was bad? She wasn't afraid of dying. She knew what awaited her on the other side. She was not afraid to go meet Him.

She was afraid she had wasted the community's money. She should have never agreed to treatment. It was too costly with no guarantee of return.

"Aren't you going to answer it?"

Ruth shook her head again. "*Nay.*"

Annie shot her an exasperated look. "Give me that." She took the phone and pressed the little button, stopping the buzzing, the silence making Ruth all the more nervous.

"Hello?"

Ruth could hear the voice of the person who had called, but she couldn't understand the words they said.

"No, it's not. This is her daughter." Annie winked at her, her confidence making Ruth's stomach hurt. It wasn't right to lie, but she was glad Annie had told the caller she was Ruth's daughter. Ruth didn't think she could hear the news of her test over the ringing in her ears.

"Uh-huh," Annie said.

She was smiling. That had to be a good sign, but still Ruth wouldn't let her spirits rise.

"Yes, sir. We appreciate all you have done for her. I'll be sure to let her know." She hit the button again and handed the phone back to Ruth.

It seemed an eternity before Annie finally spoke. "The tests came back clear. You are cancer free!"

12

The news spread like a grass fire in September. Only when his body relaxed in relief did Zane realize how concerned he'd been. He had grown close to the Fishers in the weeks that he'd been staying with them, and he wanted nothing but happiness for them. Katie Rose would have said, "God is good," or something about the power of prayer. Zane was starting to believe that she could be right. More than right.

Spot on.

The whole community had been praying for Ruth's recovery. Even he had bowed his head and asked God in his stuttering words if He could find a way to see Ruth healed. And God had answered in a big way.

Katie Rose might have said those words too, but Zane didn't know because he hadn't seen her since the Christmas pageant. He supposed she was busy getting Christmas ready for the boys and Gabriel. At least he hoped that was what she was doing, and that she wasn't avoiding him. He liked spending time with her, wanted to get to know her better. If only a little before he had to leave for Chicago.

Funny, but now the thought didn't fill him with relief like it did before. He should have been happy, ecstatic even that it wouldn't be long before he got to leave Oklahoma and the Amish ways behind. But he wasn't.

Maybe Christmas was getting to him. It never had before. Then again, he'd never given it any thought before. He'd never bought into the commercialism of trees and stockings, Santa Claus and reindeer. He'd simply gone through December the same way he would any other month.

But this year, he discovered faith in God—and that changed everything about Christmas.

Maybe, too, it was seeing the Fishers so happy over the news of Ruth's healing, excited and enjoying each other as the holiday that meant so much to them approached.

Annie was baking cookies and friendship bread, and Noni was knitting like her life depended on it. John Paul was the only one who seemed to be taking life in the same stride, yet Zane was sure it was because he was working so hard trying to provide more for his parents.

Their excitement was contagious, and Zane couldn't help letting it seep into him as well. A few days before Christmas, he borrowed the buggy and drove into town to pick up the present he had ordered for Ruth and the other gifts he'd been planning.

He had loved his time with the Fishers. Their lifestyle was gentle and unassuming. Difficult, but enjoyable. Filled with happiness and each other.

The only thing he missed was tacos.

That's how he'd give back. He would cook them all dinner. Surely there wasn't anything in the *Ordnung* about Mexican food, but just in case, Zane asked Mr. Anderson when he stopped by the general store.

"Nothing at all, son. Nothing at all," Coln had answered.

Once Zane had been given the all clear, he drove the buggy to the grocery store, walking each aisle as he tried to remember everything he would need to make the perfect taco feast.

He didn't know what kind of spices Annie and Ruth had stashed away in their kitchen, so he bought a little container of everything—garlic salt, crushed red pepper, black pepper, and taco seasoning. He also picked up fresh garlic, refried beans, tortillas, and hard taco shells. He gathered ingredients until the basket was filled.

He received a few strange looks as he walked the store. He supposed he was a curious mix of English and Amish. At least his pants didn't show his socks now, thanks to Katie Rose's expertise with a needle and thread. But his hair, in urgent need of a trim now, was still in an English cut, not the chili bowl meets Buster Brown style that the Amish preferred. He had grown a beard for sheer warmth, but instead of shaving off his moustache, as was the Amish custom, he'd left it. His clothes were exclusively Amish, though, and the cashier shook her head in confusion when he paid for his purchases with a credit card.

He smiled to himself, but didn't offer an explanation. It'd give her something to talk about later with her friends.

He loaded his purchases into the buggy. He hadn't brought a cooler to make sure the perishables made it to the house without getting warm, but that wasn't a big concern today. The sky was overcast, the wind from the north, and the old-timers were talking about an early snow.

He hoped it would snow. Unlike Chicago, he'd bet the snow here stayed whiter longer. He could just imagine how beautiful the land would look covered with a thick layer of white powder. Might even be clean enough in the Amish country to make snow cream.

The flash of a childhood memory snuck up on him. He'd forgotten about making snow cream with his parents. What a treat that had been. His heart warmed at the thought. One more good memory to add with the rest.

The ride back to the Fishers' was slow and cold, but Zane found the easy pace allowed him the time to stop and reflect on the day. To think about all that had happened, all that he needed to get accomplished. Instead of racing around and trying to speed from one place to another, Zane found that the buggy ride helped to clear his mind. Made him take a step back and see the day, the week, the month.

He passed by the driveway to Ruth and Abram's and headed on to Gabriel's place. There couldn't be a celebratory taco dinner without all of the Fisher children there. He wished he had thought about it sooner, because he might have located the elusive Megan Fisher, Ruth and Abram's long-lost daughter who'd sought greener pastures in the English world.

As it was, Gabriel and his brood needed to be there. He owed Gabriel one after the plow episode. The boys may have forgotten about it, but Zane hadn't. And he had the peppers in one of his many shopping bags to prove it.

He turned down Gabriel's drive and said a silent prayer that Katie Rose was home. It was probably unhealthy how much he wanted to see her. He knew nothing could come of it. Yet knowing that didn't lessen the desire to look into her eyes. Not one bit.

His heart gave a happy thump as she came out onto the porch, wiping her hands on her apron and smoothing her fingers over her hair.

"Hi," he said, setting the brake and hopping down from the buggy.

Katie Rose beamed him a smile, then brought it down a few degrees. She took a deep breath and nodded toward him. "Hi, to you."

"I've come to invite you to dinner."

The words had barely left his mouth before she opened hers in protest. "I do not think that is a wise idea, Zane Carson."

"No, no, no, I came to invite *everyone* to dinner. I'm cooking tonight."

"*Jah?*"

"I thought I'd make tacos to celebrate your mother's good news."

"That is very kind of you, Zane."

He smiled. "You just called me by my first name."

Katie Rose hoped she could blame the pink in her cheeks on the cold or the wind. And she further hoped that he didn't notice the extra color at all.

"You can come, right? To dinner?"

"Is that an invitation?"

"It is. For all of you—Gabriel, Mary Elizabeth, the boys. Even John Paul is going to be there."

"He got the night off from work?" She covered her mouth with one hand, her eyes wide.

He cocked his head. "How do you know that John Paul has a job?"

"Everyone knows but *Dat.*"

Zane nodded. "I pinned him down one night when he came in."

"Please don't tell *Dat*. He means well tryin' to get John Paul to experience his run-around time without distractions, but my *bruder* needs to do this to feel like he's helpin' the cause."

"I take it he's not a good pickle chef."

"Zane Carson. Promise you won't tell."

"Of course I won't. If you promise to come to dinner."

Katie Rose wrinkled her nose at him, but didn't remind him that blackmail was a sin. "That is a lot of tacos."

"I'm prepared." He held up the biggest package of ground meat she had ever seen. "I've got two of these."

"It's not easy cookin' for so many people."

"I was hoping that I could talk Annie into helping me."

Katie Rose shook her head. "Annie can only cook what me and *Mamm* have taught her. I'm not sure she will be a help to you in the kitchen."

"Mary Elizabeth?"

"She cannot cook at all."

He opened his mouth in mock surprise. "That's a terrible thing to say about your niece."

"'Tis true. Cookin' is not where her heart lies."

"I thought all Amish women could cook."

"She can go to the kitchen and prepare food to eat, but I don't recommend that you ask her to do so."

Zane laughed. "Well, Ruth's out. Even if she had the energy, the party is for her. And that only leaves . . . you."

"Oh."

He tilted his head to one side, and Katie Rose had to tamp down the urge to cup her hand over his cheek.

"Well? Would you help me prepare this taco feast?"

The thought of working in the kitchen side by side with the handsome *Englischer* was tempting indeed. She couldn't turn him down. The party was to celebrate her mother's victory over cancer, after all. She had to help. It was the Christian thing to do. But that was the only reason she would do it. It had nothing at all to do with being so close to the brown-eyed man who had somehow become such a part of her life.

"I will," she said. She just hoped the decision was the right one to make.

⋙⊙ ⊙⋘

Katie Rose arrived early to her parents' *haus*. Too early. She had been so excited at the prospect of seeing Zane Carson again that she couldn't help herself. She knocked on the door and let herself inside, finding no one in the front room or the kitchen. Once again everyone was out and about, with the exception of perhaps Noni. But if Ruth and Annie had taken her with . . .

"Zane?" she called, her voice hesitant in case her mother was still in the house. "Zane Carson."

Surely he hadn't gone too far. She was early, but not that early. Maybe he'd gone to town or over to see old Ezekiel Esh. The two of them seemed to be very close these days.

She smiled. What an unlikely pair—the old deacon and the *Englischer*. Sounded like one of those paperback novels she had read in her *rumspringa* years.

There was only one way to know if everyone was gone, so she stepped off the porch and made her way to the barn. Her family had three buggies. Well, two buggies and a wagon. John Paul's car was missing from its place across the road, so if the buggies were gone as well, then it was a fair bet that her family had taken the afternoon to visit.

The barn was dark and cool when she entered, and she pulled her shawl around her shoulders. She should have brought a coat, but the day was so beautifully sunny and the shawl was her favorite. It was black like all the others, but the stitching so tiny and delicate. It was old, one of the first ones Noni had made for her. When Katie Rose wore it, she felt wrapped in the love of the generations.

Her notions were silly, but she didn't care. The shawl repre-
sented everything good and holy that she believed in—family, love,
God. She was far pressed to remember that when she was around
Zane Carson for too long.

Once in the barn, she heard his voice coming from one of the
stalls. It sounded almost like he was singing. Though she had never
heard him sing, she would know his voice anywhere.

"Zane?"

"Back here."

She stepped through the fall of hay, following the sound of his
crooning.

She saw him shake his head as she rounded the corner. "What
are you doin'?"

"I have no idea. But I think she's in trouble."

Katie Rose's gaze fell to the beautiful black horse her father
had bought last year at the summer auction. Her belly was huge,
round with the colt struggling to find its way into the world.

She looked to Zane. "How long has she been this way?"

"I don't know. I came out here to check on things, and found
her like this. Your father left early this morning, right after the
milking, and she was all right then."

Katie Rose knelt down and rubbed a soothing hand down the
neck of the horse.

"If you'll stay with her, I'll go across the street and call your
dad. Maybe he can come back and—"

"And how do you propose to do that, Zane Carson, my *dat*
doesn't have one of those fancy *Englisch* phones."

"But your mother still has mine. If she took it with her—" He
ran his fingers through his hair. "You're right. Bad idea. But—" He
looked down at the laboring mother, and Katie Rose was certain
she had never seen a more helpless look on anyone's face. "I don't
know what to do for her."

"This is her first colt," Katie Rose said, dropping to her knees in the hay. "The horse sometimes gets confused and panicked. She'll be fine."

The horse's wild eyes calmed a bit, her snorts of distress becoming soft huffs of pain.

Katie Rose ran a hand over the hump that was the mare's belly, gently pressing, soothing, but at the same time trying to determine if the colt was right. Everything seemed in order. The colt seemed to be positioned correctly, but there was only one way to be certain. She glanced back at Zane, only to find his brow furrowed and his bottom lip trapped between his teeth.

She'd check later and only as a last resort. Zane looked so nervous she didn't think he could handle any more than what was absolutely necessary.

His brows knit together. "Do you know what you're doing?"

"Calm yourself, Zane Carson. Your fears are doing nothin' but makin' her nervous."

"But . . ."

She shot him a look over her shoulder.

He took a deep breath.

"She's goin' to be fine. She's just scared is all. The colt is comin' fast."

"So what do we do?"

Without thinking, she grabbed his hand and pulled.

Her motion was so unexpected that he stumbled forward, not able to catch himself as he fell to his knees beside her. "We pray," she said, taking his hand and placing it on the mound of the horse's belly.

"Pray. Of course." He put his other hand on the horse without being prompted, then bent his head.

"Out loud," she requested.

He gave a slight shake of his head. "I'm not sure I can do it right."

"There is no right or wrong way to talk to the Lord. Just open your heart and let the worlds flow from there."

Zane closed his eyes.

"Dear, Lord." His words were shaky, his voice held the warble of anxiety. "I—we ask that you help this horse." He continued on, adding in the colt and the fact that neither of them knew what they were up against.

Katie Rose didn't bother to correct him. She stayed on her knees, her hands splayed across the horse's distended belly, echoing his every word inside her head.

The horse was going to be fine, she knew it. Zane on the other hand, she wasn't so sure about. He needed this prayer almost as much as the horse. He needed to feel that the situation was in God's hands, and that was a fine place to be.

His words continued to grow in strength and confidence as he prayed, asking for God to take the horse in His hands, for Him to give them wisdom and patience, calmness and clarity. For someone who had only started praying a few days ago, he did it like an old hand.

"Amen." He finished, opening his eyes cautiously, as if somehow right then the horse would be transformed. With a sigh, he stood, warily watching the mare for any sign of change.

The horse still labored, and Zane looked decidedly disappointed.

"Prayer takes time, Zane Carson. Look. See how her breathin' is slowin' down. She is calmin'. The colt is comin'. All is well." She sat back on her bottom, and reached out to stroke the horse once again.

"She could kick you if you're too close."

Katie Rose shook her head. "But she won't."

"How can you be sure?"

She shrugged. "God. How did you know to come check on her?"

"Something told me to come out here."

Katie Rose nodded. "God."

"God." He said the word with wonderment in his voice, as if it were the first time he'd ever heard it, ever said it.

"That little voice belongs to God, the voice that tells you to give someone a hug, or to go check on your neighbor."

"And how do you know it's God?"

"Faith."

"I don't—"

"Yes, you do, Zane Carson."

Her words seemed to linger in the air. He frowned as if contemplating the idea of having faith.

One thing was certain, when he left Oklahoma, he would be different from when he had come. A changed man—changed for the better. That's all she could ask for, because she knew he was going back. Just as she knew she had to stay.

One thing was for sure and for certain—he wasn't the only one who'd walk away different from before.

It seemed like they had been in the barn for hours, but it couldn't have been more than an hour. Tops.

He had stopped wearing his watch right after he'd arrived in Oklahoma. The Amish lived at a pace that wasn't kept by a thousand-dollar timepiece.

The Tag Heuer had been a present from Monica, and he hadn't wanted to damage it. So he'd placed it on the nightstand by his bed until the time came to return to Chicago. For now he was living on Amish time.

"The colt is coming." Katie Rose's voice held excitement, and the hushed tone of prayer.

"How do you know?"

She was crouched down beside the horse. "See how her belly keeps tightening?"

"Yeah."

"That means her time is near. Come here and help."

"I don' know nothing about birthin' no babies."

She shot him a confused look.

"It's from a movie." He grinned nervously. "Sorry. I tend to do that when I—"

"Will you get down here?"

She used that "teacher voice," and he immediately walked to the back end of the horse and dropped down in the hay beside her.

"This is a big baby," Katie Rose said. "Just make sure the back feet are comin' out first and that his head doesn't drop too hard onto the ground. Are you ready?"

Zane swallowed hard. And to think that he'd been worried about delivering a human baby. At least then he would have been able to communicate with the mother, talk her through whatever. If only he had his phone. He could look up how to deliver a baby horse . . . pony . . . *colt.* That's what a baby horse was called. A colt. Instead he had to rely on Katie Rose to tell him what to do. He snuck a look at her puckered forehead, her intense focus on the animal. "Have you ever done this before?"

She shook her head. "I've always helped, but this is my first birth to be in charge."

He nodded, wondering how she could act so much in control when she had to be as nervous as he.

"It's just that this colt means so much to *Dat.*"

"Oh, yeah?"

"He is planning to sell it to a man in Dallas. Someone Annie knows who trains horses to race."

He paused. "Isn't that against the Amish rules, betting on horses?"

"Bettin' is, but there's nothin' that says we can't breed horses for crazy *Englischers* to waste their money on."

True enough, he supposed.

"And the money will go a long way into helpin' with the doctor's costs."

It simply amazed Zane at the resources the Amish used to work together for the cause of one. Pickles, horses, covert jobs. He shook his head. The Amish were nothing if not capable.

"Here he comes." She ran her hands down the horse's belly and gently pushed.

All of a sudden, Zane could see feet. So far, so good.

The horse managed to get the colt out a little farther, until Zane could see knee joints. That's when the labor stalled. He stared at the knobby little knees of the colt for too long, and that wild light returned to the mare's eyes.

"What do we do now?" His earlier trepidation disappeared in the light of necessity.

"We help her." Katie Rose straddled the horse. "I'll push." Her full skirt hid the horse from his view, and Zane figured that was a good thing. Not that he couldn't see the horse, but that she couldn't see him. Kinda like birth blinders. "You pull," she said. "On my count, *jah*?"

He nodded.

"*Eens . . . zwee . . . drei.*"

Zane grasped the slippery legs of the colt, praying as he did, but it was like trying to pull rain through a straw. The mare fought them, as if tensing against the pain. How could he find fault with the new mother? Giving birth was a miracle, a gift from heaven.

But it was also messy and painful and hard. It looked really, really hard.

"Again," Katie Rose panted. "*Eens . . . zwee . . . drei.*"

Katie Rose counted down twice more before Zane felt the colt move.

"One more time," he said, wiping his forehead on his sleeve to keep the sweat out of his eyes. He adjusted his hold on the colt's legs as Katie Rose counted off.

"*Eens . . . zwee . . .*"

He started to pull early, then as pretty as you please, the colt slipped from its mother's body onto the soft hay.

The mare jerked.

Katie Rose jumped to the side, getting out of the way as the mare bent her head down to bite at the birth sack. The colt was beautiful. The most beautiful thing he had ever seen. Well, next to the woman who'd helped him deliver it.

He looked up at her, tears formed in her eyes. "He's beautiful."

And he was. From what Zane could see, the colt was solid black with four white feet and a blaze of white down his muzzle.

"He's so little," she said in wonderment.

"I don't think she shares your sentiment." Zane laughed as he said the words, his joy quickly morphing with the emotions raging inside him. His own tears threatened to spill over the edges of his lashes. He sniffed them back and used his sleeve to erase the evidence.

She picked her way across the stall and came to stand beside him. He wrapped his arms around her, pulling her close.

Her arms were hesitant, then strong as they slid around his waist. She laid her head on his shoulder. He buried his face in her neck, the fine tendrils of hair that escaped her bun brushing against his cheeks and getting trapped in his beard. Instinct told him to pull her closer, draw her to him, and never let her go. Kiss her, meld with her until they were one.

But those were English instincts, and they had no place in her world.

He breathed in deeply, memorizing the scent that was all Katie Rose, the lavender of her soap and the pure, sweet woman.

Reluctantly he put distance between them, unable to stop himself for wishing for another time and place.

Katie Rose seemed to sense the electricity between them. She straightened her dress, adjusted her apron and prayer *kapp*, her efforts to tidy herself marred by the fact that she was covered with blood from the birth.

He looked down at himself. He wasn't in any better shape.

The two of them looked like they'd starred in a horror movie, but they hadn't seen something die—they'd seen something live. And the miracle was amazing.

⊰⊱

After they were both satisfied that the colt was strong, the mother capable, and their services no longer needed by the bonding pair, Zane led Katie Rose toward the house. Neither of them said a word about their heartfelt embrace. If she wasn't going to mention it, then neither was he. It was only natural, after all, for them to turn to one another after the miracle they had witnessed.

Zane could barely remember the rabbits he'd had at the cooperative. They'd had babies once, and he could remember the excitement when all of a sudden one rabbit became many. It was a fun time for him, but nothing compared to this—helping bring another life into the world. Maybe nothing needed to be said. They walked up the porch steps one after the other and stepped through the front door.

"I'll just . . ." Katie Rose pulled at her ruined apron. He didn't have the heart to tell her that her prayer *kapp* was also smeared with the birth blood from the colt. It seemed insensitive somehow.

"Yeah." He nodded.

She turned and made her way down to the bathroom off the kitchen, while Zane climbed the stairs.

Annie was going to shoot him, Zane thought with a smile. He'd better get into town and get some kind of stain remover to get the blood out of his clothes. First thing tomorrow.

He stopped off in the bathroom first, washing the blood from his hands, still in awe over what he had just witnessed. The other miracle was that no one was home to see what transpired between them. As old-fashioned as the Amish were, he wouldn't be surprised if Abram would insist that he marry his daughter . . . or else.

Except that by marrying Katie Rose he would be committed to living with the Amish for the rest of his life.

Zane stopped in the middle of drying his hands on the rough towel hanging by the sink. That wasn't such a bad thought . . . living with God-loving, God-fearing people who believed in peace above all else, helping one another, and being faithful to their spouse. He could think of a lot worse things.

He made his way into the bedroom he shared with John Paul, shucking out of his soiled clothes and donning a clean pair of black pants and a blue shirt. He tucked in the shirt and pulled the suspenders up and over his shoulders.

Of course, their clothing left something to be desired, though he understood the need for conformity. Amish garb was a badge of honor, he supposed. Though he would miss blue jeans and music, what he would gain would be so much . . .

He pulled his thoughts to a screeching halt as he made his way down the stairs and into the kitchen. Why was he even thinking about that? It wasn't like he could really stay here. He had a life to get back to, a fiancée. He had a job to do here and then he would move on to the next one.

He'd certainly never thought about staying in Pakistan or Afghanistan or any other of the war-torn countries he'd visited. Even though Oklahoma Amish territory was totally different from those violent, dusty places, he couldn't stay. This was just a stepping-stone. It wouldn't be long, and he'd be on his way to Juarez and to the drug-torn streets of the border town.

He shook his head at his own foolishness then went to the fridge and started pulling out ingredients. If he was going to pull this off, then he'd better get the peppers diced first in case anyone came home and caught him before his payback was complete. The longer the salsa sat, the more punch it would pack.

He dumped the two gigantic packages of ground beef into the biggest skillet he could find. It was huge, cast iron, and could double for a weapon if need be. He turned the stove to medium heat, added spices, then set to work on the payback salsa.

Donning the latex gloves to core and chop the habaneros, he tried to make himself feel guilty. But he couldn't. What was a little burn compared to a morning of plowing with an antique? A little reverse hazing was definitely in order.

He sensed her before she appeared, knew that Katie Rose had finished changing and was ready to help. Funny how he seemed to know where she was even without looking up from dicing the fire peppers.

He turned to face her, unable to stop the smile that spread across his face at the sight of her. Katie Rose was wearing the same dress, but a different apron and cape thingie that he was sure belonged to her mother. She had pulled her hair back in place, but her prayer cap was the same one she'd been wearing before.

"What would you have me do?"

"Do you need to run home and change?"

"No, I—"

"Have blood on your, uh—" He waved a hand around toward her head.

Katie Rose lightly touched the stained white prayer cap. "*Jah. Mamm* doesn't . . ."

She trailed off, but he knew what she was going to say. That her mother wasn't wearing the traditional head coverings right now. Instead Ruth had taken to using full-fledged bonnets that covered her entire head.

"Why don't you just take it off?"

"Oh, *nay*. I could never do that. At least not before bed."

"Why not?"

"Because. Now what shall I help you with, Zane Carson?" She started breaking up the ground beef in the big iron skillet, turning it so all sides would brown. She seemed to concentrate a little too much on the task, making Zane wonder if she were uncomfortable with the conversation—or with him.

"You can start by washing the lettuce, and because *why*?"

She moved around him and pulled a colander from underneath one of the cabinets. "To wear our heads uncovered goes against the—"

"*Ordnung*?"

"And the Bible, *jah*."

He watched as she cut the end off the head of Romaine and plopped it into the colander. "How so?"

"We—"

"Meaning the women, right?"

"*Jah*, the women. We wear our hair long. A woman's hair is her glory, and all the glory belongs to God."

"Okay." He could understand that.

"The *Ordnung* tells us that we should cover our heads when we pray. This we do out of respect for God."

"But you wear it all the time." Zane plopped the sauce pan onto the stove and reached for one of the cans of refried beans he'd picked up at the grocery store.

She smiled at him a sweet, knowing smile that would put Mona Lisa to shame with its enigmatic mysteries. "But, Zane Carson, we never know when we might be moved to pray."

Zane contemplated this as he scraped the peppers into the ceramic bowl.

She pointed her knife at the start of what was to be really hot, hot sauce. "What's that?"

He couldn't stop his sheepish grin. "Um . . . salsa." It was the truth, just a watered-down version of it.

"Oh, I can't wait to try it."

"Not this, no." He pulled the gloves from his hands and tossed them into the trash.

"And why not, Zane Carson?"

When she said his name like that he felt he should stand and recite the multiplication tables. "Okay, here's the truth. Your brothers played a little joke on me right after I got here."

"Not the plow." She laughed.

"They've done that before?"

"*Jah.*"

"Then they definitely deserve this."

"What might that be?"

"Salsa—really, really hot salsa."

Katie Rose laughed once more, and Zane knew he could get used to the sound. "I hope you will also make some mild for those of us who didn't trick you into usin' my *grossdaadi's* plow."

He smiled in return, then gave her a little wink. "I'll make a special batch."

Their camaraderie continued as Katie Rose showed him how to use the hand chopper instead of an electric food processor to chop the canned tomatoes into the base for salsa. As Katie Rose worked on chopping ingredients for the mild, he continued to work on the payback salsa.

He was adding the last of the garlic and oil into both of them when everyone started to arrive.

John Paul was the first in the house. Ever starving, his nose led him straight into the kitchen. "Smells good in here."

"*Danki*," Katie Rose and Zane said at the same time.

"What's that?" John Paul pointed to the bowls of salsa just waiting for chips and willing victims.

Katie Rose slapped his hand away even as her eyes twinkled. "It's Zane's famous salsa. But you have to wait until supper's ready. Now, shoo."

He looked a bit forlorn, then backed away. "I'll just go wash up. How much longer?"

"About fifteen minutes." Zane slid the tray of taco shells into the oven.

"And don't forget to fetch Noni," Katie Rose added.

"Have I ever forgotten before, sister?"

"*Nay*," she smiled, and Zane had the feeling she was just trying to make sure John Paul stayed out of the kitchen. Or maybe she just liked bossing her baby brother. "Don't let this be the first time."

John Paul gave a curious glance from one to the other, then shook his head. "*Jah*, then." He turned on his heel and disappeared up the stairs.

John Paul had no more gotten out of sight when Abram and Ruth walked into the house. They were together, but not, a distance between them, a mental chasm, something emotional. Whatever it was, it wasn't good. Abram kept looking at his wife, the pain in his eyes clear for everyone to see. Except for Ruth, because she looked at everything but her husband. She was hurting, Zane knew, but he had no idea how to help her. It meant a lot to him to help. They had taken him in, shown him another way of life, a special existence that one couldn't find elsewhere, no matter where they searched on the globe.

Abram went back to wash his hands and "redd up" for supper while Ruth sank into one of the dining chairs, her body seeming to wilt under its own weight.

Concern flashed across Katie Rose's face, then just as quickly, it disappeared. She took a deep breath, dried her hands on a towel, and knelt in front of her mother and began to pray.

Zane looked back to his cheese, concentrating a little too seriously on grating. He needed to get dinner ready as much as they needed some privacy.

"*Aemen*." Katie Rose lifted her head and smiled at her mother.

"Katie Rose," Ruth started. "Whatever has happened to your *kapp*?"

"Oh, *Mamm*! The colt was born. Zane Carson and I helped."

So he was back to Zane Carson now, was he? He loved the intimate sound of his name on her lips, but it was for the best.

"And the colt?"

"He's so *schay*."

"Who's pretty?" Abram picked that precise moment to come back into the room, rolling his shirt sleeves down as he walked.

"Jennifer's new colt."

Zane stopped. "You named the mare Jennifer?"

"*Nay*." Abram shook his head.

"Well, somebody did."

"*Ach*, that's true," Katie Rose added, but her father was already on his way toward the door.

Zane could tell that Katie Rose wanted to slip out and go look at the colt as well, but her mother stood and grabbed her hand. "Let's get you a clean *kapp*. The Lord will not like you goin' around like that." She led Katie Rose to the back of the house.

Zane wanted to drop everything and go look at the horse himself, but he had about another pound of cheese to grate and the tortillas to warm. He continued with his work. There'd be time after supper to go check on the new addition to the barn.

In no time at all, the women reappeared. Katie Rose had on a clean prayer *kapp*, starched and crisp white. And Ruth had a bandana tied around her head. She seemed hesitant, but Katie Rose urged her to sit and relax.

Katie Rose pointed to the bowl of salsa that Zane had made especially for the Fisher sons. "That one."

Ruth nodded, a tentative smile on her face as well.

"I like your new prayer covering," Zane said, opening the tortillas and getting them ready to heat.

She reached a hand upward, then stopped. "I am unsure."

"Why?" he asked.

"I do not believe there's a provision for this in the *Ordnung*."

"Then you're not doing anything wrong."

"That is for the bishop to decide," Katie Rose added.

"And since he's not here to pass judgment, I say leave it as is."

Ruth reached up a trembling hand and touched the soft pink fabric.

Zane smiled at the sight of all those pink ribbons and at the fact that now Ruth could call herself a survivor. Even though he'd known it all along.

God is good.

That thought made his smile even wider.

"What are you grinning about?" Katie Rose asked with a smile of her own.

"Oh, nothing."

"*Ach*, that's a fine colt, he is." Abram may have been speaking about the horse, but his eyes were fixed on Ruth and her new head covering.

What was he thinking?

Katie Rose nodded. "And he wouldn't be here had it not been for Zane Carson."

Abram tore his gaze from his wife and centered it on Zane. "Is that a fact?"

Zane shrugged. "Katie Rose and I both helped."

"*Ach*, a fine colt," he repeated. "Now, what is this special dinner that you have made for us?"

"Tacos," Zane replied.

"*Dat*, you've had tacos before."

"But not like these," Zane cut in.

Katie Rose raised her eyebrows in question.

"You won't want to eat this, though." Zane pointed to the batch of extra fiery salsa.

Abram frowned. "Why not?"

Before anyone could answer, Gabriel and his bunch arrived, soon followed by Gideon and his Annie. The house was full to bursting when John Paul loped down the stairs and went on back to fetch Noni for supper.

Zane saw Katie Rose pull Mary Elizabeth and Annie aside to warn them about the salsa. Mary Elizabeth smiled, always up for a good practical joke—especially since the men were the target, John Paul included. It seemed Annie had a sense of humor as well, for her violet eyes twinkled as she heard the plan.

Once everyone had gathered around, Zane shushed them so he could speak. "As you know, this dinner is to celebrate Ruth's triumph over cancer."

Everyone cheered, but amid the whoops Zane heard a few "*aemens*." Even Noni tapped her cane on the floor to show her support.

"God is good," Katie Rose added.

Zane smiled. Amazing how they thought alike sometimes. When she shot him down after he first arrived, he never would have guessed that could happen.

Now she would be the one he missed the most.

He pushed the sobering thought of returning to Chicago to the back of his mind and continued. "I thought we might do things a bit differently tonight. We'll have our prayer and then fix our plates buffet style. That way everyone can add what they'd like to their tacos, agreed?"

A chorus of "*jahs*" went up all around, and Zane looked to Abram to lead them into prayer.

Abram shook his head. "Tonight, Zane Carson, it is upon you to lead us to God."

Zane felt his neck burn, not from embarrassment for being put on the spot, but because Abram thought him qualified to talk to God. He glanced around the room, and took a long breath. "Let's pray, then."

Everyone bowed their heads.

As Zane started his silent prayer, he felt a hand sneak its way into his.

Katie Rose.

He tried to tell himself it was because they had shared so much in one afternoon—the joy of her mother's healing, the birth of new life, and the joke they were about to play on her brothers. But he hoped there was more to her action than that.

Not that it would matter. He would be leaving soon.

He prayed for the Lord to bless the food, he gave thanks for being able to come to Amish country and meet these fine people, for his chance to get to know God, and to help a colt be born and all the other blessings he'd experienced. He finished his prayer with the hopes that John Paul, Gabe, and Gideon wouldn't be too mad at him over the salsa. He wiped the smile from his face as he finished with "Amen."

As was the Amish custom, Abram grabbed a plate for himself. Zane started one for Noni, and Katie Rose for her mother, and after that, the men gathered in to fix their tacos.

Zane showed them the best way to construct a taco starting with a shell and meat and ending with salsa. "There are two kinds of salsa over there." He pointed to the bowls. "The one on the left is mild for the children. And the one on the right has a little more spice to it."

He hid his mirth and tried not to stare as the big Fisher men added spoonful upon spoonful of salsa to their tacos.

"How much are we supposed to use?" Gideon asked.

"As much as you'd like," Zane replied. "But I have to admit that I like a lot of salsa. It just seems to make the taco."

John Paul nodded, and Zane noticed with particular satisfaction that his roommate added more spicy salsa than all the rest.

Katie Rose and Annie stepped forward to make their plates while Zane watched the brothers.

Gabriel was the first one to dig in, eating half of it in one bite. He chewed, nodded, then reacted as if steam exploded from his ears. He grabbed his water and gulped it down just as Gideon and John Paul realized the mistake they'd made as well. The brothers jumped around, fanning their tongues, talking about crazy English foods, and trying to figure out why no one else was in such pain.

Ruth cracked first, laughing until tears slid down her cheeks. Soon, everyone else joined in, though most of the kids had no idea why everyone was cackling like hyenas, unable to stop.

Zane wiped his own tears of mirth from his eyes as he poured a glass of milk for the brothers. "This will help cut the burn."

John Paul accepted his glass with gratitude, but instead of drinking it, he stuck his tongue into the milk trying to cool it as fast as possible.

Paybacks, Zane decided, were sweet.

"*Ach*, city boy," John Paul said. "What is in that devil chutney?"

Zane couldn't help one last laugh. "Habanero peppers. Only the third hottest pepper known to man."

Gideon sat, eyes streaming from laughter or tears—Zane wasn't sure which. "If that one is number three, I'll thank you for goin' no higher."

Everyone laughed again, and the Fisher brothers got back in line to make tacos without the "devil chutney."

"So, this is about the plow, huh?" John Paul spooned the mild salsa onto his new tacos, and Zane noticed he didn't use nearly as much this second go 'round.

"Bingo," Zane replied, then noticed the puzzled looks all around the table. "It's like saying, 'yes.' It's from a game, and when you win you call out 'bingo.'"

They nodded their heads as if they understood, but Zane had the feeling they secretly thought he was making things up as he went along. "You should bear that in mind next time you feel like playing a trick on someone," he said.

"It tastes just fine to me," Noni chimed in.

Zane darted a glance at the elderly woman. *Surely she hadn't . . .* Zane took in the taco she held and realized that the eldest member of the household had smothered her taco with the habanero salsa.

Noni stared back as if they'd all lost their minds, then took another bite of the taco.

Everyone laughed.

And Zane considered Taco Night a success.

His gaze locked with Katie Rose's, and she smiled in return. He looked away first, hoping she couldn't read the longing in his gaze. Man, he was going to miss her after he left. Once again the idea to stay flitted through his mind. It was possible, yet impossible all at the same moment. This was America and a free country, so there was no legal reason why he couldn't stay.

Even though this trip was an assignment, it was akin to a vacation—a *working* vacation. And though anyone would be tempted to stay in paradise, all vacationers must return to the life where they belonged.

◈

"I'd like to thank you, Zane Carson."

"For what, Ruth Fisher?"

She fought back the urge to say, *everything*, and instead concentrated on tonight. "The tacos, the laughter. I'm afraid that my cancer has put a stop to much of that. You brought it back to us."

"My pleasure, Ruth."

She opened her mouth to tell him it was more than that, but he hushed her.

"Truth is, I was craving tacos, and this gave me the perfect opportunity to have my cake and eat it too, so to speak."

She frowned. "What good is cake if not to eat?"

Zane blinked at her question, then threw back his head and laughed.

The man had a fine laugh that said he enjoyed his life. It made Ruth feel that everything was going to be just fine. It was also contagious, and she soon found herself chuckling along with him.

"That's a good point, Ruth. A very good point."

"There's something else I'd like to speak to you about, if I may." She ran her palms down her apron, suddenly unsure of how to say what needed to be said.

"Of course."

"It's none of my business other than it is happening in my house and under my nose. And I feel that I have to say somethin'."

Zane immediately sobered, his laughter dying away like the last rays of daylight. "I—"

"Hear me out. Once I've said my peace, I'll go on up to bed. But I did not miss the looks that passed between you and my daughter tonight."

His shoulders relaxed, as if relieved that he had been called out, and Ruth wondered if there were other secrets in her house.

"There's not anything." He shook his head. "I mean, I think Katie Rose is fantastic and beautiful."

Ruth nodded. She felt the same, of course. But she was the girl's mother.

A shadow of something—sadness, perhaps?—passed over his handsome face. "I'm leaving in a couple of weeks."

"I've been prayin' to the Lord that He would send someone to help mend Katie Rose's heart." Ruth leaned her head to one side. "And He sent you."

Zane started shaking his head before she even finished her thoughts. "It's not like that."

She clasped her hands around his and squeezed. "I know you are a good man. You are strong, and you work hard. You can cook and plow and milk and a host of other things." She squeezed his hands tighter. "And I know love when I see it."

His brown eyes grew wide.

"Oh, it's not just on *your* face. I see it in my Katie Rose's eyes every time she looks at you." Something twisted in her heart. It was the same way that she herself had once looked at Abram—and he at her. That was a long time ago . . .

She stiffened against the stab of pain that thought brought her and instead concentrated on the young man before her. "I know that when the time comes, what is supposed to happen will come to pass. We all live within the Lord's will." She smiled up at him. "And love is no exception."

Ruth's words haunted him all of the next day as he wrapped his Christmas presents for the Fishers. It was hard to believe it was Christmas Eve. Hard to believe that in little over a week, he'd be headed back to Chicago. To reality.

And Katie Rose would remain here.

The thought that he was in love with her was absurd. He hadn't even known Katie Rose for three months. Sure she was kind and generous, hardworking and thoughtful—and she would definitely make some strapping Amish man a good wife.

He ignored the flash of pain that shot through him at the thought.

Zane gave his head a tight shake. Just because she was compassionate and good with children, could bait a hook, and didn't shy away when he had offered her skinned rabbits for a gift, none of that meant that he should fall in love with her. Or even could. Why, he had Monica. *She* was the one with his heart. *She* was the one he would marry.

He couldn't be in love with Katie Rose. He hadn't even kissed her . . . though he'd come awfully close. It was for the best that he hadn't. She was a gentle and sensitive soul. She was smart, and she could feel the pull between them. Attraction yes, but love? Nuh-uh.

Besides, he didn't want to take advantage of her. She was different from him, pure and chaste, good and wholesome, and not of the world. Though if others were seeing the connection they shared . . .

He would do everything in his power to keep his hands to himself and not to trifle with her emotions. He was leaving soon.

He was about to get married. It was the right thing to do . . . for all of them.

❧❧ ❧❧

All day long a suspended hush hung over the farm as if every creature held its breath, waiting for Christmas to come.

Zane was caught up in that aura of suspense too. He had wrapped all of his presents and hidden them under his bed. Even though he had never celebrated Christmas before, he knew some of the typical, non-Amish customs. Without a Christmas tree, he wasn't really sure what to do with the gifts.

He was a grown man, and yet he couldn't contain his excitement. This was his first Christmas, his first "real" Christmas. His uncle had considered the day a time to rest and watch football games. There were token presents, but nothing other than what was necessary—a pair of jeans, a sweatshirt, nominal gifts to mark what the rest of the world considered one of the biggest days of the year.

This Christmas would be different. He had heard the Bible story from the Gospel of Luke, had learned how Mary and Joseph traveled to Bethlehem, and that Mary gave birth only to have to put their child in a manger instead of a bed.

The thought of a woman giving birth in a barn and laying her newborn baby in the trough where the animals ate . . . he shook his head at it all. And people thought today's times were tough.

For the Amish, Christmas Eve was a fairly typical day. There were chores to be done, meals to get on the table, darning to be completed. Everyone went about these daily tasks as though it wasn't a special day. Still, the excitement hung in the air.

Katie Rose came to dinner, and Zane wanted to believe that she came because of him. That was certainly being proud. She probably came to spend time with her family, most important, her mother.

Not many days were left for Zane and Katie Rose to spend together. Once he returned to Chicago, things would look vastly different. Maybe he would come to believe that he had simply been caught up in the charm of the Amish, the beauty of her smile, and the thought of love. That it was all just a trick of the lighting, or sleight of hand.

None of this made seeing her any less special.

The room was dark except for the flicker of the fire and the steady glow given off by the propane light. The house was quiet, creaking and popping every now and then as if to remind them they were not alone.

How had they managed to be the only two people left downstairs while everyone else was getting ready for bed? Katie Rose knew she should leave. Mary Elizabeth was probably having a dandy of a time getting the boys to lie down and settle in for the night. As they impatiently waited for the morning to come and Christmas festivities to begin, every child knew that tonight was the longest night of the year. Samuel would be especially challenging without her there.

She stood, suddenly nervous in her own home. "I should go." She had grown up within these walls. He should be the one feeling out of place, not her.

But she did. She stood to make good on her words, but Zane reached out a hand to stop her. "Stay a little while longer."

It was more of a plea than a command, softly spoken into the dim light of the room. One might even say that the atmosphere was romantic, and Katie Rose wasn't sure if she could handle the intimacy of the air alone.

"I really should get home," she whispered in return, but she sat back down, as if her knees folded beneath her on their own.

He scooted a little closer, their legs brushing. She shivered, and wrapped her shawl a little tighter around her. She was fooling herself if she thought this reaction came from the cold. "Stay," he said, reaching for her hand. "For just a little bit. I'll take you home in the buggy."

His gaze flickered down to her lips, and she licked them nervously. She had seen that look before. He wanted to kiss her. And she wanted just as much to feel his lips on hers. She had been kissed before, but never had the anticipation made her heart thump painfully in her chest. Never before had it turned her brain to mush, her breath tight.

He cupped his hands on either side of her face, and she was helpless to move away from him. Not from his hold. *Nay*, his touch was gentle as a babe. But the power of his gaze pulled her to him in a way nothing else could.

He lowered his head toward hers. She waited, her breath trapped in her throat. The fire cast shadows across his features, but there was enough light for her to see the yearning on his face. She feared her own expression reflected the same.

What difference did it make? He was with her tonight. He might be leaving soon, but for tonight he wanted to kiss her. And she wanted him to kiss her. She would sort out the details later.

Her gaze flickered to his mouth. Her lips parted in anticipation, and his sweet breath brushed against her lips. He smelled of coffee and pie and all things good.

Her eyes fluttered closed.

A loud knock sounded, exploding the atmosphere and destroying the moment. Katie Rose jumped, instinctively moving away from Zane. She pulled in a steadying breath, her gaze darting about the room, trying to locate the disturbance.

The knock sounded again. Only then did Katie Rose realize that someone was at the front door. She couldn't look at Zane, her hands automatically smoothing down her skirt.

She shook her head. What had she been thinking? She hadn't been. She had been caught up in the beauty of the night, the magic that was Christmas. She had been taken in by Zane, his handsome smile and unexpected carin' ways. *Ei, yi, yi*, she couldn't blame him for her slip. That was hers. She just had to make sure something like this never happened again. It would be all too easy for her to lose her heart to the handsome *Englischer*.

A third knock sounded before Katie Rose made her way to the door. She took a deep, steadying breath, hoping she didn't look as guilty and flustered as she felt. She ran her palms over her cheeks, hoping they weren't as red as the heat emanating from them, and opened the door.

A gasp of shock rushed from her lungs. Of all the people she had expected at the door at this time of night on Christmas Eve, there before her stood the last person on that list.

"Katie Rose." His voice was the same as she remembered, his eyes just as blue. Until he spoke, she'd wondered if she had somehow imagined that he was there. His voice, however, proved that theory wrong.

After all these years, Samuel Beachy had returned.

13

Jealously cut through Zane. Samuel Beachy. Katie Rose's long-lost love.

"I, uh . . . come in." Katie Rose stood to the side to allow the man entrance into the house.

As wary as a lion eyeing another male entering his territory, Zane watched him step over the threshold. So this was the man who'd broken her heart, who'd pledged his love, and turned away. Every muscle in Zane's body tensed.

He wanted to get up and smash Samuel Beachy's face.

But what would it prove? How was he any better than the man before him? He'd been about to kiss Katie Rose, and that was wrong on so many levels. She wasn't like the English girls. She didn't flirt and tease. She was good and honest and wholesome, and he'd been about to toy with her emotions, whether that was his intent or not. He was no better than the man who now stood in her parents' living room, dressed in English clothes, sounding all the more like a proper Amish man.

Slowly Zane relaxed, but remained alert. He might have only known Katie Rose for a couple of months, but he'd toss this Samuel Beachy out on his ear if he so much as blinked wrong at her.

Katie Rose watched him, her emotions masked. "What are you doin' here?"

"I came back this morning. I wanted to come see you right away, but I wasn't able to get over here before now." He took her hands into his own, staring into her eyes much the same way Zane had done moments before. "*Ach*, Katie Rose. I have missed you so."

She didn't ask him if he was staying. Maybe that was the question she had planned to ask when she opened her mouth, but the words never left her lips.

Abram made his way down the stairs. "*Gut himmel*! Samuel Beachy."

Zane faded into the background, now more than ever aware that he wasn't a part of the family, the community.

Abram took Samuel Beachy by the shoulders and pulled him close. He slapped the younger man affectionately on the back. "I knew you'd come back. Though I thought it've been before now."

At least Samuel had the decency to blush. Dressed in a Carhartt jacket with jeans and boots, he didn't look much different from any other English man. Samuel was tall with dark, wavy hair and piercing blue eyes.

He looked to Katie Rose but before she could say anything, Ruth came down the stairs holding onto her pink ribbon bandana with one hand and the banister with the other.

"Samuel Beachy, is that really you?"

The man had the decency to look surprised to see Ruth in such a state. "*Dat* told me what had happened with your cancer."

"She's done with all that now," Abram boasted. Zane couldn't help but notice that neither he nor his wife looked at the other.

Zane glanced to Katie Rose. She wore a dazed look as if about ready to pinch herself to make sure she was awake. He would like to think that the mere idea of kissing him had sent her into such a dreamy state, but he knew better. Samuel Beachy's return would be talked about for days, even weeks, to come.

Annie picked that moment to find her way down the stairs. She looked from one of them to the other trying to piece together the story on her own.

Samuel solved the problem by stepping forward. He held out a hand for her to shake. "Good evening. I'm Samuel Beachy."

Annie cut her violet eyes to Katie Rose, then back to Samuel. "I'm Annie Hamilton."

"Gideon's Annie." Samuel smiled. "I've heard a lot about you."

Annie smiled in return, looking a bit confused. She glanced at Zane. He tried to look unaffected, perhaps even uninterested, but knew he failed miserably.

"I know it's late," Samuel started, nodding to each of them in turn. His eyes lingered on Katie Rose, and Zane had to suppress the urge to strangle him. "I didn't mean to disrupt the entire household." He stepped toward Katie Rose and took her hands again.

Zane had to remind himself that once upon a time they were going to get married. Katie Rose was a grown woman. If she didn't want him holding her hands, she could pull away. She didn't, and as far as Zane was concerned, that said it all.

"I just had to see you tonight. It's been so long, and I just . . ."

"I think I'll . . ." Abram started back toward the stairs, then he stopped and doubled back, shaking Samuel's hand once again before bidding everyone good night.

Ruth followed Abram up the stairs. "Don't stay up too late. Christmas morning comes mighty early." Zane vaguely registered that they didn't speak, hold hands, or even acknowledge the other as they made their way back to their bed. Something was up between the two of them and he was afraid that, unlike the cancer, it could never be healed. He made a mental note to add them to his prayer list.

He turned his gaze on Katie Rose. "I guess I should be . . . going . . . to bed as well." Zane backed toward the staircase not wanting to leave, but knowing this was for the best. He had no business trying to kiss the beautiful Kate. This had to be divine intervention. He wasn't supposed to kiss her. She was supposed to be with Samuel. He was the answer to all their prayers. He had come back for his one true love, and it was for the best.

So why did his heart feel like a rock in his chest?

She spoke up. "I thought you were takin' me home."

He had promised Katie Rose that he would take her back to her house in the buggy. Before he could utter one word on the matter, Samuel jumped in. "I can take you wherever you need to go."

"*Danki*, Samuel," Katie Rose said with a slight curtsy. "I stay with Gabriel and his children now."

Samuel nodded, and Zane felt more and more like a third wheel. "*Dat* told me about Rebecca. So sad."

Katie Rose nodded. "I need to get home to help get the children all tucked in for the night."

Zane inched toward the stairs. He'd never found himself in this situation: about to kiss a girl in the middle of the night, and then having to give her up for an ex. Nope, that had to be one for the record books.

"Zane." She spoke his name, her voice stopping him before he could reach the stairs. "Good night."

He nodded, pushing his crazy emotions to the back of his mind. "Good night."

How many times had she ridden in a buggy with this man at her side? Too many to count, that was for sure and for certain. But when she walked out onto the porch, there was no shiny black buggy and waiting horse. Instead, a shiny black car gleamed like sin in the moonlight.

She stopped. "You want me to ride in *that*?"

"Isn't she beautiful?"

"She?"

Samuel sighed. "I suppose I'll have to give her up to come back and join the church, but my other interests are more than worth it."

Katie Rose blinked, trying to decide if he was talking about her or something else, and if there was any way out of riding in that sinful black car with him.

Samuel cupped a hand over her elbow and urged her down the steps toward the little automobile. There was no way out. He opened the door and nodded for her to get inside.

She was sure that Samuel was a much better driver than John Paul, but it still made her nervous. She could count on one hand the number of times she'd been in a car. She'd never gotten used to the feeling of travelling faster than the good Lord intended.

But tonight she didn't have far to go. It was less than half a mile to Gabriel's *haus*.

The windows were rolled up, tinting the world darker than midnight, still Katie Rose held tight to her prayer *kapp* as if it might fly off from the speed.

Samuel talked about what he had been doing for the last six years, but Katie Rose could barely listen. She was still too stunned that he had returned. And for good, if she was to understand what he'd been saying about his car.

He pulled down Gabriel's drive, and Katie Rose was thankful the ride was over. She would have much rather ridden with Zane in the buggy, swaying against him as the horses rocked them home. Maybe shared a kiss at the door, the first taste of his lips. The thought jolted her. That wasn't what she wanted, was it?

Samuel turned off the car, cooling her thoughts. He came around to her side and opened her door. It was a *gut* thing, too, because she couldn't tell which of the crazy levers on the door actually opened it.

"Good night, Samuel Beachy," she said as he walked her up the front porch steps. She should say how *gut* it was to have him home and how happy she was to see him after all these years, but she couldn't find the words. And she was terribly uncertain as to their truthfulness.

"I'll come by tomorrow, after supper. We've got so much to talk about."

"*Jah*," was all she could manage.

He reached out a hand, running the backs of his fingers down her cheek.

Katie Rose ducked inside and closed the door behind her, hoping she didn't appear too much like a frightened bunny running from a bloodhound, and praying that God would keep by her side through this crazy situation she'd found herself in.

She pressed her back to the door and didn't move until she heard Samuel Beachy's fancy *Englisch* car start up and drive off into the night.

$$14$$

The buzz of excitement hung in the air as Zane made his way down the stairs. It was Christmas morning, and all the English boys and girls were getting up to see what Santa had brought them. Well, a lot of them were. He was pretty sure his family wasn't the only one that didn't celebrate the holiday.

His parents and all the other families in the cooperative hadn't celebrated Christmas at all. Most of their holidays, if a person insisted on giving them a name, were more about the stages of the sun, the vernal equinox and the winter solstice, that kind of thing. Once he'd gone to live with his uncle, he hadn't celebrated anything except birthdays. If having his uncle hand him an unwrapped gift across the breakfast table could be called a celebration. Still, he had heard other children talk of their Christmas traditions. He'd been jealous of what these other children had, but he knew that life didn't belong to him. Long ago he'd tamped down those feelings of want, believing they had died of starvation. But this cool December morning those longings came rushing back.

These thoughts gave him something to think about other than almost kissing Katie Rose the night before. He couldn't say that it was better this way, to be interrupted and not to have experienced Katie Rose's lips beneath his. But to be interrupted by Samuel Beachy, the man Katie Rose had once loved . . .

Her expression, however, had been guarded, and he considered that a good sign. Samuel Beachy might win her love all over again, but at least she wasn't going to make it easy for him. Not that any of it was his business since he was leaving in a little less than a week.

After he and John Paul had fed the chickens and milked the cows, they walked silently back to the house. John Paul hadn't said one word to Zane since Taco Night, two days ago. Zane wasn't sure if he was mad, or just didn't have anything to say. Besides, he had only seen the younger man for a few minutes each day. John Paul had taken to working more and more. How he had explained his absence to his parents, Zane didn't know.

He glanced at the younger man. "You're uh . . . not still mad about the salsa, are you?" Zane's breath turned foggy in the winter air. The sky looked heavy with clouds. If he'd been in Chicago, he would have guessed that it might snow, but Oklahoma weather was as unpredictable as it came.

"*Nay*, it's . . ." The young man pulled in a deep breath and looked at the sky as if the heavy clouds held an answer.

He stood that way for so long Zane was glad that he'd worn his heavy coat. Something was bothering John Paul, and it had nothing to do with tacos.

"A girl."

"*Jah.* Bethany."

Zane shoved his freezing hands into his pockets and waited for John Paul to continue. He could sympathize. Katie Rose had him tied in knots. The need to be close to her, when he knew that nothing could ever come of this attraction that seared him.

"She wants to marry, for me to give up my job and my *rumspringa* and join the church right now."

"You're only seventeen."

John Paul continued. "It is not uncommon for Amish to get married young."

Zane couldn't imagine himself married at such a young age. He'd been hopelessly immature as a teen. But the Amish were different. John Paul, for all his fun-loving attitude, was a much more mature young man than Zane had ever been. Amish youth took on responsibilities, helped in the community, and did much more in any given day than most English kids in a week. It made them strong, steady, and dependable. Perfect spouse material. Still, there was no sense in rushing it. "I take it you're not ready to get married."

He shrugged. "I know I'm goin' to join the church, but I'm enjoyin' the *Englisch* world. I love goin' to movies and listenin' to rock and roll."

Some of the same things Zane would miss if he stayed. He pushed those thoughts away. Staying was not an option.

"I like goin' to work outside the farm."

"If you join the church, will you have to give up your job?"

"*Jah*. I won't have a way to get there. It's too far to walk or take the horse and buggy. I'd have to give up my car, and the job would follow. I'm afraid that if I give in to her demands that I'll regret it always. I love Bethany. I have since we were in school, but I don't want our marriage tainted by unreasonable demands."

Zane thrust his hands into his coat pockets. "Are you asking for my advice?"

"*Nay*. I know that I have to enjoy my *rumspringa*, that this is what the time is set aside for."

"If she loves you, she'll wait. Don't you think?" As he said the words, his mind flashed back to the night before. Katie Rose had never married, even though Samuel Beachy had been gone for six long years. Had she been waiting, or had this been just the way things turned out, like she said? Zane couldn't shake the feeling that love had its hand in Katie Rose's choice not to marry someone else. He sighed. Samuel Beachy's return was for the best.

"*Jah. Weibs leit.*"

He said the word in *Deutsch*, but Zane understood the tone perfectly. *Women.*

The smell of coffee greeted them as they stepped into the house. There were no decorations like all in the English world. No red and green wreaths, no Christmas tree. Not even a stack of presents. Zane had all his wrapped and hidden under his bed upstairs.

Annie was at the stove flipping bacon like a short-order cook. Ruth sat at the table, a coffee mug in front of her, as she sliced oranges to go with their breakfast.

Zane and John Paul hung their hats and coats on the pegs just inside the door.

"*Shayna Grischtdaag,*" Annie called.

"*Shayna Grischtdaag,*" they echoed. Nice Christmas.

"Breakfast will be ready shortly," Ruth added. "Go on and get washed. Everyone will be here in a while, and we'll exchange our presents then."

John Paul poured himself a cup of coffee and joined his mother at the table.

Zane couldn't account for his excitement. He felt like a kid, knowing that he'd get to see Katie Rose again. He also couldn't wait to give everyone the gifts he'd bought on his first ever Christmas shopping spree.

He bounded up the stairs and knelt down by his bed, reaching underneath where he had stored the presents and coming up with . . . nothing. Well, almost nothing. There was an envelope with his name printed on the outside in carefully formed letters.

Zane opened the note.

> *Dear Zane—*
> *I had to move the presents. I was afraid something*
> *would happen to them here.*
> *John Paul.*

Something did happen to them here. John Paul took them.

> *P.S. Check the bathroom.*

Zane pushed himself to his feet, mumbling about the crazy habits of the Amish. But the presents weren't in the bathroom, either. All he found was another note. This one taped to the mirror.

> *Sorry. Decided this was not the place for them*
> *either. The chicken coop is much safer.*

The chicken coop?

Zane rushed back down the stairs, rounding into the kitchen and pointing a finger at John Paul. "Where are they?"

The young man shrugged, his face impassive, and Zane wondered if he'd ever played poker. John Paul glanced at the note in Zane's hand. "Says there, in the chicken coop."

"You did not put my Christmas presents in the chicken coop."

He shrugged again. "Says I did."

Zane glared at John Paul for a full minute while he sat and drank coffee, then he realized what this was about. Paybacks for the payback.

With a low growl that was more for show, Zane pulled on his coat and hat and made his way outside.

He found just what he suspected in the chicken coop: a note telling him that the presents were in the linen closet for safe keeping.

He went back inside the house, hiding his grin as he took off his coat and hat and ran up the stairs. As he knew it would be, the linen closet did not house his presents—just another infernal note telling him that the barn was a better storage place, of course.

Zane tripped down the stairs, a little slower this time, donned his hat and coat and shot a look at the three innocent bystanders. Well, two of them were innocent.

It took him a little longer to find the note in the barn, as it was tacked onto the wall of one of the empty stalls. It stated, as he knew it would, that the barn might be a little messy for the presents, and that they were indeed upstairs in the room that Annie occupied.

Not so innocent after all.

Zane made his way back into the house, pulled off his coat and hat, hung them on their pegs and jogged up the stairs. He made it as far as Annie's door, but stopped when he found the expected note stuck to the outside.

The presents were in the buggy.

He went back down the stairs again, pulled on his coat, smacked his hat on his head, and did his best not to slam the door behind him as he made his way back out to the barn.

But the presents weren't in the buggy, just another note telling him to check in the downstairs bathroom.

He stalked across the yard, wondering how much longer John Paul could keep this up, and how much longer it would be before he ran himself ragged looking for the presents.

Zane pulled open the front door, took off his hat, then his coat, all the while watching John Paul for any sign of weakness. There were none.

Note in hand, he made his way to the downstairs bathroom

where he found another one telling him to look upstairs. He shot John Paul a look as he climbed the stairs, again. He found another note on the door to their room stating that John Paul had found the best place for hiding the presents: they were under his bed!

Zane looked, and sure enough there they were under John Paul's bed, not five feet from where they had started out. He blew out a breath, rocking on his heels. Then he pulled the presents out and made his way down the stairs.

John Paul was laughing hysterically when Zane hit the first floor.

Zane tried to act mad, but that lasted all of two minutes. He sat the presents at one end of the table and joined in.

John Paul wiped his eyes. "You should have seen your face."

"Don't push it." Zane growled.

Abram chuckled as he joined them. "That'll teach you to go around feedin' people the devil's chutney."

⚜ ⚜

They were still laughing when Annie called them to eat. Zane bowed his head and said a prayer with them, the motion as natural as breathing. He had so much to be thankful for: the feeling of family on this beautiful Christmas Day, the fact that the Lord loved them enough to send them Jesus, and had he mentioned the feeling of family? He had never before experienced anything so closely resembling a family. He hadn't really known what he was missing. Now he did. He would miss them more than they knew.

Soon after, Gideon arrived with Katie Rose and Gabriel's bunch not far behind. John Paul fetched Noni from the *grossdawdi haus*, and the celebration began.

As far as celebrations go, this one was rather subdued, but the fire crackled and everyone was together. Of course, nothing is really quiet with seven children present, yet Zane enjoyed every minute of it. He handed out his presents, more excited to see what everyone thought about their gifts than he was about opening the stack that had appeared next to his chair.

"Zane Carson, it's beautiful," Ruth said, as she carefully unwrapped the faceless nativity scene.

For Annie, he had bought a length of fabric in the most beautiful shade of purple. He'd consulted with Coln Anderson's wife, and she assured him that the fabric would be allowed by the bishop and would also match the newcomer's eyes perfectly. He'd bought the men varying sets of tools including a battery-operated drill that could be recharged at the general store. For the children he had purchased a variety of toys and candies in celebration of the day.

He held his breath when Katie Rose got to her present.

She ripped daintily at the bright red paper that covered the box. But young Samuel was having none of that. He tore at the paper with a squeal of glee. Zane wasn't sure if it was because the package, all of his packages for that matter, were wrapped in brighter paper than all of the others—they had been wrapped in old copies of the Old Order Amish newspaper, *Die Botschaft*, and brown grocery sacks. He wondered if that was part of the *Ordnung* that he'd missed, but no one seemed too concerned on the festive occasion.

Samuel ripped and tore while Katie Rose laughed at his antics. Then she grew quiet, her beautiful eyes big and round. "An entire set of *The Little House on the Prairie* series?"

Zane nodded, a lump in his throat from her awed expression.

"In hardbound copies?"

"For your classroom."

She smiled, even as she blinked back joyful tears. "*Danki*, Zane Carson."

He wanted to get up and take her in his arms, share an embrace with her like they had in the barn after the birth of Jennifer's colt, but he remained stuck to his chair. Showing her how much giving the present to her really meant to him was not necessary. Desired, but not feasible.

Annie nodded toward the pile that had slowly been building up next to Zane's seat. "You haven't opened any of your presents."

He picked the one on top, realizing for the first time that everyone else had finished unwrapping their gifts, had fed the paper into the fire, and now were waiting on him. He'd been so caught up in the giving that he had completely forgotten about the receiving end.

There were four, but considering the fact that they were his first Christmas presents ever, it seemed like a mountain of gifts to him. He tore at the corner of one.

Noni pounded her cane against the planks of the floor, her green eyes sharp and merry. "That one is from me," she said, pointing a gnarled finger. Zane couldn't imagine what the old woman had to give him, but he was excited. He tore off the paper and uncovered the most beautiful sweater he had ever seen. It was black, a thick knit that looked like something from Anthropologie for men, if there had been such a store. Handmade, each stitch near perfect, but with enough texture to keep it interesting.

Emotion constricted his throat. "*Danki*, Noni."

"It will keep you warm, Zane Carson. I hear tell that Chicago city is cold in the wintertime."

"It is." He gently wrapped the sweater back in its paper, knowing full well that every time he wore it he would be thinking of Clover Ridge.

Mary Elizabeth clapped her hands together. "Open mine next."

"It's from both of us," John Paul added.

She elbowed him in the ribs, and Zane couldn't help but laugh at their antics. Their relationship was just another something to add to the list of things that he would miss once he left.

He opened the present to find an entire box of Astro Pops. Everyone laughed. "That way you'll have plenty," Mary Elizabeth said.

"Yes, I will," he said with a chuckle.

The next present was a shirt from Katie Rose. She had made it from a pretty green-patterned fabric. Its color-on-color roses might have been considered feminine, but somehow the shirt looked worthy of Banana Republic. He'd wear it with pride. "It's beautiful. *Danki*."

Katie Rose nodded.

Their gazes locked and held, and for that moment, everything seemed to stand still. A cliché, maybe, but that was what it felt like. He and Katie Rose alone, yet connected. Everyone else faded into the background, and it was just the two of them.

Then someone coughed.

"Open the last one," Ruth requested softly.

Zane picked up the last present, this one wrapped in newspaper decorated with drawings of the Northern star, a cross, and the outline of what could only be a manger.

He tore at the paper, anticipation rising.

The Holy Bible.

Warmth flooded his hands, and they tingled as if the book were alive and vibrating its energy into him. He looked up in wonderment.

"It's from all of us," Ruth added.

"I-I don't know what to say."

"Say you'll read it." This from Abram.

"Every day," Zane promised, turning the book over in his hands. Never before had anyone given him such a special gift. No one but this Amish family, who hadn't known him at all until three months ago. This family, who took him in and taught him about God, fed him both literally and spiritually.

Tears sprang to his eyes, and he lurched across the room, pulling Ruth into a one-armed embrace. The other hand still held the Bible, and he was unwilling to let it go.

After the gift giving, the younger children went out to check the new colt with Abram. Annie went to the kitchen to start another pot of coffee. And somehow Zane found himself sitting on the couch next to Katie Rose.

"I cannot thank you enough for the books, Zane Carson."

So they were back to that, huh?

He gazed at her. "I'm glad you like them. Hopefully all of the children will enjoy them."

"How did you know?"

"That *Little House* was on the approved reading list, or that you wanted them?"

"Both."

Zane smiled. "Coln Anderson helped me in ordering them. He's the one who told me they were okay for you to have."

"The bishop does try to shield us from the sins of the world. It's hard sometimes, but we all know and understand that it is for our own good."

"In the world, but not of the world."

Katie Rose's eyes twinkled as he said the words. "*Jah*. But how did you know I wanted them?"

Zane tilted his head to one side and studied her. "You told me. That very first day you allowed me to have lunch with you."

"I don't remember."

"Well, I do."

"It would seem so."

Zane looked down at the leather-bound Bible in his hands. "I still can't believe this."

Katie Rose just smiled, her version of the enigmatic Mona Lisa. Zane both loved and hated when she did that. He loved her smile, but hated that this particular one cut him off from guessing her thoughts. "It might be prideful to say, but I picked it out for you."

"I love it."

"We wanted you to have somethin' beautiful to take with you next week."

"I have a lot of beautiful to take home with me."

"We wanted you to be able to pack it in your suitcase."

Zane nodded. There wasn't much more for him to do. He was leaving in just a few short days. He'd be home by the first.

The idea had grown less and less appealing the longer he stayed with the Amish. But with Samuel Beachy's return the night before, Zane knew it would be next to impossible for him to stay. Katie Rose was more than half the reason he loved it here so much. Everything about her made him a better man. Like he could do God's bidding, succeed in anything he tried. But she didn't belong to him. She had given her heart to another long ago and now that other was back to claim it.

The fact didn't make the desire to hold her in his arms lessen. It didn't make the need to kiss her disappear. It would be so easy to lean into her, press his lips to hers as they sat there together. But Annie was just a few feet away. Besides, Zane was afraid that if he kissed Katie Rose even once, he'd go on kissing her forever.

A knock sounded on the door. It was Christmas Day and not the day for visiting, but Zane knew whoever it was would be welcomed inside to join in the family gathering. That was the Amish way. He just hoped it wasn't Samuel with the preacher intending to marry Katie Rose no matter what the season.

"I'll get it." He stood bracing himself for whatever was to come. He couldn't take many more surprises, as he was still reeling from the last one.

He opened the door, and a familiar dark-haired woman stood on the other side, fur coat pulled up around her neck, diamonds sparkling at her ears.

"Monica?"

"Surprise!" She smiled, holding up her left hand and flashing the deep red ruby he'd offered her so long ago. "I accept."

15

Surprise was right. Monica was the last person he'd expected to see. Not only was she in Oklahoma, she had somehow found her way to the Fishers'.

She threw her arms around him and pressed herself close, her lips naturally finding his. Instinctively he braced his hands on her waist. Too stunned to do anything else, he half-heartedly kissed her back.

She pulled her lips from his, but kept her arms anchored firmly around his neck, thankfully not seeming to notice his inattentiveness. "Oh, I've missed you. It's crazy for us to be apart." She gave him one last hard kiss on the lips, then pulled away.

Zane was too stunned to do much else but remove her hat and smooth down the static in her hair.

"Daddy got married."

"Again?"

"Again." She nodded. "Number five. He and his new wife decided to honeymoon in the Caribbean. They left yesterday.

So . . ." she dragged out the word, running a finger suggestively down his lips. "I decided to come see you."

"Wow." *Eloquent, Carson.* But he didn't know what to say. He was all too aware of Katie Rose watching their every move. All too aware that moments before his fiancée had arrived, he'd been contemplating kissing another.

"Plus, I wanted to give you the good news in person. Aren't you going to invite me in?"

He stepped back, allowing her into the house. "Good news?"

In lieu of an answer, she held up her left hand and waggled her fingers as she stepped inside.

Oh. Yeah. The good news.

Her sharp blue eyes flickered around the room. He imagined her noting the crackling fire and the lack of anything modern. Zane had thought it quaint and unassuming, but Monica would find it backward, maybe even barbaric.

Katie Rose stood, her gaze darting between the two of them. The Mona Lisa smile was back, and Zane felt like an outsider.

Monica's voice interrupted the stillness. "Aren't you the cutest thing!"

Inwardly, Zane cringed, until he realized Monica was talking to him and not Katie Rose.

She flipped a hand toward his barn-door pants and suspenders, then rubbed her palm down the side of his face. "And this beard. I like it. So manly."

He was scum. He hadn't called her in weeks, hadn't made any attempt to contact her, hadn't thought about her as he should. He'd been too wrapped up in the here and now. He had taken a vacation from reality, and his real life had come knocking on the door—literally.

Zane stood between the two women. "Monica, this is Katie Rose Fisher. Her parents are my host family."

Monica stepped forward and took Katie Rose's limp hand into her own. She gave it a girlie handshake squeeze. "It's so nice to meet you."

"*Danki.*" Katie Rose nodded. "Thank you."

Monica smiled, and Zane relaxed. She was cordial and collected around Katie Rose, and he knew that she didn't consider the Amish woman to be a threat. His secret was safe.

Lord, please forgive me. I've not been the faithful man I am supposed to be.

Zane pointed to the kitchen where Annie was drying her hands on a dishtowel. "That's—"

"Avery Ann Hamilton." Monica's voice rose. "So the rumors *are* true."

To his surprise, Annie smiled. "Monica."

Zane turned to Monica. "You know Annie?"

"Yes, silly. And you do too."

Annie spoke up. "We met at the Dunstan Pro-Am a couple of years ago. I never mentioned it because I didn't think you remembered."

So that's why she looked so familiar. What was a Dallas socialite doing in Amish country Oklahoma? Then it struck him. Love. He had seen the way she looked at Gideon. The way Gideon looked back at her.

Had love been the only reason, or was God at work here too?

Monica returned her gaze to him. "You didn't answer your phone the other day. And you didn't call me back." She gave a pretty pout, and once upon a time, he thought the action cute. Now he found it annoying.

Or maybe he was just upset that, once again, his opportunity to kiss Katie Rose was gone. Maybe, too, he was upset with himself for forgetting all the things that he needed to remember . . .

That he was engaged to another.

That he'd be leaving soon.

That he'd be in Mexico before President's Day.

It was better this way. He didn't need to be kissing Kate. He was leaving in just a few days. After that, he'd never see her again. There was no sense starting something that neither one of them could finish.

Annie snapped her fingers. "You're Zane's fiancée!" Then she frowned and shot a glance at Katie Rose.

Katie Rose tilted her head. "Fiancée?"

"That's right." She passed him a loving look over her shoulder and hooked her arm through his. "Zane asked me to marry him just before he came here."

He saw the hurt flash through her jade green eyes. He wanted to go to her, to explain, but stayed where he was. He'd done enough. More than enough.

Katie Rose stood, and ran her hands down her apron. "I think I'll go to check on my Samuel."

Zane wasn't certain if she meant Gabriel's son or the one who belonged to the bishop. Either way, it was time to let her go.

Helpless, he watched her stumble toward the door, not even bothering to put on a coat to fight back against the cold December air.

Annie hurried behind her, grabbing a coat for each of them off the pegs by the door. "I think I should . . . go help Katie Rose."

Monica watched her close the door and turned back to Zane. "They seem like very nice ladies."

Around the lump in his throat, he choked out, "She is." Too nice to deserve how he'd treated her. He owed her an apology. A big one. But he had the sinking feeling that he wouldn't see Katie Rose again.

Katie Rose let the screen door slam behind her, realizing only when she was halfway across the yard, that she'd forgotten her coat. It didn't matter. The heat in her cheeks would be enough to keep her warm.

"Katie Rose."

She turned at the sound of her name. Annie hurried across the yard toward her, jacket in hand. "I, uh . . . didn't want you to get cold."

"*Danki*." She took the garment from Annie and quickly pushed her arms into the sleeves.

"You want to talk about it?"

Katie Rose shook her head. "There is nothin' to talk about."

"Seems like there's a lot to talk about, if you ask me."

And what would she say? That she thought she was special to Zane? That she'd fallen hopelessly in love with him? Or that she'd harbored a little dream that he would stay and join up with the Amish? Maybe even marry her? And they would be happy for the rest of their days?

It was only a dream. Their real lives had come calling. And next week the dream would end forever.

"There is not. I am just bein' foolish."

"Love can do that to you."

"I'm not—" She stopped, unable to tell the lie upon her lips. "It doesn't matter. He loves another." All things for a reason. She had been taught that her entire life. Still she couldn't ignore her breaking heart.

"I'm no expert, but he doesn't look like he's in love to me. At least not with Monica." Annie shot her a pointed look.

Katie Rose chose to ignore it. It was better this way. No sense in getting her hopes up when she knew nothing would ever come of it. "I'm goin' to check on Samuel." She had left him behind a lot lately, spending more and more time with Zane. But now it was time to reclaim her place. He'd grown so independent. Maybe that was why God sent Zane Carson, to allow her to let go of little Samuel so he could grow. She just wished her heart had been spared.

⚜

He guessed correctly, and Katie Rose did not come back into the house. He couldn't very well go chasing after her with Monica at his side. So he had to let Kate go, in more ways than one. He'd just gotten caught up in the romance of the situation. Being in Amish country, away from all the hustle and bustle of Chicago, he'd fallen into a trap of his own making.

He owed Katie Rose an apology. He hadn't realized what he was doing, had lost sight of where he was, and who he was dealing with and how fragile she might be. He'd seen an independent woman who loved God and her family, who was beautiful inside and out, who he wanted to get to know better. He discounted the fact that she had been raised so differently from he. That she was a kind and loving person who would look upon his actions with eyes different from the women he'd known.

And now that Samuel Beachy had returned . . . well, Zane couldn't imagine that she would do anything other than fall right back into his arms. They would probably be married before the end of January, wedding season or not.

"Zane?"

"Hmm . . . ?" He stirred the straw around in his drink, unable to lift his gaze to Monica's.

"Is something bothering you? You've been so quiet tonight."

"No," he lied. "Of course not." He forced a smile and finally met her inquisitive blue eyes. "I'm just . . ." He waved a hand around toward the few patrons in the hotel restaurant. It was one of the few places open in small-town Clover Ridge on Christmas Day. He settled his eyes on her. "Monica, do you want children?"

She made a face. "What is wrong with you?"

"Nothing. It's a simple question. After we get married do you want to have a baby?"

"Zane, it's Christmas," she said quietly. "Can we talk about this some other time?"

Reluctantly, he nodded. Why children had been on his mind so much he wasn't sure, but they had been. He'd watched Samuel and the other kids play this morning, everyone enjoying each other and being together. He couldn't imagine going through life without that. Yet he couldn't imagine bringing a child into his crazy reporter's life.

"I bought you something."

He cupped his drink with his hands. "For me? Why?"

"For Christmas, of course."

"Of course," he murmured. They had never exchanged presents before, choosing instead to take a trip if he wasn't overseas or just Skype if he was.

"It's nothing big," she said, pulling a small wrapped box out of her purse.

"I didn't . . ." He felt awful. He had bought presents for all the people he'd known for less than three months, but not for the woman he was soon to marry.

She pushed the box across the table toward him. "It doesn't matter."

"*Danki*," he said.

Monica blinked.

"I mean, thank you."

She smiled. "Merry Christmas."

Zane opened the box. Nestled inside was a silver key ring engraved with his last name and next year's date. It was beautiful, but confusing. "I don't understand."

"It's a key ring."

"I know that."

"I bought it for your house key. See, I've got one just like it." She pulled her key ring out of her bag and laid it alongside his.

"My apartment key?"

"Your house key. Daddy bought us a quaint little cottage in Waukegan. Part Christmas present, part wedding gift. I think he's feeling guilty that he's gone right now."

"A house?" Flabbergasted wasn't the word.

"I know, right?" Monica smiled so prettily, so excited, that Zane couldn't express the myriad of conflicting emotions coursing through him. A touch of confusion, a lot of anger, and a bit of disbelief. What were they going to do with a house?

He didn't even want to think about it right now. He pointed to her plate. "Are you finished?"

She nodded.

Zane signaled the waiter for their bill, paid the tab, and walked with her out into the lobby. "I'll see you to your room."

Her brows lowered. "Aren't you staying here tonight?"

Zane shook his head as they stepped into the elevator. He pushed the button for her floor and watched the doors close, trying his best not to cave to the inviting light in her eyes. "I don't think I should. I am supposed to be working." Truth was, he hadn't even thought about it. After living with the chaste and honorable Amish, the idea seemed cheap somehow. But he wasn't sure Monica would understand. Better to deflect right now and fight that battle another day.

"I understand." Her eyes told a different story, one of hurt and confusion. "My flight leaves early tomorrow. I just thought—"

"Do you want me to come to the airport with you?"

She shook her head. "That seems kind of silly, don't you think? I mean, I have a rental. There's no sense in you making the trip in a separate car." Her explanation was sound, but her expression wistful.

He nodded. The elevator doors swished open, and together they stepped into the carpeted hallway.

Instinctively, Zane clasped Monica's elbow and steered her toward her room. They stopped at the door, and he waited patiently while she dug around in her purse for the key card.

"It's just that . . . well, I've missed you so much." She raised up on her tiptoes and covered his mouth with her own.

Zane pulled her away from him. "No, Monica. I think we should wait."

She pouted, no doubt hoping to tempt him with the shape of her lips. "Wait until you get home?"

He shook his head. "No. Wait until we get married." *Where had that come from?* Suddenly, though, it seemed like the most natural thing in the world.

She took one hard step back, her eyes meeting his steady gaze. "Are you serious?"

"Very." And he was.

She continued to stare at him. "You've really changed."

He shrugged. "I guess I have."

She paused and cocked her head to one side. "Well. It's not a bad thing."

"I think it's good."

Monica smiled, and pressed her lips to his one more time. "I'll see you in Chicago."

"Next week," he promised, as she closed the door behind herself.

He'd drop the bomb about church on her once she got used to the idea of abstinence.

～◯ ◯～

Ruth hesitantly pushed the door open, hating the creak of the hinges. The last thing she wanted to do was disturb Abram. He'd been so worried about her of late, worry she couldn't dispel. Worry that she had caused.

Quietly she stepped into the room and gently pushed the door shut. One step, then two, a couple of more and she'd be to the bed that she had shared with her husband for over thirty-five years.

She exhaled as she slipped out of her house shoes and shucked out of her thick robe. Never before had she owned such luxuries, and she silently sent up a prayer of thanks to the Lord for sending Zane Carson their way. She needed a warm robe and fuzzy shoes intended only for the house. Truly she did, as the treatments for the cancer had drained away the last of her body's stores of fat. She found these days that she was shivering even when standing directly in front of the fire. And the beautiful nativity scene. She would cherish it always.

She hung the robe on its peg and automatically reached up to pull the pins that held her prayer *kapp* in place. Her hand stilled, and she dropped it back to her side. There were no pins. There was no prayer *kapp*. A lump as hard as stone formed in her chest and worked its way up into her throat. Even the news that she was cancer free couldn't ease the ball of ache. Heartache. She'd won. She'd fought the good fight, and the Lord had led her to triumph. *But at what cost?*

A sob snagged in her throat.

The figure on the bed stirred. "Ruth?"

The sound of his voice was her undoing. One sob came, and then another. And another until her shoulders shook in the dark.

She heard the creak of the bed. "Ruthie, my Ruthie. What's wrong?"

His arms slid around her, warm and comforting. On any other night she might have pulled away, banished him to his side of the bed, the room . . . their life. But she didn't have the strength to fight anymore.

She laid her head on his chest, the steady thump of his heart soothing her wounded spirit.

He allowed her to cry, standing there in the dark, her arms folded in front of her, his wrapped around. His big calloused hands ran up her spine, not stopping at each bump and valley left by the weight loss. Just a smooth, steady stroke, like in the early days.

Finally her sobs turned to hiccups, and her hiccups to whimpers as he continued to hold her.

"Are you goin' to tell me what troubles you, Ruth Ann?"

"*Nay.*" She pulled herself away from him like she had every day and night since she'd found the lump that changed all their lives. "Go back to sleep, husband. It is nothin' to concern yourself over."

Accustomed to the darkness of the room, Abram watched as she pulled back the covers on her side of the bed and slipped in between. He stood there in the night, disbelieving the words in his ears. He had been understanding, he had left her to her feelings, allowed her to hide her worries, permitted her to deal with the changes they'd faced in the way she saw fit. But tonight Abram had lost his feelings of generosity.

He wanted his wife back.

"*Nay.*" His voice quavered with emotion. "You tell me that it doesn't concern me, wife, and then you wet me with your tears. If it concerns you, then it concerns me as well."

He'd hoped to solve this in a different way, had hoped that once he brought up the subject she would allow him into the parts that haunted her.

But she turned away from him, facing the inside of the bed.

Abram stormed to the other side and dove beneath the covers before she could turn away a second time. "Look at me," he commanded, holding her face in between his palms and forcing her gaze to his. "Look at me and tell me what causes you such heartbreak on the day our Lord was born."

"I . . . I." Tears welled in her eyes again.

He wanted to shake her as she faltered, force the words from her lips.

"The cost was too high," she finally choked out.

He released a deep sigh. "When we started this, we vowed that we would pray about the money, just like we prayed for direction. Hasn't the Lord provided all that He said He would?"

A large tear broke free from one eye and slid down her cheek. It caught the light of a stray moonbeam and glittered for a moment before falling off the edge of her chin. "It's not about the money."

"I don't understand, wife. What else is there?"

"The price was *me*. My earthly body."

He held his breath, not yet able to comprehend what she was saying.

"*I* am the price. My hair, my body, my strength. I am no longer the woman I was, and I don't know how to be the woman I have become. I have no strength to hold up my end of the bargain we made the day we wed. I have no hair, I have no breasts. I feel as if my womanhood has been stripped away. And I wonder how long it will be before you resent all that's been taken from me and all that you will no longer have."

He shook his head fiercely. "I'll never leave you." He barely got the words past the lump in his throat. *Was that what this was all about?* She thought he might have wished her dead instead of healed the way she was?

"I know. It is the Amish way. But I want more than the *Ordnung* to keep you at my side." She drew a ragged breath and raised her eyes to meet his. "I want your love."

"You have it." He released her face to grab her hand and place it over his chest. "My heart beats for you, Ruth Ann. It always has."

"Even with a body that is less than what it was? I am as God made me no more."

He moved their joined hands, brushing his fingers across the front of her nightgown, across the chest as flat and smooth as that of a young child.

"There might be less of you here." He brushed the back of her hand across her surgically altered body. "But there is more of you here." He placed his hand over her beating heart. "You are still the way God made you, Ruth Ann. Because He made you for me."

16

The day after Christmas, Zane decided that Katie Rose was never going to speak to him again. He couldn't leave it like that. He had grown to care for her over the last couple of months. She was a good woman and deserved better than what he had offered her. Still, in another time, or perhaps another place, things might have been different for them. As it was, other people depended on them, and there was no way around it.

He pulled the buggy down the drive that led to Gabriel's house, deciding it was too cold to walk it. There had even been some talk of snow, but Zane couldn't tell for sure, as he'd been unable to read the Oklahoma sky since his arrival.

He saw a shadow in front of the window as he pulled to a stop. Someone knew he was there. If he knew Katie Rose at all, she would forgive him, but she wouldn't make it easy on him.

Zane hopped down and walked the horses toward the shelter the barn offered. He didn't know how long he'd be and a man couldn't take too good of care of his horses. Or another man's horses, as in this case.

Once the beasts were settled, he loped across the yard and up onto the porch. He knocked on the door and shoved his hands into his coat pockets to keep them warm.

"Who is it?" Katie Rose's voice was muffled by the thick wood of the door.

He rolled his eyes. "You know who it is," he growled.

She must have waited a full ten seconds before opening the door. Or maybe it just seemed that way because he was trembling inside. She stood in the doorway, looking as fresh and lovely as ever. Maybe he had overestimated the hurt she had displayed the day before.

Her eyes flashed at him. "Where's your girlfriend today? Or should I say fiancée?"

"Where's yours?" The words slipped out before Zane could stop them. He had no right to be angry with her, but she had every right to be mad at him. He furrowed his brow. "I didn't mean that."

"Then what did you mean?"

He pulled one hand from his pocket and leaned it on the doorframe. "Can we start over?"

"*Jah*," she said, and closed the door in his face.

He waited for her to open it once again. When she didn't, he reminded himself that she wasn't going to make this easy for him.

He knocked.

"Who is it?"

He chuckled. "Zane Carson. I've come to apologize."

She opened the door, her face a mask of sweetness. "Continue."

"Well, it seems that I may have given you the wrong idea."

"I may have misunderstood."

"And I wanted to say how honored I am to have known you these past few weeks."

Her dimples flashed, and Zane's heart lurched. He was going to miss her. "As am I, Zane Carson."

He hated it when she used his entire name, but it was for the best. It put a distance between them that they needed to honor.

"I'm leaving at the end of the week. I know you'll be in school with the children."

"Won't you stop and tell them all good-bye?"

"I'll do my best, but I'll be with the driver."

"Just promise Bill some extra pickles, and he'll do whatever you want."

Zane smiled at the truth of the statement. The Mennonite would do just about anything as long as they paid him in Fisher family pickles.

Her winsome smile faded some. "I'm glad I got to meet you, Zane Carson. I was worried at first when you came, but I know now, God sent you. You brought laughter back into our fold. And for that I'm eternally grateful."

"Me too, Kate, me too."

But he was walking away with much, much more.

Zane adjusted his jeans, feeling strange dressed in Englisher clothes after these months in Amish garb. He glanced around the room once again. Satisfied that he'd not forgotten anything, he closed the door behind him and made his way down the stairs.

Annie, Ruth, Abram, and John Paul were standing in the living room talking to the Mennonite driver, Bill. Gideon had come over as well, offering Bill some wool from one of his prize alpacas, part of the first "crop" from his new livestock.

"Are you all packed?" Ruth asked, her eyes running over him in true motherly form.

"I think I got everything."

"You got your Bible?"

Zane smiled. "You know it. Thank you for everything." He bent down and kissed her cheek, then thought better of it and pulled her into a one-armed hug. He was going to miss her.

"God bless you, Zane Carson."

"And you too, Ruth Fisher."

He released Ruth and moved down the line. "Abram." He reached out a hand to shake and instead found himself in a hug. Something had happened between the Fishers since Christmas. Something that had chased the lines of worry from Abram's weathered face and added the sparkle back into Ruth's eyes. Somehow Zane knew God was at the root of it, and he was happy to see it there.

He continued to say his farewells to the Fishers, even hugging John Paul and slapping him on the back in camaraderie. "Don't go crazy out there," he said. "Make the decision God tells you is right for you."

John Paul nodded.

Bill took Zane's last suitcase and loaded it into the back of his minivan.

"You won't forget to write," Ruth said.

"Of course not. And I'll send you a copy of the magazine when it comes out."

"Better send one to the bishop too," Abram added.

Zane laughed. "Good idea." He turned to Bill. "Katie Rose said that if I promised you some extra pickles you would take me by the school on our way out of town. I'd like to say good-bye to the children."

Bill smiled. "That Katie Rose always was a smart cookie."

"Will two jars get me a swing by Ezekiel Esh's place?"

"You know it."

"I need to tell him good-bye as well." He'd miss the old man.

"No time like now." Bill shook Abram's hand, then climbed inside the cab.

Zane crawled in beside him, and rolled down the window, his heart both heavy and light at the same time. He'd gained so much from this visit, found new friends, an understanding of God, and he learned what goodness was all about.

"Bye," the Fishers called, waving their arms in farewell.

As Bill backed the car and turned it around, Zane called out, "John Paul, if you're looking for your keys, you'd better get a move on. Check the cookie jar first." It would take him half the afternoon to find them. He grinned and rolled up the window, laughing as John Paul patted his pockets then took off toward the house.

Zane chuckled as he drove away, a much better person than when he arrived.

17

The Davenports are having a party, but so are the McMillians."

"Uh-huh." Zane tried participating in the conversation, but he was just so tired. Maybe it was the travelling, or maybe because he had become used to going to bed early. It was eight o'clock on New Year's Eve and all he wanted to do was climb underneath the covers and not come out until the cows needed milking. Or he had to meet up with Jo.

"Are you listening to me?" Monica took her eyes off the road for a brief second and flashed an irritated glance his way.

"Of course." It had definitely been a good idea to have her meet him at the airport. He hadn't gotten his car out of storage since his last assignment. It had remained there after his surgery and recovery, so he'd simply left it there when he'd gone to Oklahoma. No sense getting it out now, since it wouldn't be long before he left on assignment again. Normally the thought filled him with excitement and adrenaline. Now, it just . . . didn't.

"I don't know which one we should go to."

"We?"

"Yes, 'we.'" She flashed him another look.

"Oh, Monica. Do I have to go too?"

"I'd like for you to."

"I know, but do I *have* to?"

She pressed her lips together. "I guess not. I just . . . well, you just got home, and I wanted to spend some time with you."

"And attending a party with a hundred other people is going to be our quality time?"

She sniffed. "When you put it like that, it doesn't sound like such a good idea."

"It's not. How 'bout we order a pizza and watch all the hoopla on TV?"

She gawked at him. "Are you serious?"

"Yes."

"I've already told the McMillians that we'd be there."

He leaned his head back against the seat and closed his eyes, already tired of the argument. "That's great, because I'm not going to be. I'm surely not going to speak for you, though."

He couldn't see her expression, but her tone conveyed it all—frustration, anger, and resignation. "I understand. I shouldn't have accepted the invitation for you too."

"That's right."

She paused. "Do you mind if I go without you?"

"Not at all."

"I'll miss you, you know."

"I know. I'll miss you too."

Yet Zane was asleep even before the ball dropped in New York City.

The morning of January 6 dawned bright and cold. Old Christmas. For the Amish it was a quiet holiday filled with visits and friends. Presents had already been exchanged, but this was still a time for reverent celebration. Gabriel had packed up the buggy and taken the children to his parents' house, but Katie Rose couldn't rustle herself in time. She had pleaded a headache and watched as they drove down the road.

She had tried to push all thoughts of Zane Carson from her mind, but they kept surfacing time and again. She pictured him fishing, opening his Bible, and at the schoolhouse saying goodbye. That had been one long week ago. The longest of her life. She could never remember feeling like this when Samuel left, so bereft and sad. But she must have been. How could she care more for an *Englischer* she had barely known for three months than she did the bishop's son, whom she had known all of her life? She had promised that when she felt better she would walk down. The day was sunny and cold, so as long as the wind didn't pick up too much she would be just fine. If she kept these ruminations up, she would find herself in bed with a rag over her face, instead of spending the afternoon with her parents.

A knock sounded on the door. Katie Rose jumped, pressing a hand to her heart to slow its beating. "Comin'."

Who could that be on Old Christmas? Only one person she supposed. *Jah.* Samuel Beachy stood on the other side of the threshold, looking more like the man she fell in love with than he had since he returned. Black coat, black hat, and scarf that she supposed Noni knitted for him. Though his hair was still in the *Englisch* cut, she reckoned that under his coat he wore a blue shirt to match his eyes and a black *for gut* vest.

She nodded her head. "Samuel."

"Katie Rose." He bent his head and brushed a sweet kiss on her cheek. He smelled of sandalwood and mint toothpaste, but she couldn't raise even the slightest thump of her heart over the familiarity.

"I told you I was here to stay."

"That you did." Had he? She couldn't remember.

"May I come in?"

"*Jah*, of course." She stood back and let him enter.

He pulled off his coat, scarf, and hat and hung them on the peg inside the door. Underneath were the shirt and vest, just as she predicted. Who was it that said the more things change, the more they stay the same? They certainly knew Samuel Beachy.

He warmed his hands by the fire, then settled himself on the couch.

She hovered by the door, not sure what to make of this visit.

"Come." He patted the seat next to him. "Sit by me. We have a lot to talk about."

"We do?"

"*Jah*."

Katie Rose moved to sit next to him, wondering at the wisdom of the decision. She perched on the edge, able to pop to her feet if need be.

"Why are you acting so skittish?" He chuckled. "It's me, Katie Rose. I came back for you."

"W-what?"

"I know I hurt you in the past. If I had thought you would have gone with me, I would have taken you along."

"I might have. If you'd asked."

He sat looking a bit dumbfounded at this news.

"Are you surprised? I loved you so much."

He swallowed hard, his confidence slipping. "You say loved— past tense. Does that mean . . . ?"

"Love doesn't die easily, Samuel Beachy." It was the best answer she could give him. She didn't know how she felt anymore. She had loved him once upon a time, and she thought that love to be stronger than anything in the world. Turned out she was wrong.

"I never stopped loving you, Katie Rose. Never stopped wishing you were at my side. It's taken me a long time to get to the truth, and the truth is, if I can't have you in the *Englisch* world, then I'll come back to the Amish world for you."

She stood, shaking her head. "*Nay*, it should not be like that. You should want to be here for God, your family, all the other pillars we stand for, not for me."

He was on his feet in a flash, cupping her face in his hands and turning it toward him. "That's the beauty of it, don't you see? Here I can have everything: God, my family, you. It took me leaving to know what I had."

She opened her mouth to protest, but he kissed her instead.

She pulled away, but he held her close, his mouth inches from hers. "We can have it all. A family, everything that we planned before will be ours now. Marry me, Katie Rose."

How many times over the last six years had she wished for him to say those words to her? Countless. But now that he had? She wasn't sure how to respond.

He pressed his cheek to hers. "We can tell our families tonight." He wasn't asking. He was taking it for granted, assuming that she had been waiting for him all of these years.

You have been.

But it was different now. And yet it wasn't. Zane had gone and had taken with him a big chunk of her heart. This was her chance at happiness and family, a home of her own, the children she had secretly longed for her entire life.

Zane was gone, and Samuel was here. What choice did she have?

18

What do you think? This one"—Monica pointed to two different patterns of china on display—"or this one?"

At least he assumed they were different. Zane could barely focus on another plate. And he certainly couldn't tell the difference between the two white, gold-rimmed choices presented to him. "Uh-huh."

"Zane, are you listening?"

He met Monica's eyes. "Of course I am." He hated the lie that slipped from his lips, but he didn't want to hurt her feelings. He hadn't been listening. He'd been back in Clover Ridge, wondering how Ruth was faring, if John Paul's driving had improved any. And if Katie Rose had agreed to marry Samuel Beachy.

Monica studied him, her blue eyes intense as they searched his face.

Zane said a little prayer that she wouldn't see the truth there, the fact that he would go back tomorrow if given half the chance. Clover Ridge hung like unfinished business around him. Called to him. Made him wonder if his life could be different—*should* be different.

Zane averted his gaze first, staring across the room toward the big round clock on the wall. Wherever did they get a clock that size?

"I think you could use a break."

"Hmm." Definitely. They had been looking at house stuff all morning, registering for the wedding they hadn't even set a date for yet.

"We'll finish another day," Monica told the obviously disappointed clerk. She pushed her arms into the sleeves of her coat.

"There's a coffee shop just down the corner," the ever helpful, commissioned clerk said as Zane pulled on his coat. The way it flapped around his knees annoyed him. Funny, but he'd never noticed that before.

"Thank you." Monica smiled at the clerk, then looped her arm through Zane's and nudged him outside.

The coffee shop was three stores down from the department store, the kind of place that served double mocha nonfat lattes, but frowned if a person ordered a regular coffee. The weather being what it was—cold—the place was crowded. Zane placed their orders and paid for their coffees as Monica found them a table.

"I don't think it's Avery." She snapped her fingers, then gave a knowing nod. "Maybe that blonde. Katie Rose. She is very pretty. Every girl I know would kill to have skin like that. And those eyes."

Zane sat back. "What are you talking about, Monica?"

She took a tentative sip of her coffee and eyed him over the rim of the oversized mug. "You're in love, of course."

"Of course," he repeated, hiding the fact that his heart plummeted to his feet as she said the words. He hid his reaction, staring into his coffee and stirring it as if his life depended on it.

"With the Amish girl."

He looked up. "No."

"Zane, something's going on. We've known each other too long to not be honest now."

He shook his head. "I don't know what you're talking about."

"I'm talking about love. This month's issue of *Talk* is how to tell if you're in love."

"Of course I'm in love. We're getting married, aren't we?"

She flashed him a patronizing smile as she pulled her iPad from her bag. "Not with me."

"Listen." He took a deep breath and let it out slowly. This conversation was getting way out of hand. "I'll admit that I got a little caught up in the simplicity of their life, but I did not fall in love with anyone while I was there."

"Uh-huh." She busily tapped the screen on the tablet till she got to the page she wanted. "*How to Tell If He's Still in Love with You or If He's Set His Sails for a Different Shore.*"

"Seriously?"

She shot him another quelling look. "Number one: moony-eyed. Uh-huh."

"Moony-eyed? It really says that?"

"Easily distracted. Check. Defensive." She dragged out the word as if she were a lawyer for the prosecution. "Definitely."

"Monica." His voice was low with warning. Or was he being defensive?

"Then kiss me."

He straightened. "What?"

"You haven't kissed me once since you got back."

"Sure I have." Had he?

Monica shook her head with a tiny little smile. "Kiss me."

"Right here?"

"Yeah."

"But there are a ton of people in here."

"So?"

"Any of them could be from the newspaper or the tabloids."

"Good publicity."

He couldn't refuse, even though he wanted to. He pulled her to her feet and angled his head for the kiss.

There was no flash of excitement—only annoyance—which had to be blocking his true feelings. Of course he was excited about kissing Monica. He lifted his head. Or maybe later he would be.

Monica was staring at him.

"See?" he said.

"Yeah. I do."

"What does that mean?"

"You're definitely in love."

"Toldja."

"Just not with me."

He dropped his arms to his sides. "Monica."

So the kiss was not a set-the-world-on-fire kind of kiss. That didn't necessarily mean anything.

Monica pressed her lips together as if she were smoothing out her lipstick. Like she could taste his intentions. "Nope, not in love. At least not with me."

"That's insane, Monica." He stood and grabbed his coat off the back of the chair. He'd had enough of this strange conversation. "If you want to call this off just say so."

She shook her head, her eyes filled with sadness and regret. "I don't want to break up, but I don't want a marriage of three, either."

<hr/>

Zane did his best to ignore Monica's words pinging around in his head at the least opportune time—like constantly. He was not in love with Katie Rose. How could he be? He hadn't even kissed her.

And thankfully, Monica hadn't brought it up again. Not even when he asked her to go to church with him on Sunday.

"Really? You want to go to church?"

"I think it would be a very good way to restart our relationship."

She dipped her chin and frowned, but in the end, she agreed.

Sunday dawned with an excitement like he'd never felt before. He walked into the Methodist church amazed at the beauty of the building alone. High-arched ceilings of polished oak; long, padded pews to match; and brightly colored stained glass windows added to the overall beauty. The sanctuary was awe inspiring, and he knew God was there. How could God not want to be in such a beautiful place?

At the end of the service everyone stood, then the pastor called for those who wanted to know more about Jesus and the changes He could make in their lives.

Zane's legs flinched as if they wanted to walk down that aisle with no direction from him. But he was uncertain. Should he go? Would they laugh at him because this was his first time in a church? Or would they understand that religion usually came from a person's upbringing, and that he hadn't experienced anything other than earth worship.

He wouldn't go. Monica was sitting closest to the aisle, and several people sat on his other side. No sense disturbing them. How could he mess up their church experience by pushing past them to get down front?

Seconds ticked by. He stood still, pushing down the urge to move. Finally, Monica stepped into the aisle, then reached for his elbow. He stepped into the aisle with her, and with a knowing smile, she led him down to the altar and to the waiting deacon.

He stood there for a moment, unable to speak, and then the words tumbled out, one by one. So many thoughts, questions. It felt amazing to talk to someone about Jesus. Even better to bow his head and pray to invite Jesus into his heart. A warmth like he had never known filled him, and he walked out of the church that day a changed man.

Or maybe he had been changed in Clover Ridge, and he was just now accepting it. He'd have to give that some thought.

Monica had waited for him, listening to everything the deacon said, nodding her head occasionally. At the end of their talk, Monica shook his hand right alongside Zane and promised they'd be back for next week's service.

Funny, Zane had never known Monica to be a religious person. She never mentioned church or God. On the flip side, she never used foul language. When he asked her about it, she just shrugged and said, "I did mention it right after we met, but you told me you weren't interested."

"But we . . . you know." Why couldn't he say the words?

"No one's perfect, Zane. Not even Christians."

When it came to baptism and joining the church, Zane didn't think he was ready for that. Jo would be calling soon, and he'd be off again. Some lessons would have to be postponed until another day. A little voice inside his head kept whispering that he was stalling, but he continued to push it aside.

Zane spent the following week getting things ready to leave: passport, mail forwarding, and vaccination boosters. He was expecting Jo's call any day. Monica hadn't mentioned anything more about him being in love, and for that he was grateful.

He had proposed to Monica. He intended on marrying her. And that was that.

~⚬ ⚬~

It was almost February when Jo finally called.

"You want to explain to me why there are no pictures with your articles?"

"There are plenty of pictures."

He could hear the papers shuffling in the background, most probably the eight-by-tens he'd printed up to get her off his back.

"I see a picture of a big red barn, a brand new colt, and a passel of dogs. Where are the shots of the family?"

Zane sighed. When it came down to it, he'd kept the drawings he had made for himself. He couldn't let those intimate moments be printed for all the world to see. "I told you, they don't allow their pictures to be taken. They consider it vain, at best."

"And at worst?"

"A graven image."

Jo let out an aggravated growl that she had surely perfected as an assistant editor. "I sent you there to get what no one else has. Everyone has pictures of their barns."

"And I told you I wasn't going to violate their beliefs."

"What is wrong with you?"

"You know, Jo, you never asked me to go against the customs of the Afghanis. Why is it okay to ignore the wishes of the Amish?"

The other end of the line went so quiet that he wondered if she'd disconnected. "Something happened to you there."

A lot happened to him there, but that wasn't any of her business.

"Something even more life-changing than getting shot."

"I have integrity, Jo. There's nothing wrong with that. In fact, it's what keeps me alive."

She growled again, only this time more softly. "I suppose so."

His stubbornness, he figured, had ruined his chance at Mexico.

Jo sighed. "You win, Zane. Pack your bags. You're leaving for Juarez in three days."

❧ ❧

Three days. Zane should have been excited, but he couldn't muster even the faintest shadow of happiness. This was what he wanted. Wasn't it?

He didn't have time to think about it. He had too much left to do than to dwell on his emotions. His counselor would say it was a natural reaction to getting back into the hot zone, but this was like getting on the horse that bucked him off. He'd never know if he could do it again unless he, well, did it again. Unless he got back out there.

What other choice did he have?

❧ ❧

"You're really leaving?"

Maybe it had been a mistake to invite Monica over to help him pack. He didn't have much time with her until he left, and unlike the Amish trip, she couldn't just pop down for the weekend. Well, she could, but Mexican tourism had nearly ground to a halt as the result of the drug runners so close to the border. He wouldn't want her anywhere near all that conflict.

"It's time to go." He folded another shirt and put it in his soft-sided nylon case.

"But . . . but you just got home." She laid her hand on his arm, stilling his jerky movements.

Why was this so hard? It was like any other assignment. Then again, maybe getting shot had affected him more than he realized. He exhaled heavily, stilling his nerves as he turned to face her. "It's all part of the job. You know that."

"But what about our engagement?"

"I can't go to work and be engaged?" A bark of sardonic laughter escaped him. Or maybe it was that nervousness back again.

"That's not what I mean. I just thought things would be different now."

He reached for another shirt. "Different how?"

She turned her face away. Instead of looking at him, she toyed with the end of her sweater. "I've been thinking about what you said. About having children."

Zane became motionless once again. "Oh yeah?" All at once he felt as if it a huge weight had been lifted off his shoulders, but transferred to his heart. That was what he wanted, wasn't it? Someone to carry on his name. To live forever even though his mortality had been crammed in his face by way of a stray bullet from an insurgent drive-by?

"This month's *Talk* says I have a greater chance of getting shot by a terrorist than having a baby."

"Did you make up that statistic?" This conversation was getting way too heavy.

"No! Maybe. But it made me wonder, and . . . you know."

"I know." Once again seriousness descended between them.

"I've thought about it and . . . I do want to have a baby. A little girl to dress and braid her hair, a little boy with your eyes and skinned-up knees from pushing a toy truck all over the driveway . . ."

He wanted to jump up and down and shout to the heavens. Instead he raised one eyebrow and waited for her to continue. "But?" he prompted.

"Your job is so dangerous."

"I know that. You think I don't know that?"

"Then tell me how we're going to make this work?"

He plunked another shirt into his suitcase. "Like everyone else does. We've already got a house. We'll have ourselves a couple of kids, buy a dog . . ." his words trailed off as she shook her head.

"You really think it's okay to bring a child into this crazy life? What am I supposed to tell them when you get shot again?"

"I'm not going to get shot again."

She wrapped her arms around her middle, hugging herself. "You don't know that."

She was right, but dwelling on such things was not how to deal with it. "It's my job, Monica. It's the only thing I know how to do." That wasn't entirely true. He'd turned out to be mighty fine Amish farmer.

"You could go to work for Daddy."

Zane stifled a snort. "I am not working for your father."

"So what are you going to do? Just go back to the Middle East and pretend you don't have a wife waiting on you in the States?"

"I'm going to Mexico. Juarez."

Her hands stilled, her voice barely a whisper. "Zane, they are killing people left and right down there."

"And that's why I need to be there to uncover the truth."

"When were you going to tell me?"

He shrugged. "You knew what my life was about when you decided to wear my ring. Why do you want to change me all of a sudden?"

"I have needs too."

"I know that."

"I can't be married to you, here raising your children, when you're putting yourself in harm's way for a headline."

He cocked his head. "Is that really how you feel about it?" She was the one person he thought understood his need to cover the dangers of their world. Evidently, he'd been wrong.

"I nearly died when I heard you'd been shot. I can't go through that again." She blinked, sending tears down her cheeks. "This Amish thing . . . I thought that might be something new for you. Something safe."

"It was Jo's condition . . . so I could have Mexico."

She took a deep, shuddering breath. "I guess it's better that we discovered this now before we brought a child into this mess." She pulled his ring from her finger. Tears filled her eyes once more as she took his hand and placed the ruby in his palm before closing his fingers around it.

"Monica, I—"

"It's okay, Zane. I'll be okay. And maybe one day, you'll find someone who can make you forget about your adrenalin rush. But it doesn't seem I'm that woman."

She kissed him on the cheek and walked to the door.

Zane didn't stop her as she let herself out.

"Are you ready?"

Jo's words brought Zane out of his reverie. "What? Oh. Yeah." How long had he been sitting there, staring off into space while she outlined the details of his assignment?

Her brows knitted over shrewd hazel eyes. "You were a million miles away."

Not quite a million. More like eight hundred. "Just thinking."

Jo came around the desk, the motion further emphasizing her diminutive stature. Barely topping five feet in her three-inch heels, Jo was still a force to be reckoned with, a dynamo of energy and power capped off with an impossibly dark pageboy. Zane always suspected she dyed her hair from blonde to black in order to be taken seriously in her male-dominated industry. "We have a contact there. He goes by Jesus, though I doubt that's his real name."

Zane nodded, mentally coaching himself to stay attentive. This information was highly valuable. He couldn't keep letting his mind slip back to Clover Ridge, to wondering what Katie Rose was doing now.

"I trust your Spanish is in order?

"*Mi espanol es muy bien.*"

She leaned against the desk. "Good, good."

"*Danki.*" The word just slipped out.

Jo's eyebrows nearly disappeared into her hair. "Beg pardon."

"It's Pennsylvania Dutch."

"Oh, I know that." Her brows lowered, and she dropped her gaze back to the file folder she held. "You'll be working closely with the border patrol. A Captain Vance. He's your main contact and—*Are you listening?*"

"Of course I am. Captain Vance. Got it."

Jo closed the file and tossed it onto her desk. She took off her glasses and without the filter studied him intently. "How are things with Monica?"

"What?"

"You heard me."

"What does Monica have to do with anything?"

"You're very distracted and about to go on what could be the most dangerous assignment of your career." She paused. "I know she gave you back your ring."

Zane sat up a little straighter in his seat. "How do you know that?"

"A good reporter never reveals her sources. Are you sure you're up for this?"

"Yes, yes. Monica and I parted on good terms. It's not like I'm heartbroken. I'm fine."

Despite his reassurances, she continued to study him.

"What?" His voice sounded more defensive than he would have preferred.

"If you're not upset about Monica, why do you still look like a lovesick teenager?"

"I don't know what you're talking about."

"This month's *Talk* had an article about how to tell if your man is in love, and you, my friend, are showing all of the signs."

"Oh, not you too."

She pinned him with a glare. "What do you mean by that?"

Zane shifted uncomfortably. "Monica said almost the same thing. She has this cockamamie idea that I'm in love with—never mind."

"In love with whom?"

Zane laughed and waved a dismissive hand. "It's not important."

"My top reporter comes back from an assignment staring off into space and using words like 'cockamamie.' I'd say that's important."

He sighed. They just had to go down that road. Better to get it over with so they could continue their briefing, otherwise he might not ever get out of Jo's office. She was a bulldog once she set her mind to something. True or not. "I met an incredible woman while I was in Oklahoma. She's kind and gentle and beautiful. She takes care of her brother's children and teaches school, and does the laundry for the bishop, and . . ."

"And you love her."

Zane scoffed. "That's impossible. I didn't even kiss her."

"Do you believe *that* has anything to do with love?"

"Of course. What am I saying? Do you even believe in love?"

He was surprised by the dreamy look that overtook Jo's usual mask of hard-nosed reporter. Her expression held a faraway quality while her hazel eyes filled with regret. "I loved a boy once." She shook her head. "I won't bore you with all the details. But I loved him with all my heart and soul. Still do."

"What happened to him?"

"Last time I heard he was happily married, living in Michigan with his stay-at-home wife and four great kids. See, I chose my career over him, and he went on without me."

"She's going to marry Samuel Beachy."

"And you're just going to let her?"

"I told you, I never even kissed her."

"That should tell you something, Zane."

He shook his head.

Jo walked around her desk and picked up the phone.

"What are you doing?"

"Changing your flight. Mandy, get American Airlines on the phone. I need you to change Zane Carson's ticket. He's going back to Oklahoma."

His heart lurched, thumping hard in his chest. Just the thought of seeing Katie Rose again made his mouth dry, his hands tremble. Was this love?

Jo smiled as she hung up the phone.

"You're slipping, Jo. Your romantic side is showing."

"It's too late for me, Zane, but not for you. Go kiss your girl. Mexico can wait another week."

"And if . . . and if I . . ." he tried to say "stay," but the word wouldn't form. "If I don't come back?"

"Then I'll give the assignment to Talbert. He's been itching to stretch his legs a little."

Zane nodded. The thought of the assignment going to his number-one competitor should have had him packing his bags for Mexico. But all he could think about was the sweet face of Katie Rose Fisher.

Jo's smile was gentle. "Life's too short not to grab all the love you can."

And that's just what he planned to do. He just hoped he wasn't too late.

Valentine's Day was always fun for the children. It gave them something to look forward to during the cold winter months when farming had slowed and it was too cold to stay outside for long. The best part was that all the scholars could take place in the exchange. There were so few projects that the entire school could do together.

Katie Rose pulled a stack of red construction paper from the supply cabinet. "Matthew, can you hand everyone a sheet of this, please?"

Her nephew stood without question and walked to the front of the classroom to retrieve the paper.

Katie Rose found the stash of pink paper. "Jodie, will you hand this out for me, too?"

"Yes, Katie Rose." The young girl stood and came to the front as well.

As the older scholars walked around handing out the paper, Katie Rose continued to dig in the cabinet retrieving more items for them to use: glue, lace, and beads. She wanted this to be fun for all the children. Once they all completed their Valentines, she would let them go out and play while they dried. It was so hard on them to be cooped up all day, especially with a couple of inches of new snow on the ground. Fortunately, no ice was involved, and the roads were clear. Though Katie Rose suspected she'd have to break up a snowball fight or two.

Adding safety scissors to the pile of accessories on her desk, Katie Rose turned and faced the children. "Now, scholars. This is a free project. There will be no grade. You may make a Valentine for one person or as many people as you like, *within the time we have.* Now you have forty-five minutes. Ready, go."

As the children worked not-so quietly, Katie Rose graded papers. She'd already made a Valentine for each of her students and dropped them in the box by the door, ensuring that everyone received at least one note of love. Everyone deserved a Valentine.

"How come you're not makin' a heart, Katie Rose?"

"Cuz, she's already got a Valentine, silly."

"*Dat* says now that Samuel Beachy's back, we'll have a weddin' to go to out of season."

"*Jah*," the students chorused.

She opened her mouth to protest.

"Is that true?"

Katie Rose swung around at the sound of his voice. It was no trick of her hearing. There he stood in the flesh looking so much like he had the first time she'd ever seen him.

"Zane Carson!" The children didn't ask for permission, getting up from their seats and clambering around him.

"Children. Children!" She banged her hand against the solid wood of her desk. It hurt like all get-out, but at least she had their attention back. "Kindly return to your seats, and allow Zane Carson a chance to breathe."

In truth, she was the one who needed air. Just one sight of him and all the oxygen left her lungs. He looked even better than she remembered. He'd shaved his beard, and there were dark circles under his eyes, but he was still the most handsome man she had ever seen.

She wanted to run to him, throw herself at his feet, and beg to know why he had returned. But as his eyes scraped over her, she maintained control.

"Is it true?" he asked again.

She lost her concentration as soon as she looked into those chocolate-brown eyes. "What?"

"That you already have a Valentine?"

"*Jah*." She could only whisper the word.

Zane shifted uncomfortably from one foot to the other. He

looked so out of place, standing there in his *Englisch* clothes. He took a deep breath and let it out noisily, running his fingers through his hair as if he desperately needed something to do with his hands. "I see," he finally said. "I guess I'm too late, then."

"Too late for what?" she asked, so aware that the children had completely stopped making their Valentines and instead were watching them like a fox watches a hare.

One of the girls giggled.

Zane glanced toward the class as if only then he remembered that they had a captive audience. "Can I, uh, talk to you alone?"

"After school?"

He shook his head. "Outside."

Katie Rose stood and rushed to the door, only slowing down as she neared the threshold. "Children, continue to work on your projects, I expect to see lots accomplished when I return."

Without bothering to get her coat, she followed Zane out into the school yard. They walked across the playground, and Zane looked as if he were gathering his thoughts. Katie Rose remained silent, allowing him time to say his piece.

When they reached the big oak, he stopped and turned to face her.

Katie Rose shivered in anticipation. Or perhaps it was the north wind cutting through her dress like a knife.

"You're cold."

Before she could answer, he had slipped out of his wool coat and wrapped it around her. It smelled like Zane, but different. Zane and store-bought aftershave. She inhaled deeply, loving the scent and the warmth of him wrapped around her as it was.

"I think I might be in love with you."

Katie Rose blinked. "You don't know?"

"I'm confused. See, I've never been in love before."

"What about your intended?"

He shook his head. "I never loved Monica. At least not romantic love. I only thought I did."

"Oh."

"She gave me back my ring. We've parted as friends."

Katie Rose swallowed hard. Best not to let her hopes rise. He thought he was in love with the pretty *Englisch* brunette, but it wasn't true. Now he was saying that he might love her . . .

"She thinks I'm in love with you, but then—it doesn't matter. Never mind. You're marrying Samuel. I should have never come here." He started to turn and walk away, but Katie Rose put a hand on his arm to stop him.

"Why did you come?"

He shoved his hands into the pockets of his dungarees as if he didn't have anything better to do with them. Then he shrugged, as the wind ruffled his wheat-colored hair. "It's silly," he said with a shake of his head.

"Tell me."

"I came to kiss you."

Katie Rose couldn't help the sigh that escaped her. His words were like something out of the romantic movies she had watched during her *rumspringa*. At the time, she had thought they were nothing but made-up stories. After all, she had been in love with Samuel Beachy, and he had never treated her like the men in the movies treated their women. But now Zane Carson had travelled hundreds of miles just to kiss her.

She took a steadying breath. She couldn't lose her head. Not with her heart already on the line. "And what happens after that?"

He shrugged again. "I don't know. If it is . . . love, then I suppose I should go talk to the bishop about staying. If not, then I walk away and never bother you again."

The thought of never seeing him again hurt her heart.

"Okay," she said, expelling a heavy sigh.

How could she not say yes? She had been wondering the same thing. When Samuel had kissed her the few times they had found themselves alone since his return, Katie Rose had to remind herself that it was what she wanted. Samuel had always been what she wanted. To be married. Have children.

"I've never asked to kiss a girl before."

Katie Rose waited patiently as he took a step closer, and braced his booted feet farther apart. He seemed even more nervous than she. He took a breath, then placed his hands on either side of her face and tilted her mouth up to meet his.

The touch of his lips was like everything beautiful and perfect rolled into one. Sunshine and green grass, freshly fallen snow, and the smell of wood burning in the wintertime. Katie Rose had never felt love like this, had never felt so *loved* like this.

His lips clung to hers, warming her against the cold. She wrapped her arms around his neck, knowing full well that the children were most probably pressed against the windows of the schoolhouse watching with wide eyes. She couldn't help herself. She had waited so long.

When Samuel left she had been waiting, waiting for the man God had set aside for her. Waiting for Zane.

He pulled his mouth from hers, his thumbs brushing her checks. She said a little prayer that he felt the same about her. If not, she was certain her heart would never heal.

"Please don't marry Samuel Beachy." His voice was thick with emotion.

She wanted to be coy like the actress in the movie and say something pithy, but all she could do was pull his lips back to hers.

"*Nay*," she said so many minutes later. "I'll not be marryin' Samuel Beachy. You see, I never told him yes."

Relief took hold and spread across Zane's handsome face. "And me? Will you marry me?"

"What about the bishop?"

"I don't want to marry him."

Katie Rose laughed, then immediately sobered. "What if he denies your petition to join the church?"

"Then I'll stay in town. I'll buy a house. I'll show him how much you and the community mean to me. This is where I'm supposed to be. God led me here, to you, and I'm not going anywhere." With God on their side how could they lose? "Somehow, we'll find a way."

"*Jah*," Katie Rose said, holding him tight. She laid her head on his chest, the steady thump of his heart easing her uncertainties. "True love always does."

Glossary of Amish Words

Ach	Oh
Aemen	Amen
Aenti	aunt
Allrecht	all right
Bruder	Brother
Bu, buwe	Boy, boys
danki	thank you
Dat	Dad
Dawk	day
Deutsch	Pennsylvania Dutch
Die Botschaft	old order Amish weekly newspaper (*The Budget*)
Dochder	daughter
Ei, yi, yi	My, oh, my
Elder	parents
Englisch	non-Amish person
Fisch	fish
Frack	Dress
geh	Go
goedemiddag	good afternoon
grossdaadi	Grandfather
grossmammi	Grandmother

grossdawdi haus	a house usually built onto the back where the grandparents live
gut	Good
guder mariye	Good morning
Gut himmel	Good heavens
gut nacht	Good night
haus	House
Jah	yes
Kapp	prayer covering, cap
Katfisch	catfish
Kinder	children
Mach schnell	hurry up (make quickly)
mamm	Mom
mudder	Mother
natchess	supper
nay	No
nichte	niece
onkle	Uncle
Ordnung	Amish rules written and understood
Red-up	clean up
Rumspringa	running around time (starts at 16)
Schay	pretty
Schveshtah	sister
Shayna Grischtdaag	Nice Christmas
vatter	father
Wie geht?	How are things?
Weibs leit	women

Counting—

1	eens
2	zwee
3	drei

Dear Reader—

My name is Katie Rose Fisher, and I live in the Old Order Amish community of Clover Ridge, Oklahoma. For almost as long as I can remember, I knew what I wanted out of my life: to live in the Amish tradition, join the church, and marry Samuel Beachy, the bishop's son. But before he could bend his knee and give his life to God, Samuel decided to stay in the *Englisch* world long after his run-around time.

I'll admit, I was heartbroken, but it seemed that God had other plans for me. When Gabriel's wife died, I went to live with my brother to help take care of his brood of six. I found myself teaching the young scholars in our district. God has provided me with a fulfilling life. Even if it isn't with Samuel. Even if I do not have a husband or children of my own.

The news that our mother had breast cancer devastated the entire Fisher clan. As usual, we pulled together and did everything in our power to help pay for the medical costs, including inviting an *Englisch* reporter to come and live with us. The hope is he will write articles for his fancy magazine and bring business and tourists to our little community.

I think allowing Zane Carson to come to Clover Ridge is a bad idea. He is worldly and handsome and has no idea of the ways of the Amish. He isn't even sure if he believes in God, but he is willing to learn how we live, dress like us, ride in a horse and buggy, even farm the earth. When so many others tend to scoff at our ways, his acceptance is refreshing. And I think maybe he has even found his way to the Lord.

But there is so much more to Zane Carson as I soon discover. His presence alone makes me wish for things I cannot have—a husband, children, and for Zane to stay among us and live out his days as a Plain man. He has had these thoughts himself, for I can see the confusion and longing in his eyes. But whether that want is for me or a closer relationship with God, I do not know.

I may never know, for as soon as I think I understand the man underneath the English exterior, Samuel Beachy returns, throwing my dreams of something more into a tailspin.

But has Samuel come back for me or for his family who has shunned him? Do I give him another chance? And what of this handsome *Englisch* reporter who walks away with my heart? It is not an easy choice to make.

Love to you always—

Katie Rose Fisher

Discussion Questions

1. How does Zane's lack of religious/spiritual background affect his views of the Fishers? Have you ever had the opportunity to talk to someone who knows little or nothing about the story of Jesus?

2. Are Zane's reasons for asking Monica to marry him sound? How does her lack of an answer affect him during his stay with the Amish?

3. Zane is stunned the first time he meets Katie Rose. Do you believe in love at first sight? Have you ever felt an instant connection with someone, be it romantic or platonic? How did that relationship pan out for you?

4. Zane was raised in a "hippie" commune by very liberal parents. How do their earthy ways help him learn to live with the Amish?

5. Zane feels that the danger he faces as a war correspondent helps him feel alive. What is it about the peaceful ways of the Amish that has him feeling the same way when he's in Clover Ridge?

6. Katie Rose has been living with Gabriel since his wife died. How has this relationship hindered her from finding a husband? Is her reasoning sound or has she been waiting for Samuel to change his mind and return to Clover Ridge?

7. When Ruth asks Zane to pray with her, she tells him to thank God for his blessings. Zane finds there are too many to count. How do you feel these prayer instructions affect Zane's thoughts and behaviors as he continues to live with the Fishers?

8. Katie Rose demands Zane pray aloud over the colt's birth. Is this request helpful to Zane? Does it aid in his acceptance of the ways of the Lord?

9. How do you feel about John Paul having a job even though his father has forbid him to work during his *rumspringa*? Have you ever gone against someone's wishes because you thought it was the right thing to do?

10. How does Megan Fisher's leaving the community affect Abram's view of his family and his treatment of John Paul's *rumspringa* freedoms?

11. How has Ruth's surgery affected her relationship with God? What about her relationship with Abram? Is her reasoning sound? Or is she simply grieving over the loss of her "normal" life?

12. In this book, the reader gets to catch up with Annie from *Saving Gideon*. As an Englisher among the Amish, how does Annie help Zane understand their ways?

13. Zane knows from the first time that he meets her that Katie Rose is different than any other woman he's known. How do these differences affect the way Zane treats Katie Rose?

14. How does Zane's inability to completely leave Katie Rose alone and his reluctance to pursue a relationship with her show the power of love? Have you ever loved anyone whom the world thought wasn't right for you?

15. Even though he won't admit it, Zane is in love with Katie Rose when he returns to Chicago. Do you feel this determination to marry Monica is noble or is it irresponsible?

If you enjoyed *Katie's Choice*, you can
read more about the wonderful people
of Clover Ridge in *Saving Gideon*.

A disillusioned Dallas socialite breaks down on the outskirts
of an Amish community and begins to find herself thanks to a
widowed young man who has lost his faith in God.

978-1-4336-7752-6, $14.99

Amy LIllard

@AmyWritesRomnce

AmyWritesRomance.com